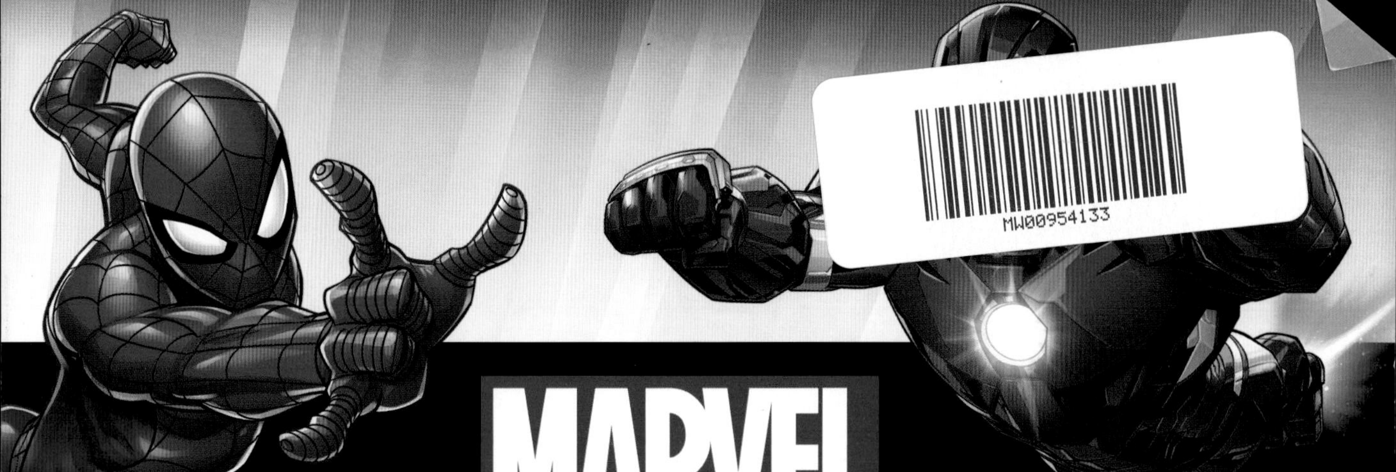

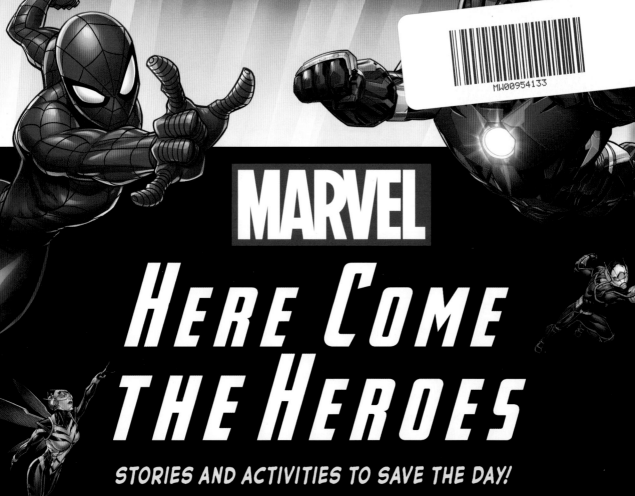

MARVEL

HERE COME THE HEROES

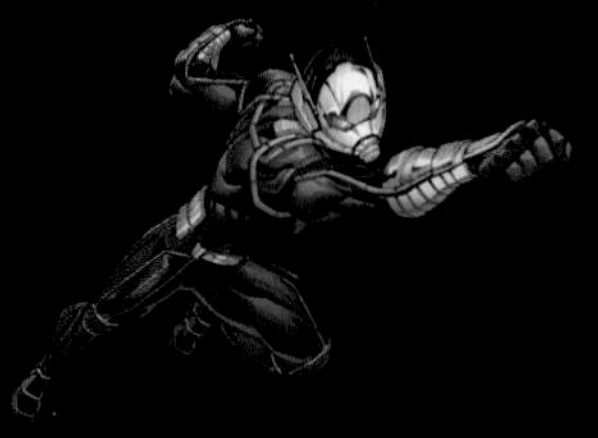

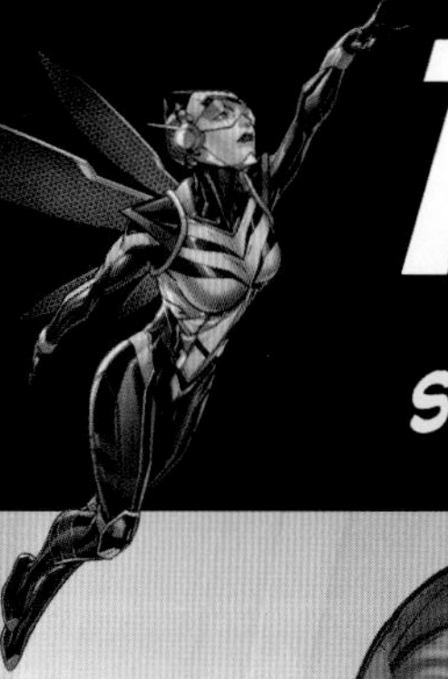

STORIES AND ACTIVITIES TO SAVE THE DAY!

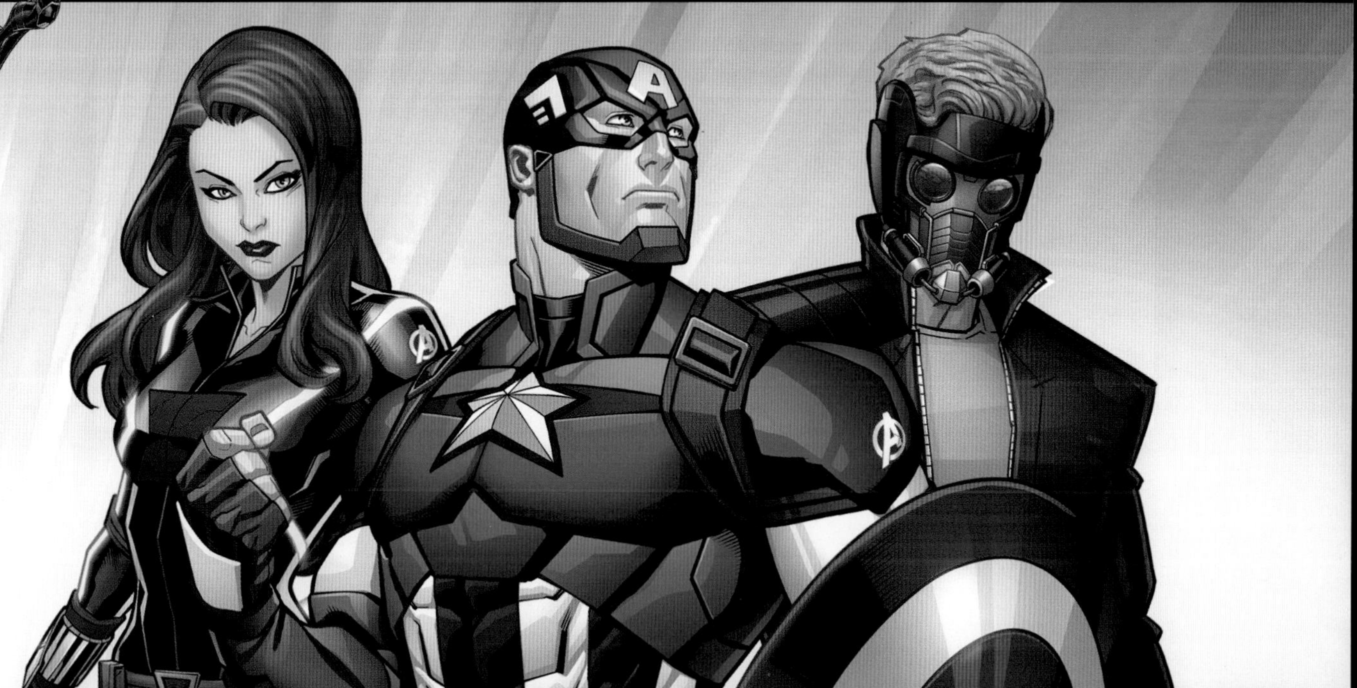
A

we make books come alive®
pi kids® Phoenix International Publications, Inc.
Chicago • London • New York • Hamburg • Mexico City • Sydney

Customer Service: 1-877-277-9441 or customerservice@pikidsmedia.com

Published by Phoenix International Publications, Inc.
8501 West Higgins Road   59 Gloucester Place
Chicago, Illinois 60631   London W1U 8JJ

PI Kids and *we make books come alive* are trademarks of
Phoenix International Publications, Inc., and are registered in the United States.

Look and Find is a trademark of Phoenix International Publications, Inc., and is registered in the United States and Canada.

www.pikidsmedia.com

ISBN: 978-1-5037-5455-3

TABLE OF CONTENTS

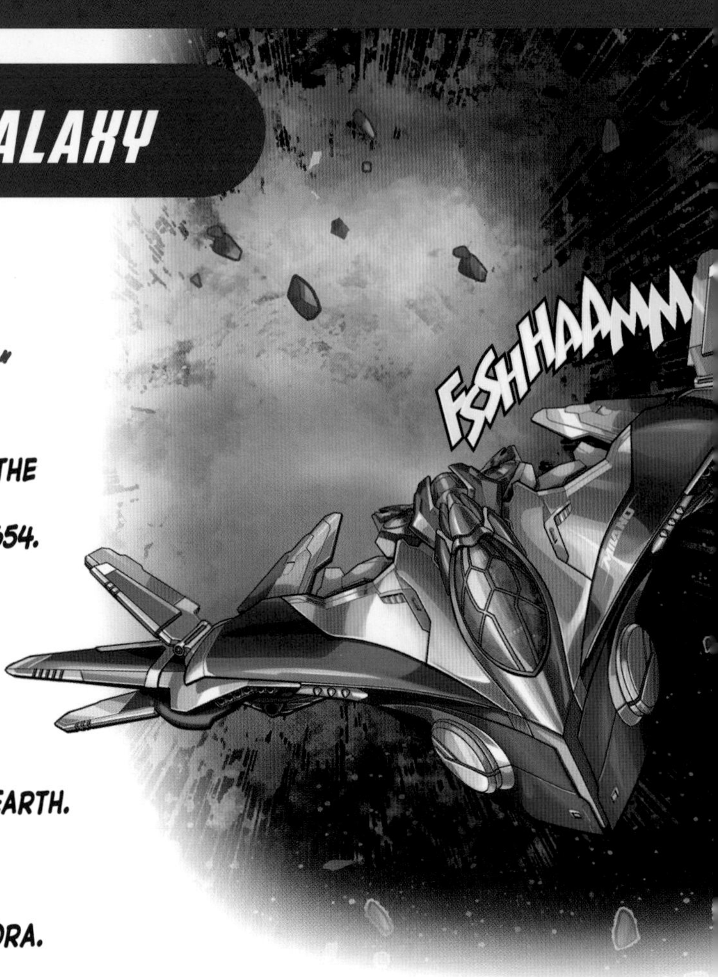
FSSHAAMM

ALIEN INVASION

"A LITTLE GOOD, A LITTLE BAD, ALL GUARDIAN!"

SOMEWHERE DEEP IN SPACE, THE GUARDIANS OF THE GALAXY NOTICE STRANGE ACTIVITY IN QUADRANT 7654.

"THAT'S EARTH!" SAYS STAR-LORD. WITHIN MOMENTS, THE MIGHTY STARSHIP *MILANO* IS HURTLING TOWARDS EARTH.

THE GUARDIANS ARRIVE ON THE OUTSKIRTS OF EARTH. THERE, THEY SEE SEVERAL ALIEN SPACESHIPS.

"THOSE SHIPS BELONG TO THANOS," SAYS GAMORA.

"I AM GROOT," SAYS GROOT.

"EVIL ALIENS SENT FROM THANOS?" SAYS ROCKET. "AND I WAS WORRIED THIS WOULD BE BORING."

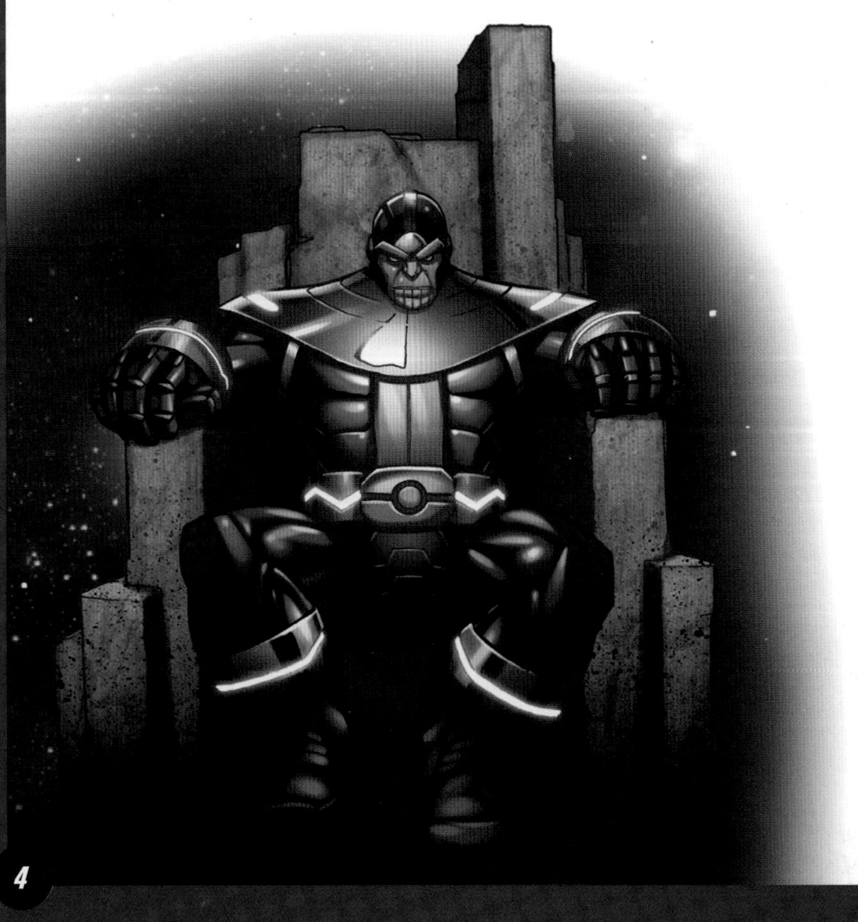

THE GUARDIANS PREPARE FOR BATTLE.

THANOS'S EVIL ALIEN ARMY ATTACKS. THE GUARDIANS OF THE GALAXY FLY OUT TO STOP THE INVASION!

A SWARM OF ALIENS MOVES TOWARD GROOT, BUT ROCKET USES HIS LATEST INVENTION TO BLAST THROUGH IT.

"I AM GROOT," SAYS GROOT.

"YOU'RE WELCOME, BUDDY," SAYS ROCKET.

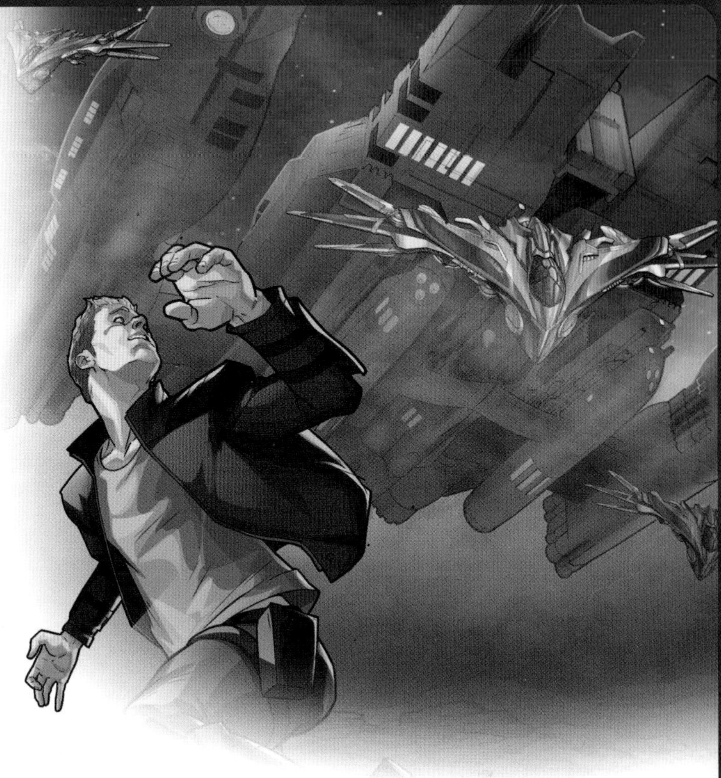

MEANWHILE, DRAX THE DESTROYER IS LIVING UP TO HIS NAME. HE RIPS THE FRONT OFF AN ALIEN SPACESHIP AND THROWS IT AT THE INVADERS!

THE GUARDIANS BATTLE THE INVADERS BACK TO THEIR LAST REMAINING SHIP. ROCKET THINKS THE BATTLE IS OVER, BUT STAR-LORD ISN'T SURE.

"I'VE GOT A BAD FEELING ABOUT THIS," HE SAYS.

SURE ENOUGH, THE ALIEN SHIP GLOWS BRIGHT BLUE AND FIRES A GIANT LASER AT THE TEAM.

"I. AM. GROOT!" SAYS GROOT. HE GROWS TO AN ENORMOUS SIZE AND SHIELDS THE TEAM FROM THE BLAST.

THE BLAST BOUNCES OFF GROOT AND DESTROYS THE ALIENS' SHIP.

"WELL SAID, BUDDY," SAYS ROCKET.

THE EARTH IS SAFE AND THANOS'S PLANS ARE THWARTED, THANKS TO THE GUARDIANS OF THE GALAXY!

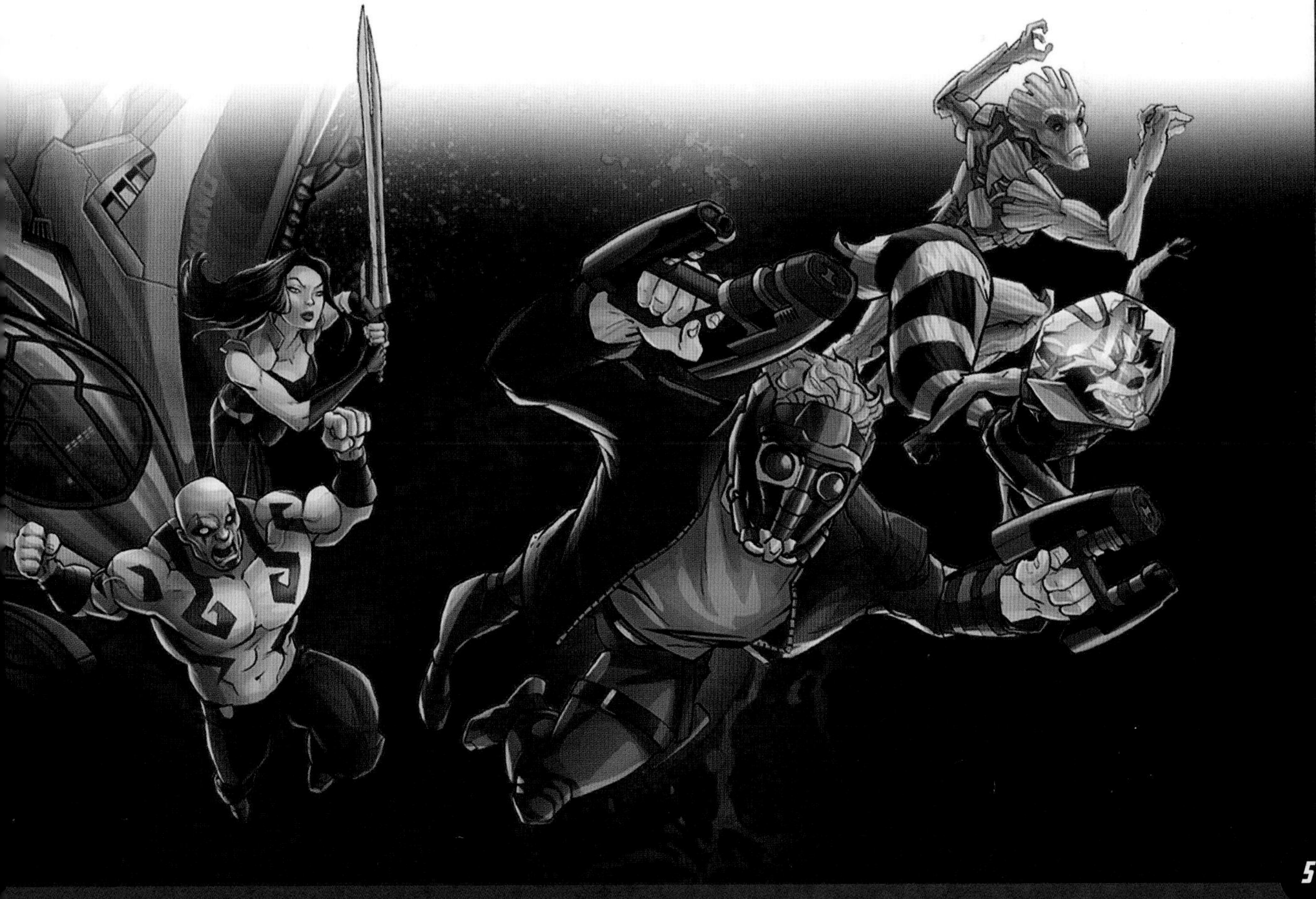

XANDAR IS UNDER ATTACK! THE GUARDIANS OF THE GALAXY ARRIVE TO SAVE THE PLANET AND ITS PEOPL
FROM RONAN'S EVILS. AS STAR-LORD AND FRIENDS BATTLE RONAN'S ARMY, HELP THEM KEEP AN EYE OUT
FOR THESE SOARING SPACESHIPS AND ADVERSARIAL ALIENS:

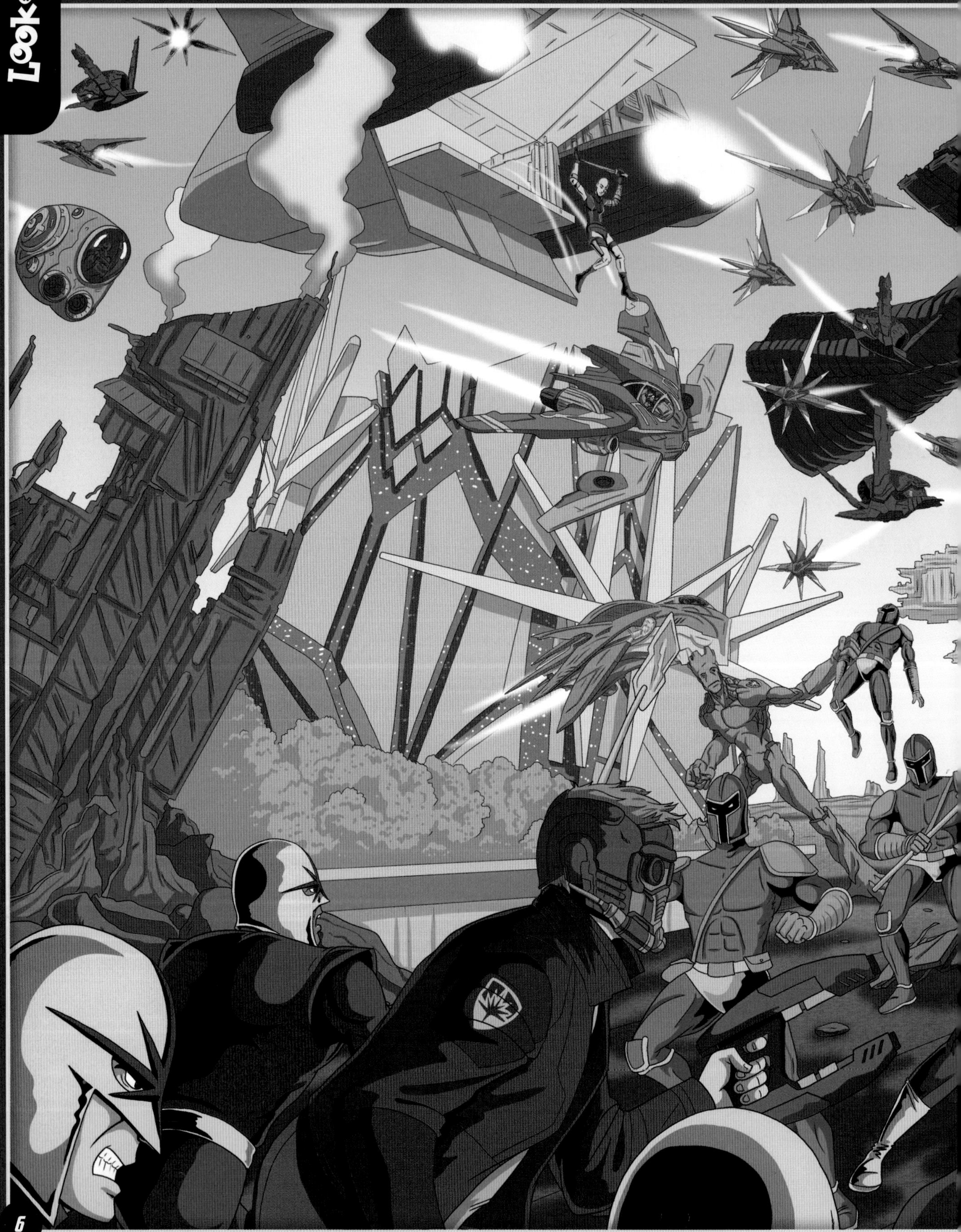

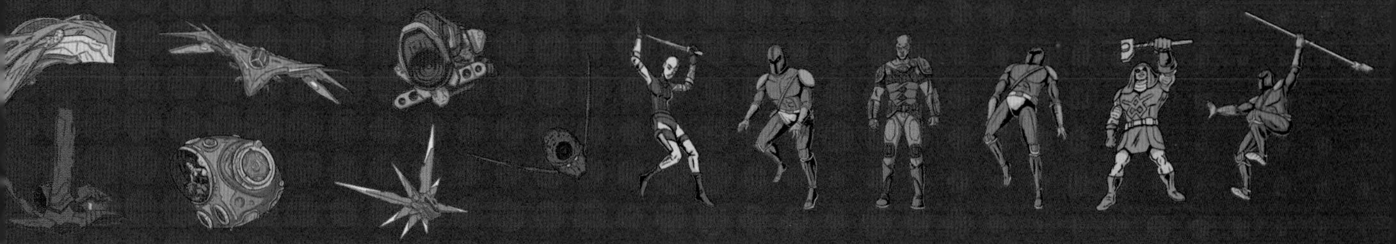

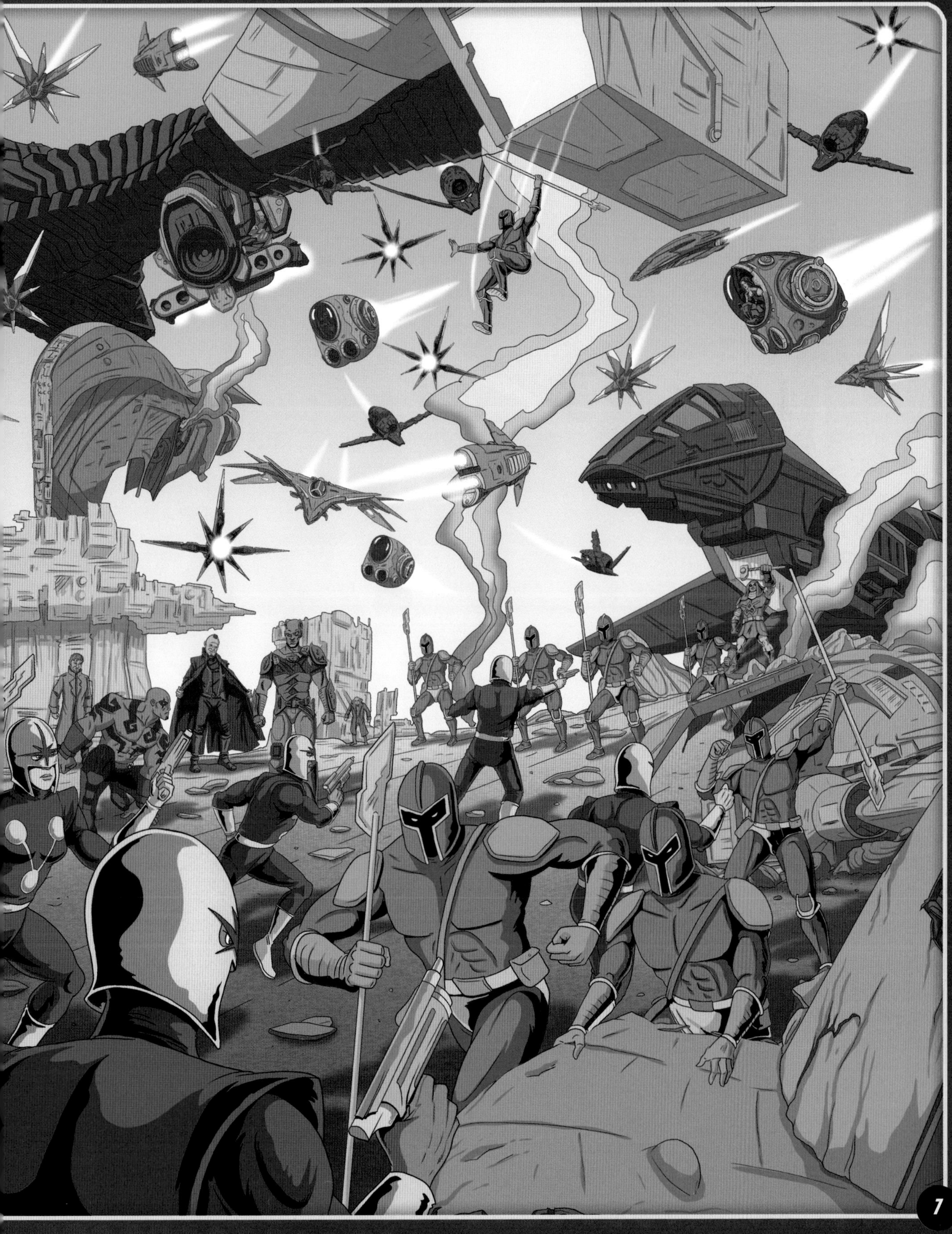

Picture Puzzle

Help set things straight in Xandar!

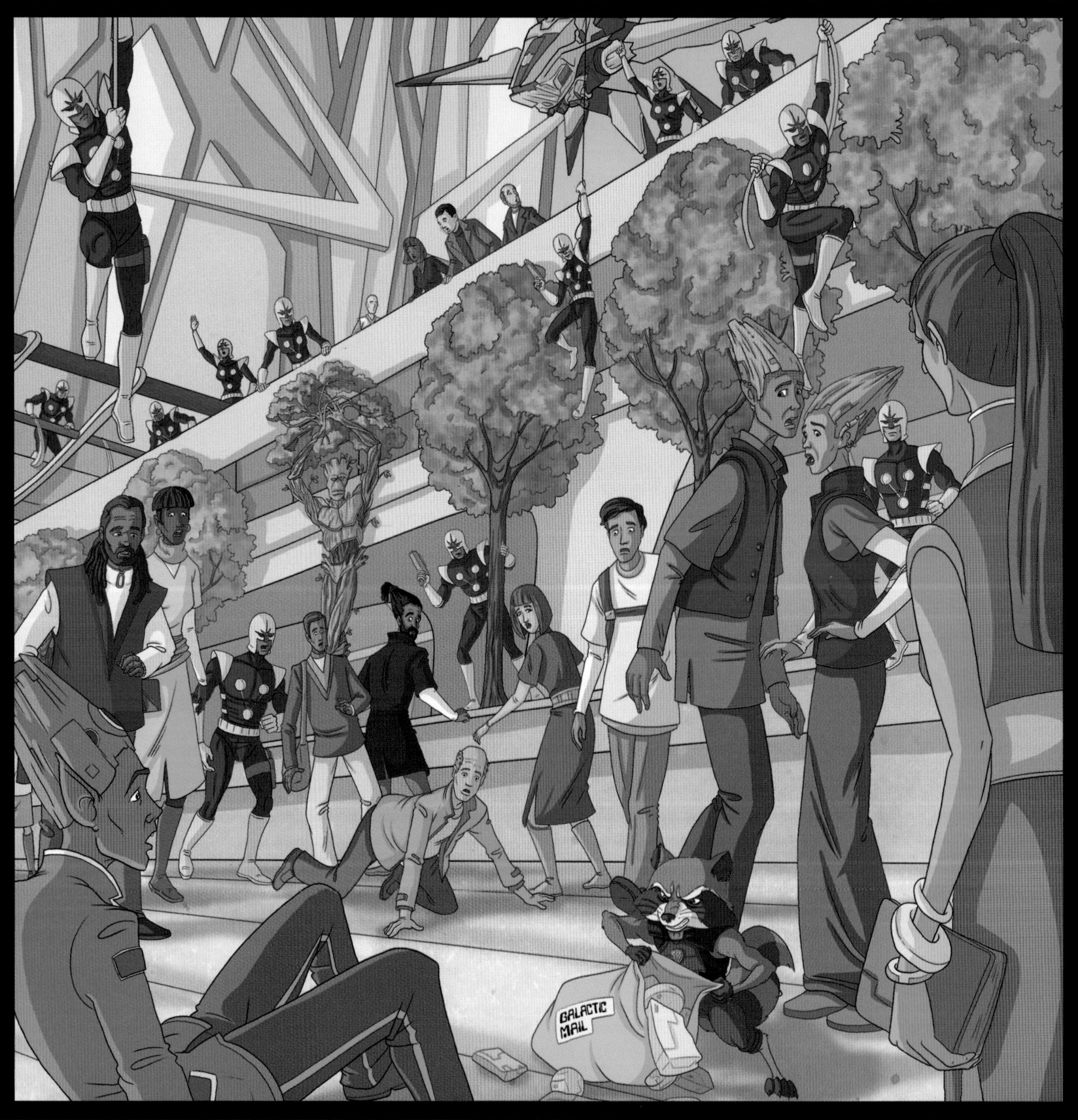
GALACTIC MAIL

FIND 10 DIFFERENCES BETWEEN THESE SCENES.

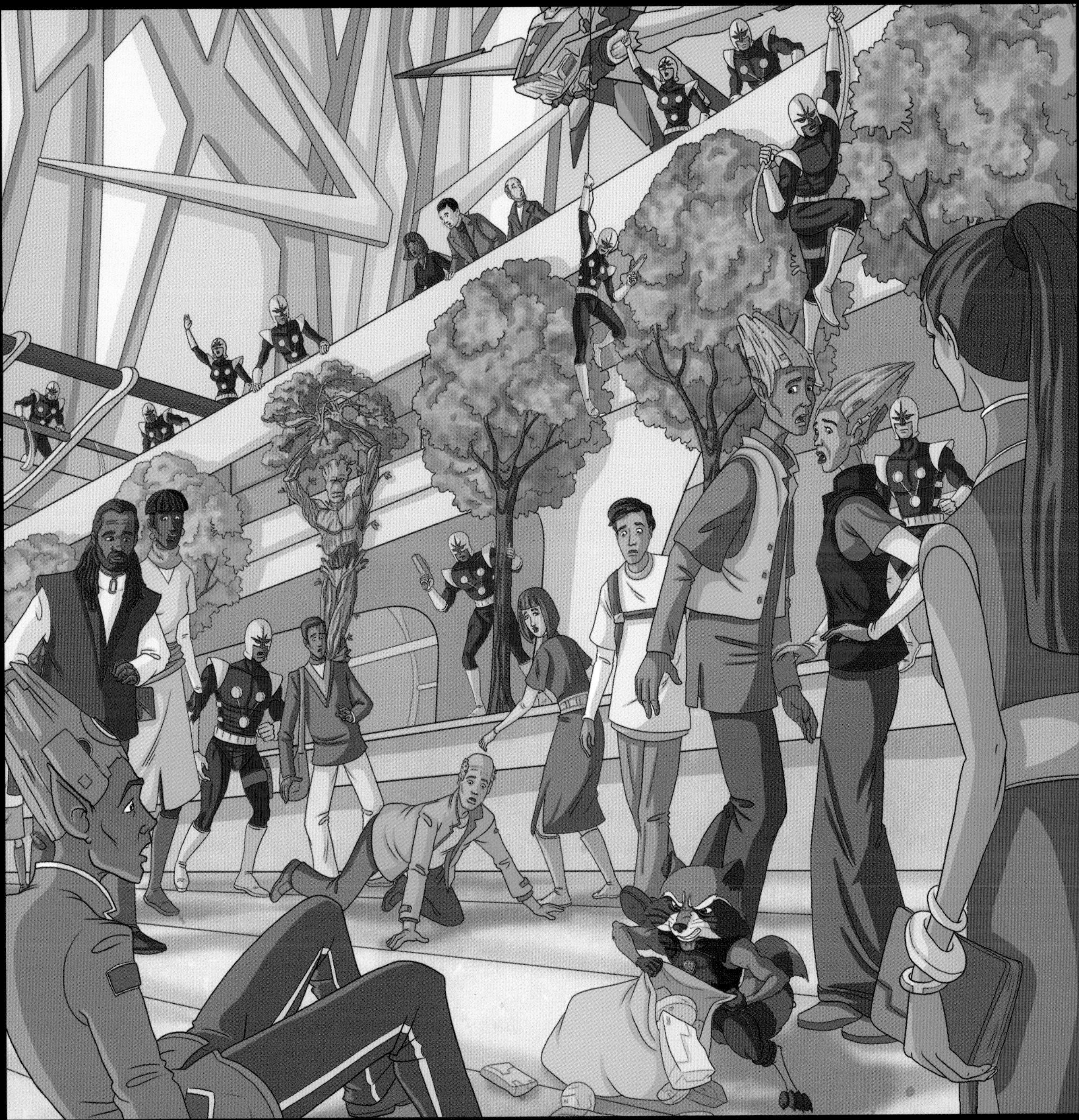

Answer key: top left guard, alien on balcony, man in red jacket, color of fallen alien, dangling guard, blue vest shade, galactic mail label, climbing guard's buttons, sitting alien's pants, space ship wing color

DOUBLE TROUBLE
"LET'S ROCK!"

THE GUARDIANS OF THE GALAXY ARE HAVING A QUIET NIGHT ON THE *MILANO*.

"I'M TIRED OF SITTING AROUND," ROCKET COMPLAINS. "I WANT SOME EXCITEMENT!"

"I AM GROOT," GROOT AGREES.

JUST THEN, THE GUARDIANS GET A MESSAGE FROM NOVA CORPS:

"SOMEONE HAS STOLEN DANGEROUS WEAPONS FROM OUR LAB. CAN YOU HELP US FIND THEM?"

"NOW THAT'S MORE LIKE IT!" ROCKET SAYS.

"WHERE WOULD YOU GO WITH STOLEN WEAPONS?" STAR-LORD ASKS THE CREW.

GAMORA'S SISTER NEBULA IS A THIEF. "IF THEY'RE LIKE NEBULA," GAMORA SAYS, "THEY'LL HIDE ON MORAG."

THE PLANET MORAG IS FULL OF UNDERGROUND TUNNELS, MAKING IT EASY FOR A THIEF TO DISAPPEAR. THE GUARDIANS NEED TO GET THERE FAST, BEFORE THE TRAIL GOES COLD.

IN THE TUNNELS OF MORAG, GAMORA HEARS A FAMILIAR VOICE.

"THIS THIEF ISN'T JUST *LIKE* NEBULA," GAMORA SAYS. "IT *IS* NEBULA!"

SHE RACES AHEAD AND FINDS NEBULA HOLDING A STOLEN WEAPON. AND THE VILLAIN LOKI IS THERE WITH THE OTHER DEVICES. THEY'RE WORKING TOGETHER!

GAMORA DRAWS HER SWORD. SHE'LL HAVE
TO CATCH NEBULA WITHOUT GETTING ZAPPED
BY THE STOLEN WEAPON.

GAMORA GETS THE JOB DONE, BUT
STAR-LORD REALIZES THAT LOKI SLIPPED AWAY
WHILE NEBULA AND GAMORA WERE FIGHTING.
ROCKET AND GROOT ARE ON THE CASE!

ROCKET CREATES A DISTRACTION WHILE GROOT
GIVES CHASE. HE RUNS INTO THE TUNNELS AFTER
LOKI, DODGING ANGRY ALIENS TO CAPTURE THE
MASTER OF MISCHIEF.

TOGETHER, THE GUARDIANS BRING NEBULA, LOKI, AND THE WEAPONS THEY STOLE BACK TO NOVA CORPS.

"I'M READY FOR A QUIET NIGHT IN," ROCKET SAYS.

"I THOUGHT YOU WANTED MORE EXCITEMENT," STAR-LORD REPLIES.

"TWO VILLAINS IS A LITTLE *TOO MUCH* EXCITEMENT FOR ME," ROCKET SAYS.

"I AM GROOT," GROOT AGREES.

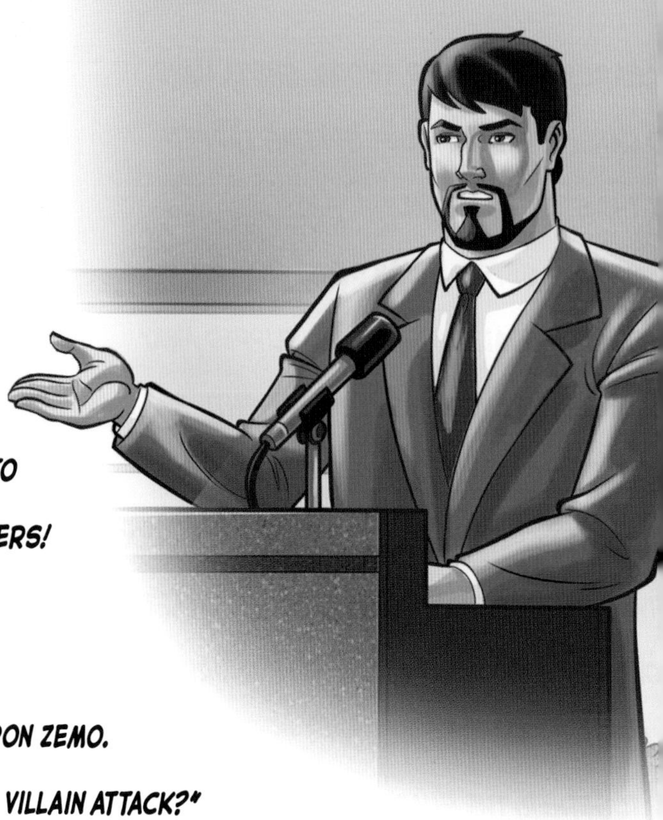

SCIENCE FAIR SURPRISE

"WE ARE THE AVENGERS!"

TODAY IS THE ANNUAL STARK SCIENCE EXPO. SCIENTISTS FROM AROUND THE WORLD HAVE GATHERED TO UNVEIL THEIR LATEST INVENTIONS...AND MEET THE AVENGERS!

SUDDENLY, ULTRON, THE ENCHANTRESS, KLAW, AND BARON ZEMO CRASH THE PARTY.

"THESE INVENTIONS NOW BELONG TO US!" SNARLS BARON ZEMO.

"CAN'T WE HAVE ONE SCIENCE EXPO WITHOUT A SUPER VILLAIN ATTACK?" ASKS TONY STARK AS HIS IRON MAN ARMOR ZOOMS ONTO HIS BODY.

KLAW TRIES TO STEAL A WEATHER MACHINE, BUT IRON MAN STOPS HIM WITH A REPULSOR BLAST.

THOR AND BLACK WIDOW TEAM UP TO STOP THE ENCHANTRESS FROM STEALING A SONIC RAY FROM A SCIENTIST.

ACROSS THE ROOM, HAWKEYE FIGHTS OFF A WAVE OF ULTRON SENTINELS, WHILE CAPTAIN AMERICA PROTECTS A GROUP OF SCIENTISTS FROM BARON ZEMO.

"GET TO THE EXIT!" CAPTAIN AMERICA TELLS THE SCIENTISTS.

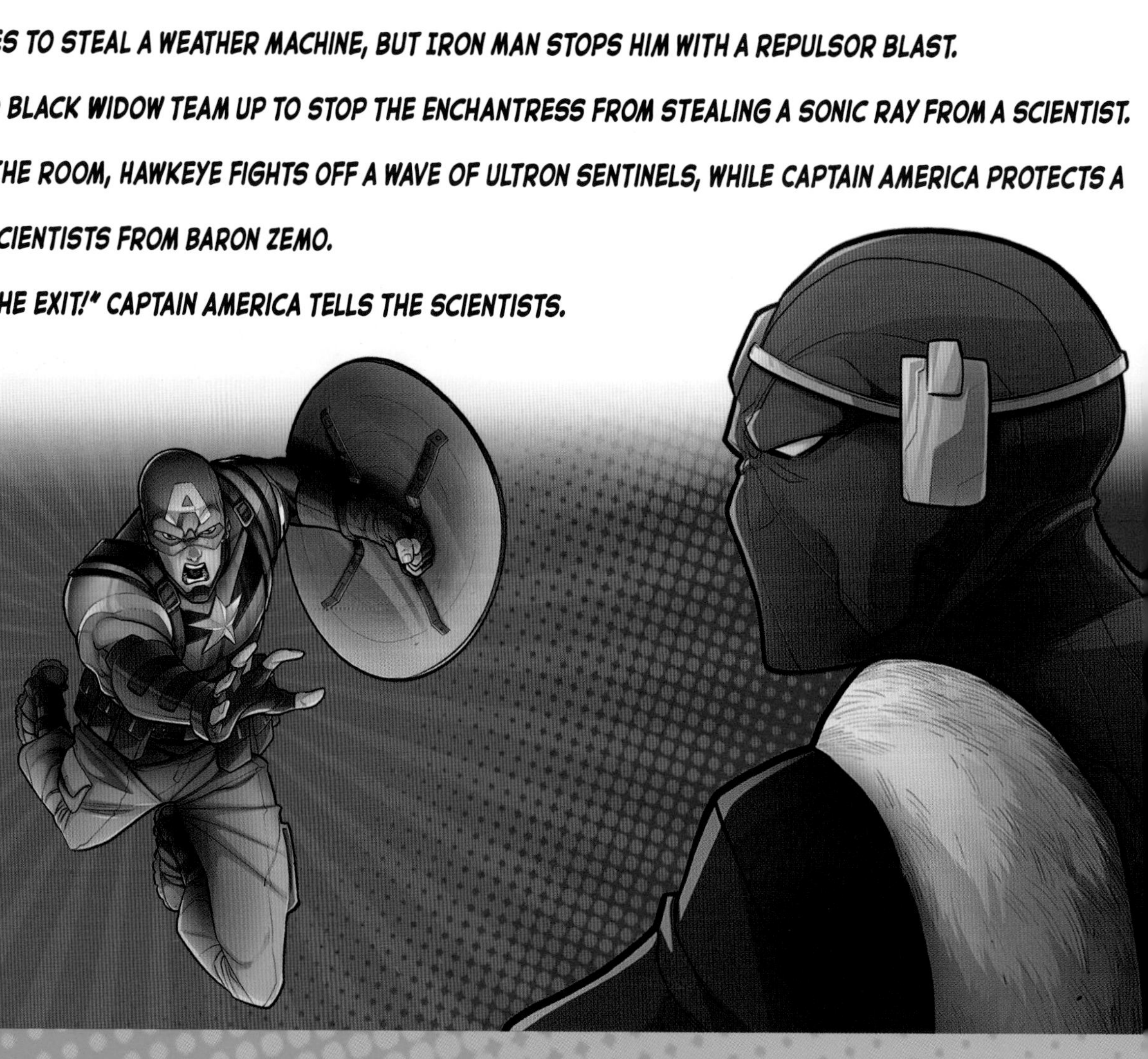

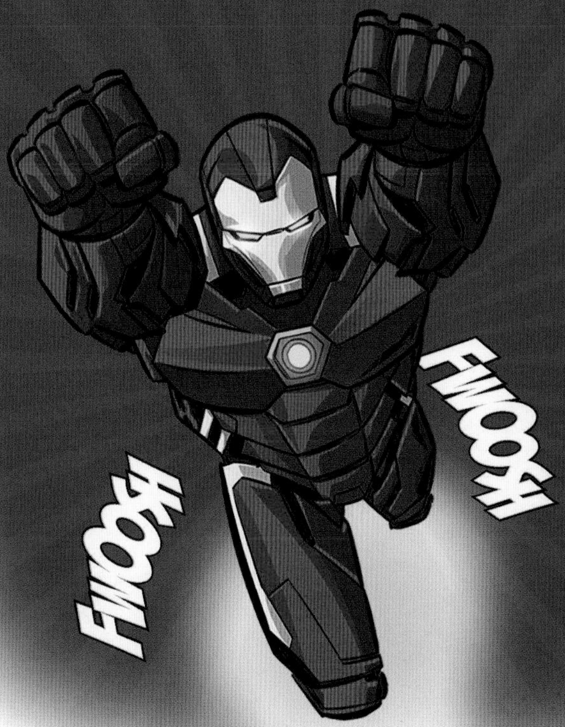
FWOOSH
FWOOSH

ONE SCIENTIST, DR. BRUCE BANNER, DOESN'T RUN FOR THE EXIT. INSTEAD, HE GETS ANGRY. AND WHEN BRUCE BANNER GETS ANGRY, HE BECOMES THE HULK!

THE HULK AND THE REST OF THE AVENGERS BATTLE ULTRON'S SENTINELS. MEANWHILE, THE SUPER VILLAINS RACE TO ESCAPE!

THE VILLAINS REACH THE EXIT, BUT THE SCIENTISTS BLOCK THE WAY WITH THEIR AMAZING INVENTIONS!

"PARTY'S OVER," SAYS IRON MAN.

IRON MAN THANKS THE SCIENTISTS AND APOLOGIZES FOR THE INTERRUPTION.

"DON'T APOLOGIZE," SAYS ONE OF THE SCIENTISTS. "WE GOT TO SHOWCASE OUR INVENTIONS AND HELP THE AVENGERS SAVE THE DAY. THIS WAS THE BEST EXPO EVER!"

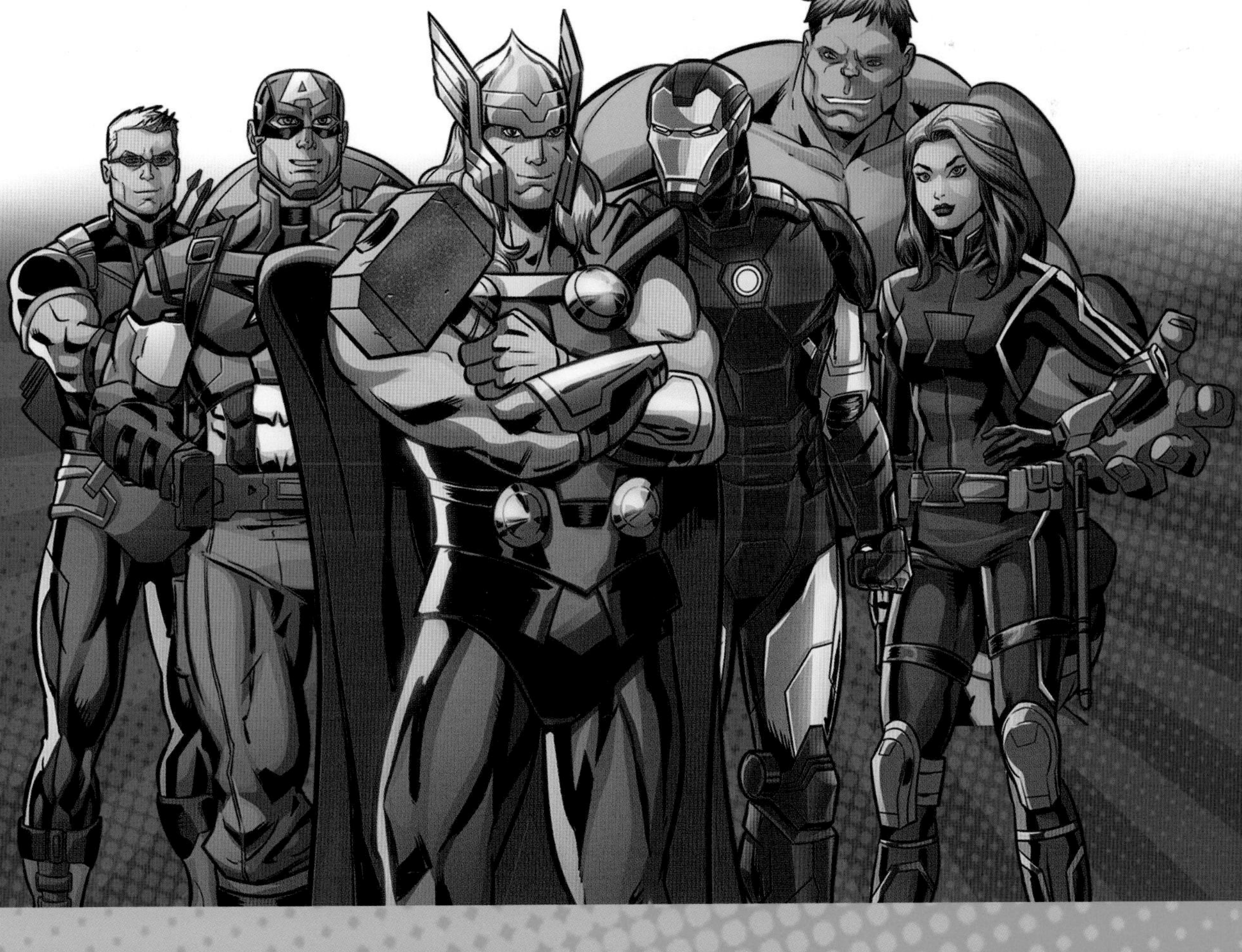

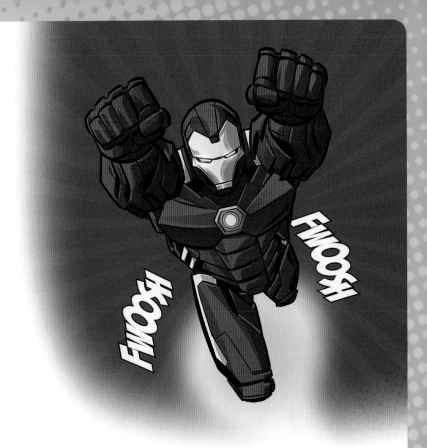

A GROUP OF THIEVES AND THUGS HAVE BROUGHT THEIR CRIMINAL WAYS TO THE WHARF—AND ONLY THE AVENGERS CAN STOP THEM! SIFT THROUGH THE ACTION AND FIND OUR HEROES, THEN HELP THEM SPOT THE LURKING VILLAINS AND OTHER THINGS AROUND THE DOCKS:

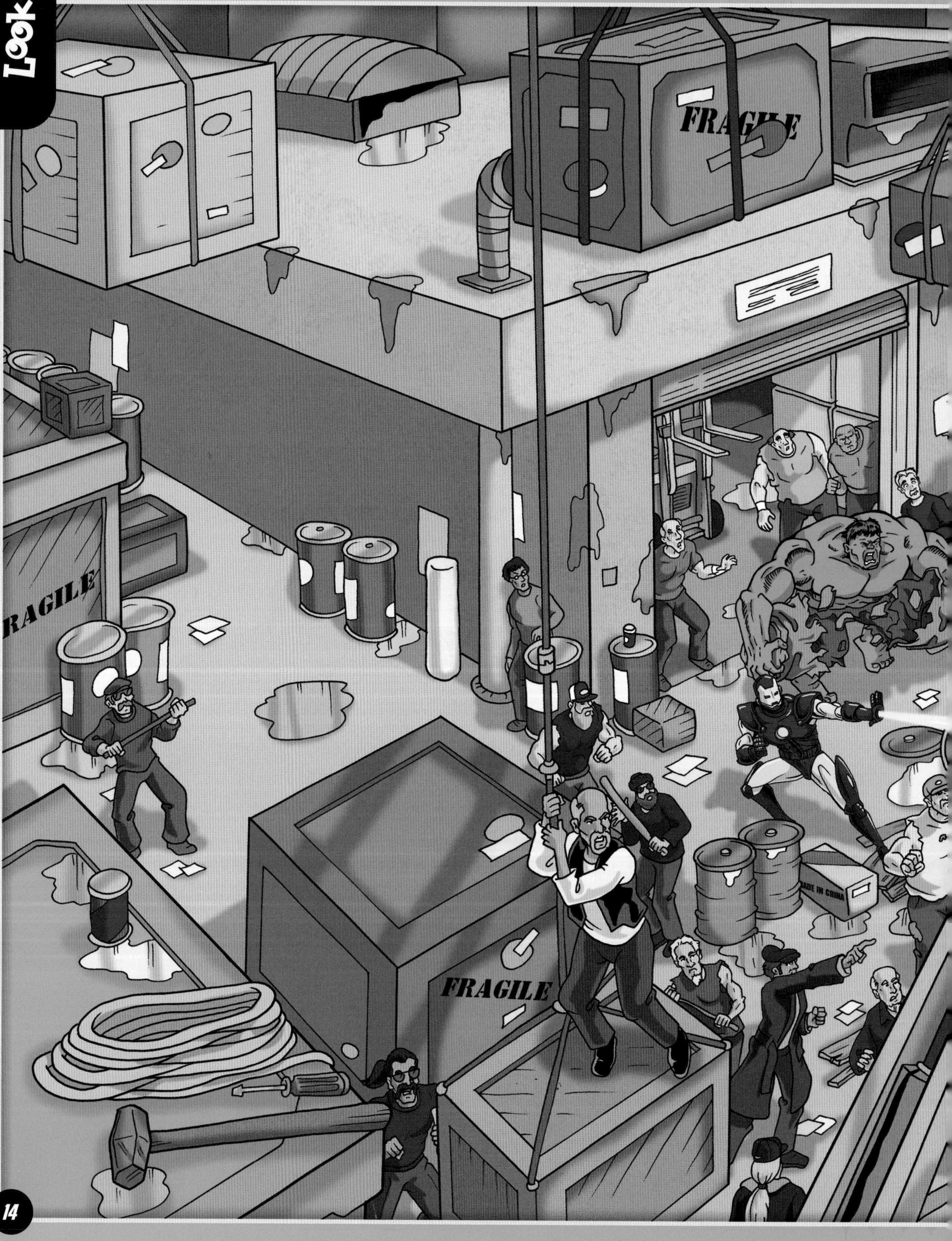
FRAGILE
FRAGILE
FRAGILE
MADE IN CHINA

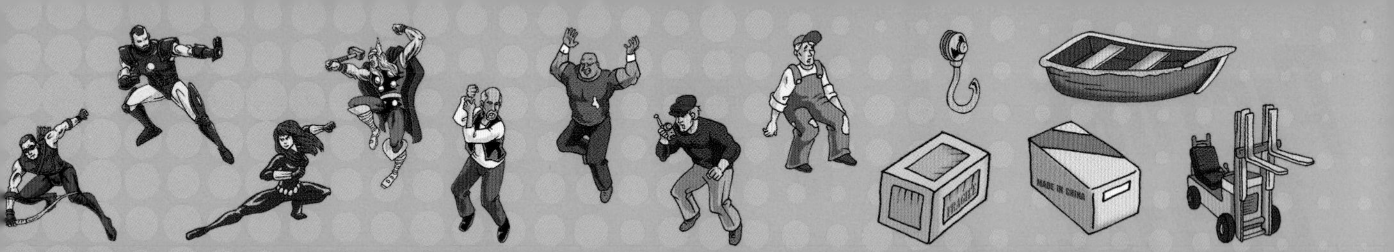
FRAGILE
MADE IN CHINA

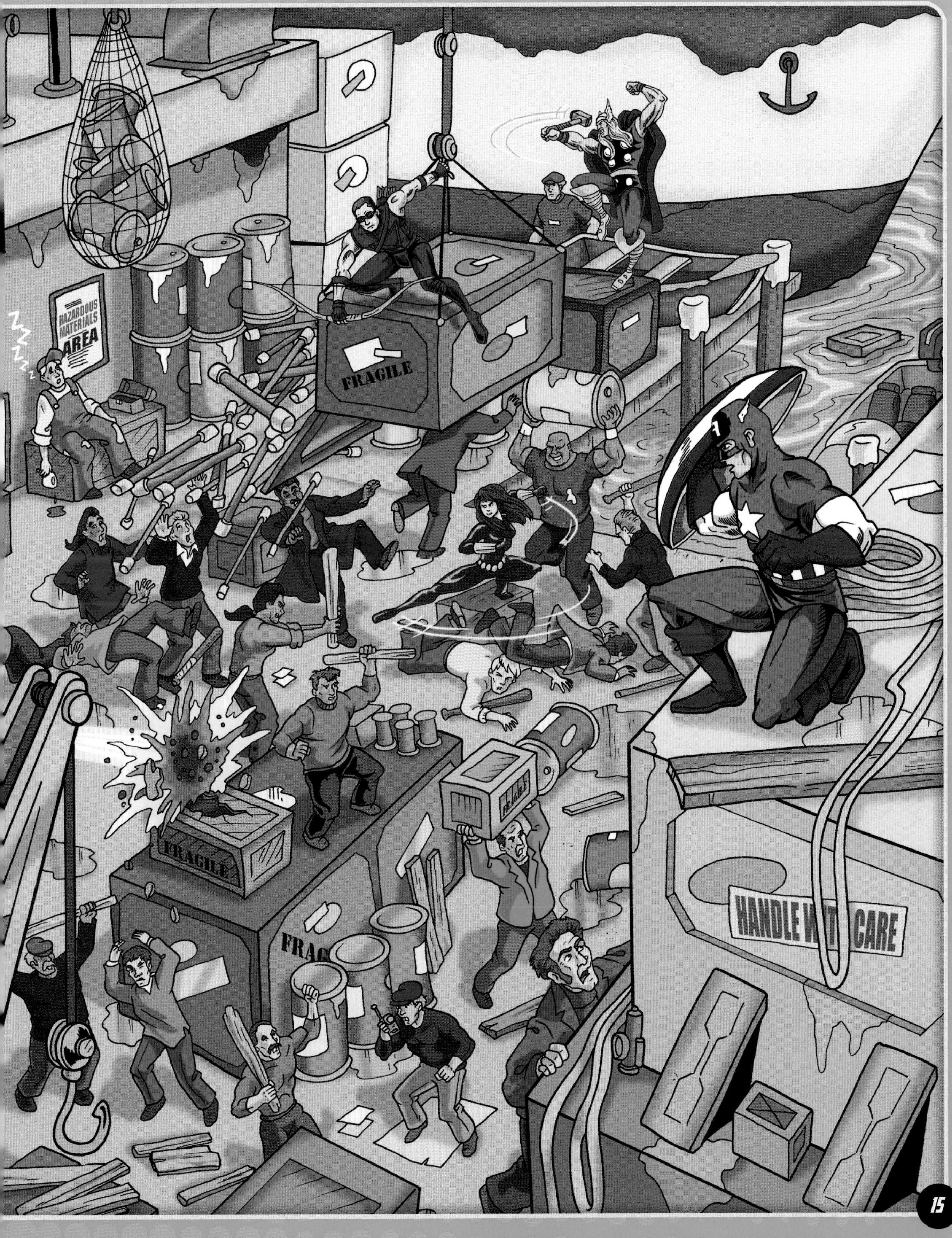
HAZARDOUS MATERIALS AREA
FRAGILE
FRAGILE
FRAGILE
FRAG
HANDLE W CARE

Picture Puzzle

These grouchy ghouls do not want to be disturbed!

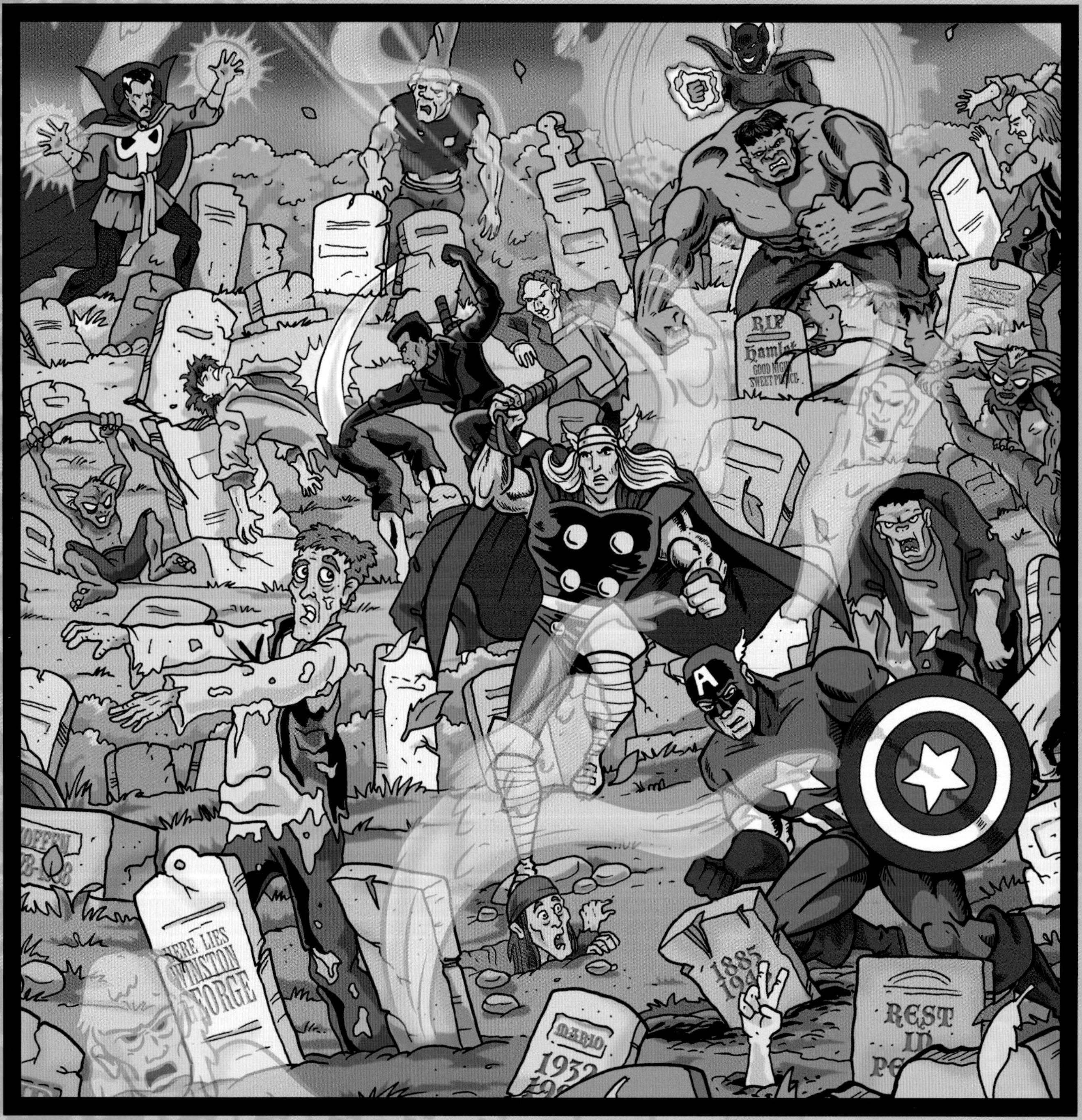

RIP
GOOD NIGHT
SWEET PRINCE
MARIO
REST
IN

HELP KEEP THE PEACE BY SEARCHING FOR 10 DIFFERENCES BETWEEN THESE SCENES.

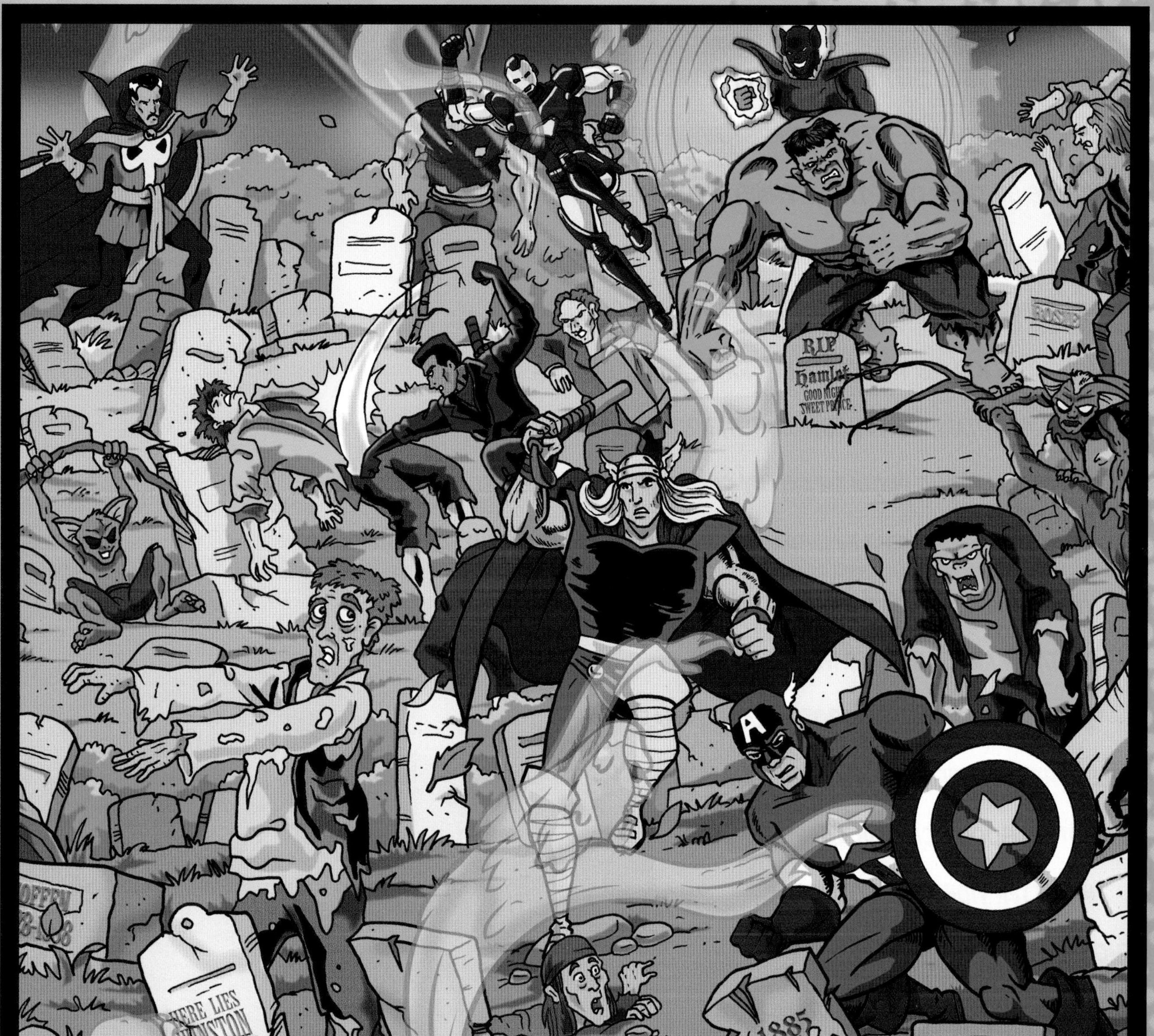
RIP
Hamlet
GOOD NIGHT
SWEET PRINCE
HERE LIES
WINSTON
GEORGE
MARIO
1932
REST
IN
PE

Answer key: Doctor Strange's magic, Iron Man, goblin's eye color, ghost by Frankenstein's monster, monster's shirt color, Thor's buttons, gravestone behind Thor, zombie's pants, star on Cap's shield, rest in peace hand

CAPTAIN IN ACTION

"THIS MIGHT GET MESSY."

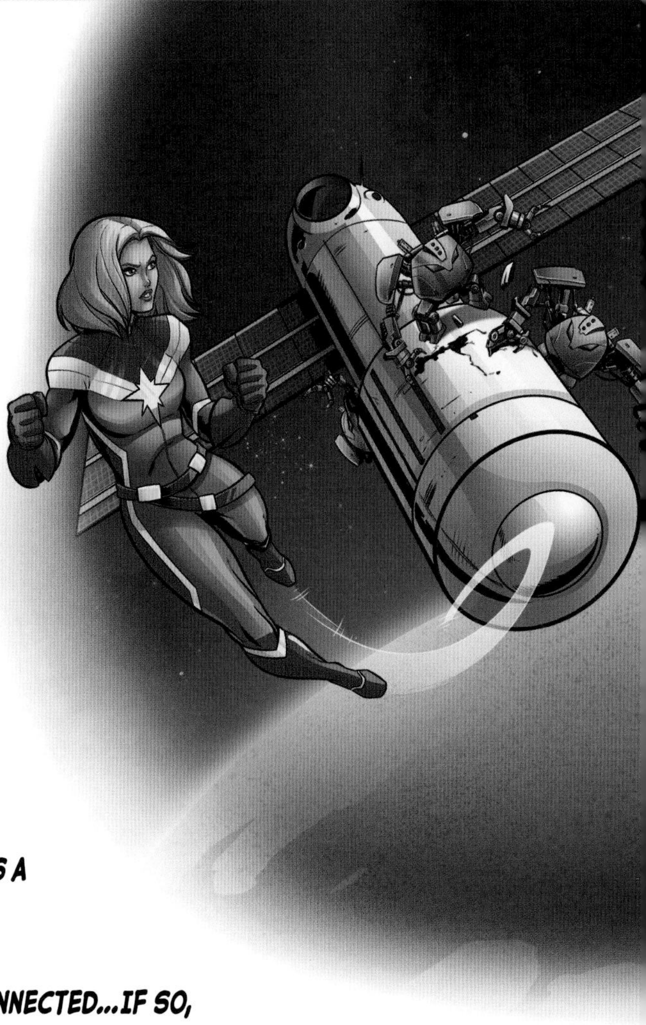

SOMETHING WEIRD IS GOING ON.

IN OUTER SPACE, CAPTAIN MARVEL HAS TRACKED A MYSTERIOUS SIGNAL TO A SMALL ARMY OF SPACE ROBOTS. WHERE ARE THEY FROM? CAPTAIN MARVEL DOESN'T KNOW, BUT THEY'RE CLEARLY UP TO NO GOOD.

BACK ON EARTH, THE AVENGERS ARE HAVING SOME PROBLEMS OF THEIR OWN. THE INTERNET IS DOWN—EVERYWHERE ON EARTH.

THE AVENGERS SEND A MESSAGE TO CAPTAIN MARVEL.

"A VIRUS IS KILLING THE WHOLE INTERNET? YEAH, THAT'S A PROBLEM." CAPTAIN MARVEL LOOKS AT THE ROBOTS.

"I WONDER IF YOUR PROBLEM AND MY PROBLEM ARE CONNECTED...IF SO, MAYBE DESTROYING THESE EVIL SPACE ROBOTS WILL BRING THE INTERNET BACK. AND IF NOT, HEY, FEWER EVIL SPACE ROBOTS!"

CAPTAIN MARVEL GETS TO WORK.

"WELL, I SMASHED THE ROBOTS," CAPTAIN MARVEL TELLS THE AVENGERS. "HOW'S THE INTERNET?"

"NOT SO GOOD," CAPTAIN AMERICA SAYS.

"MY KITTEN VIDEO WILL NOT LOAD," THOR SAYS.

"I'M ON MY WAY," CAPTAIN MARVEL TELLS THEM. "MEET ME AT ALPHA FLIGHT HEADQUARTERS. IF ANYONE CAN TRACK THIS VIRUS, IT'S US."

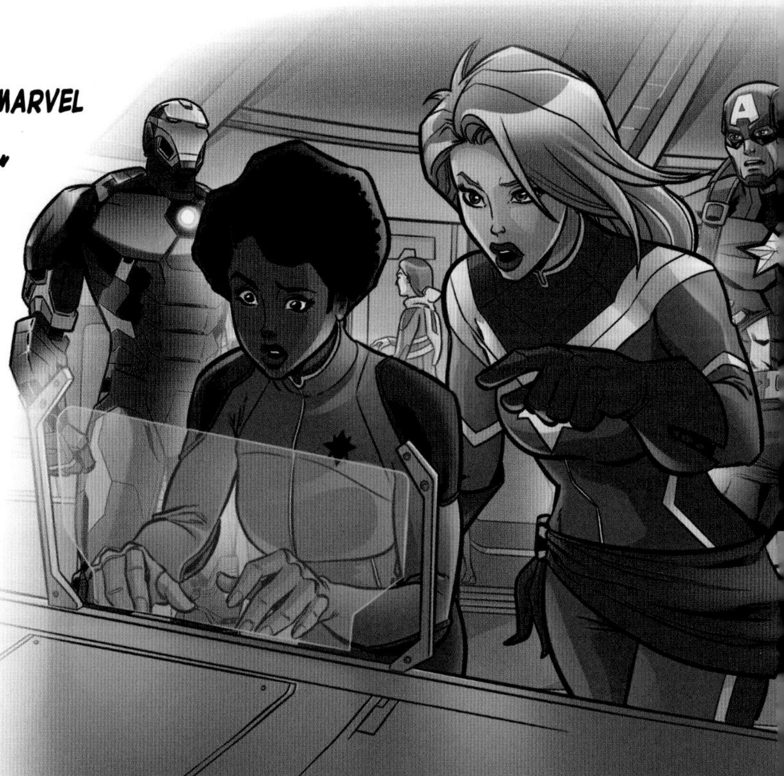

AT ALPHA FLIGHT, THEY TRACE THE VIRUS BACK TO A FAMILIAR SOURCE.

"OF COURSE ULTRON IS BEHIND THIS!" CAPTAIN MARVEL SAYS.

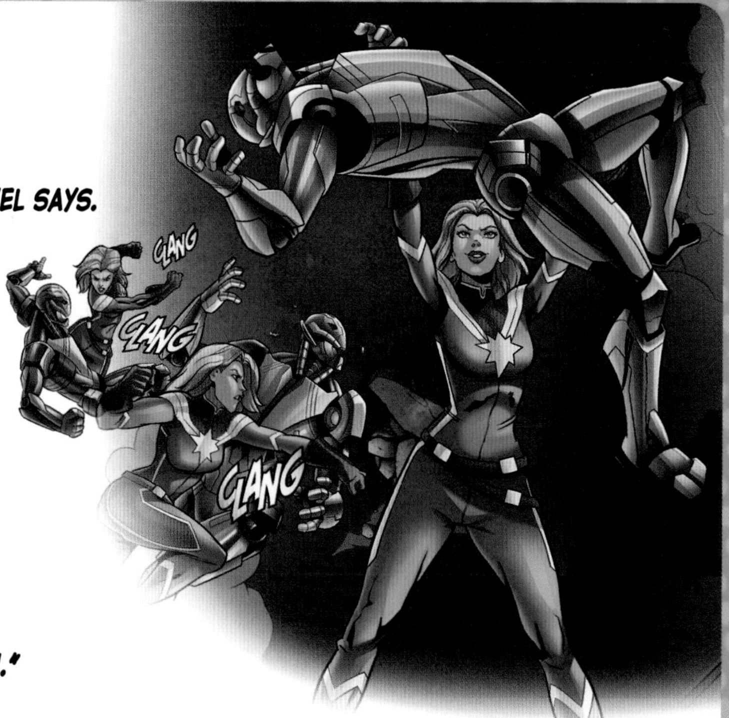
CLANG
CLANG
CLANG

"HE'LL SEE WE'RE FIGHTING HIS VIRUS," IRON MAN SAYS, "AND HE'LL COME HERE TO STOP US."

"HE'S WELCOME TO TRY," CAPTAIN MARVEL SAYS—JUST AS ULTRON BURSTS IN.

"YOU PATHETIC HUMANS THINK YOU CAN STOP ME?" ULTRON SNEERS.

CAPTAIN MARVEL LAUGHS. "I'M NOT *ENTIRELY* HUMAN." SHE POWERS UP FOR A FIGHT.

CAPTAIN MARVEL HITS ULTRON SO HARD THE IMPACT SENDS HIM INTO SPACE!

IN THE BACKGROUND, A COMPUTER DINGS.

"OH GOOD," CAPTAIN MARVEL SAYS. "OUR CODE IS DONE WITH ULTRON'S PROGRAM."

"THE INTERNET'S BACK UP!" IRON MAN SAYS. "TIME TO CELEBRATE."

"MEET YOU AT AVENGERS TOWER?" CAPTAIN MARVEL ASKS.

"PERFECT," SAYS IRON MAN. "AS LONG AS YOU LIKE KITTEN VIDEOS."

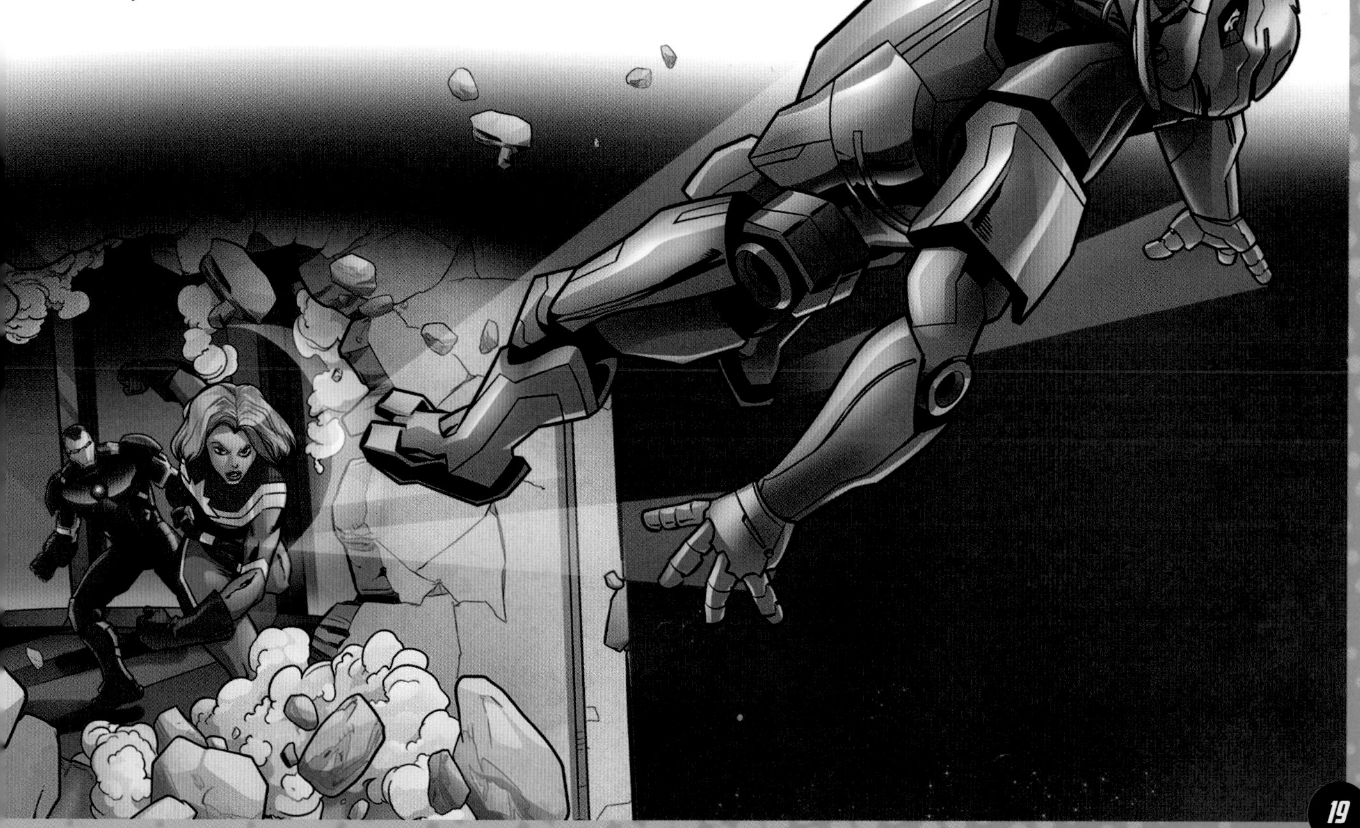

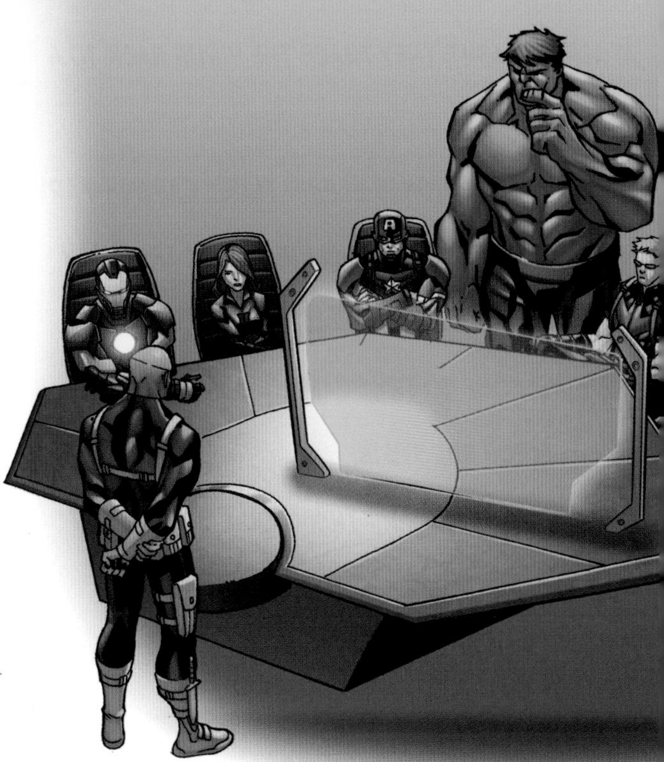

THE MOON MENACE

"IRON MAN ARMOR: ACTIVATE!"

NICK FURY HAS BAD NEWS FOR THE AVENGERS.

"WE HAVE TWO CRISES THAT REQUIRE IMMEDIATE ATTENTION," FURY SAYS. "FIRST, COUNT NEFARIA IS ROBBING AN ART MUSEUM."

"WE'LL TAKE CARE OF IT," SAYS CAPTAIN AMERICA. "WHAT'S PROBLEM NUMBER TWO?"

"THERE'S BEEN EXPLOSIVE ACTIVITY ON THE MOON," SAYS FURY. "ONE OF YOU SHOULD INVESTIGATE IMMEDIATELY."

"WE'D BETTER SPLIT UP," IRON MAN SAYS. "BESIDES, I'VE BEEN MEANING TO GIVE MY FANCY NEW SPACESHIP A SPIN."

WHILE THE AVENGERS ARE OCCUPIED WITH COUNT NEFARIA, IRON MAN FLIES TO THE MOON AT LIGHT SPEED. HE'S SHOCKED TO LEARN THAT THANOS AND HIS ARMY OF OUTRIDERS HAVE LANDED ON THE MOON AND ARE PREPARING TO TAKE OVER EARTH.

THIS JOB IS TOO BIG FOR ONE AVENGER, IRON MAN THINKS.

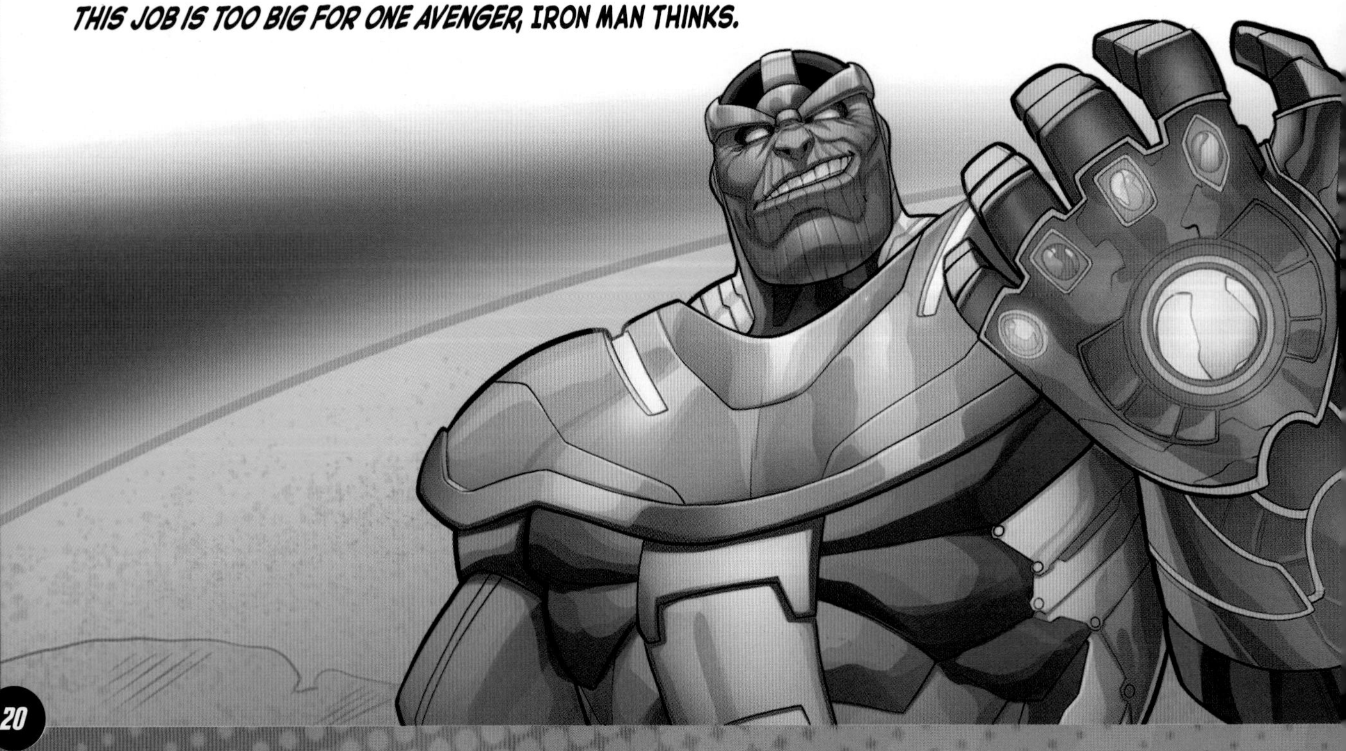

HE CALLS IN HELP FROM THE GUARDIANS OF THE GALAXY.

WITH A BOOST FROM NOVA CORPS, THE GUARDIANS TELEPORT TO THE MOON IN THE *MILANO.*

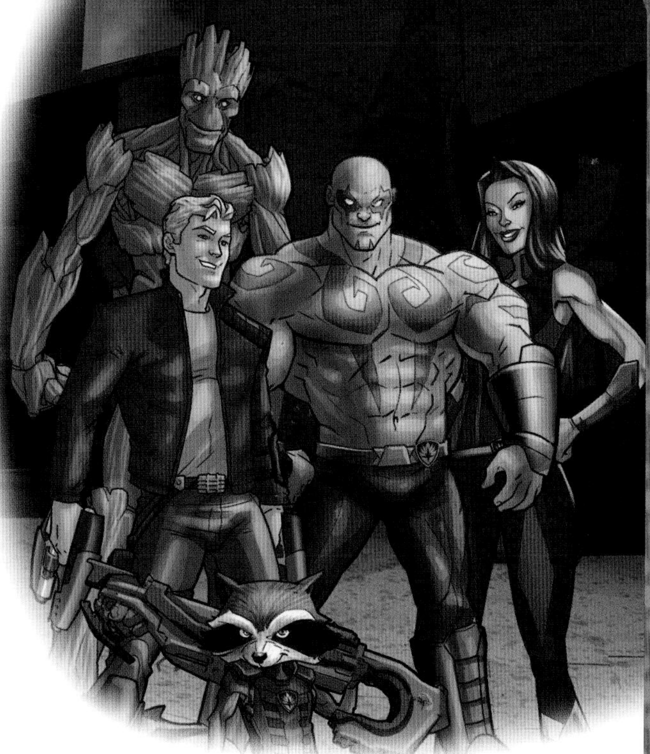

"HOPE WE DIDN'T MISS THE PARTY!" SAYS GAMORA. THE GUARDIANS AND IRON MAN FEND OFF THE OUTRIDERS UNTIL, TO THEIR SURPRISE, THE REMAINING AVENGERS ARRIVE IN THEIR QUINJET.

TOGETHER, THE HEROES EASILY DEFEAT THANOS AND HIS ARMY.

"YOU GOT HERE FAST," IRON MAN TELLS THE AVENGERS.

"COUNT NEFARIA WAS A PIECE OF CAKE," SAYS HAWKEYE.

"PLUS, WE THOUGHT YOU MIGHT NEED SOME BACKUP," CAPTAIN AMERICA CHIMES IN.

"WHAT?" SAYS IRON MAN. "YOU THINK I CAN'T HANDLE AN ENTIRE RACE OF ALIEN WARRIORS WITH CLAWS AND RAZOR-SHARP TEETH ALL BY MYSELF?"

CAPTAIN AMERICA JUST ROLLS HIS EYES.

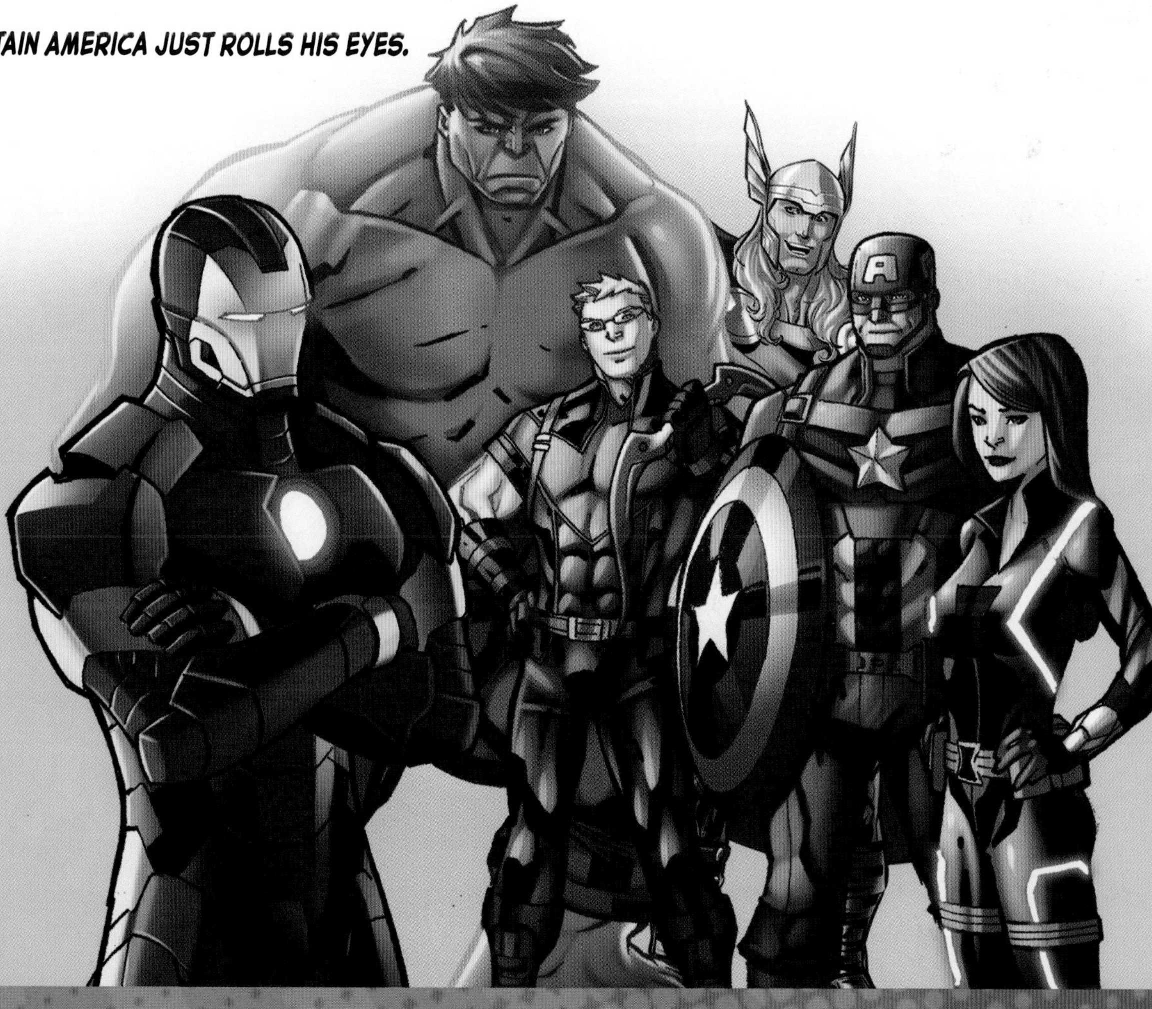

COUNT NEFARIA AND MADAME MASQUE ARE MAKING TROUBLE, AND THEIR GOONS ARE LOOTING THE STREETS OF ROME. THAT'S A LOT FOR IRON MAN TO HANDLE ALONE, BUT LUCKILY THE GUARDIANS OF THE GALAXY ARE IN TOWN, AND THEY DON'T MIND STOPPING IN TO HELP SAVE THE DAY. HELP MAKE ITALY SAFE BY CATCHING THESE BAD GUYS COMMITTING CRIMES AND IDENTIFYING THE ITALIAN ART THEY'VE FORGED

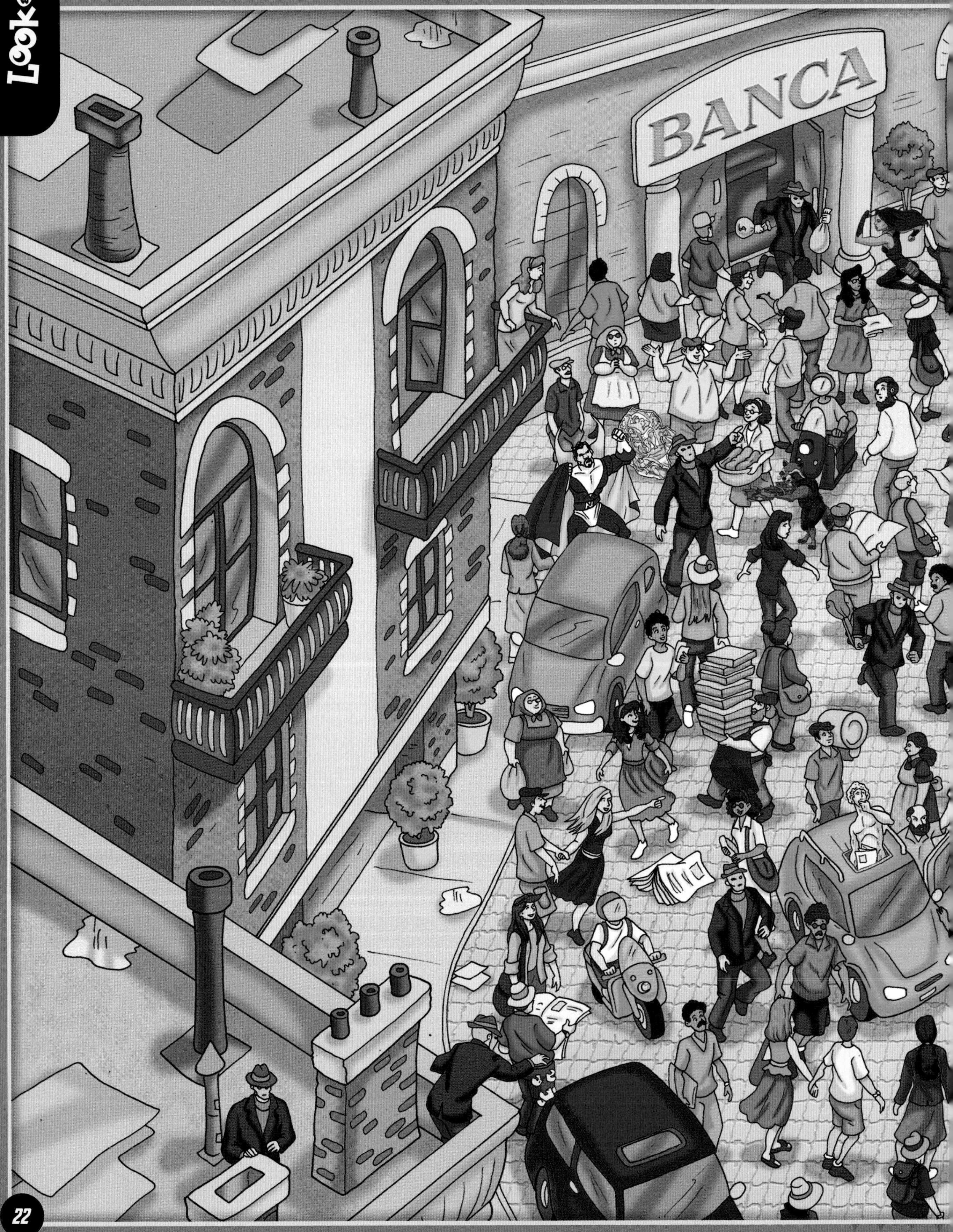
BANCA

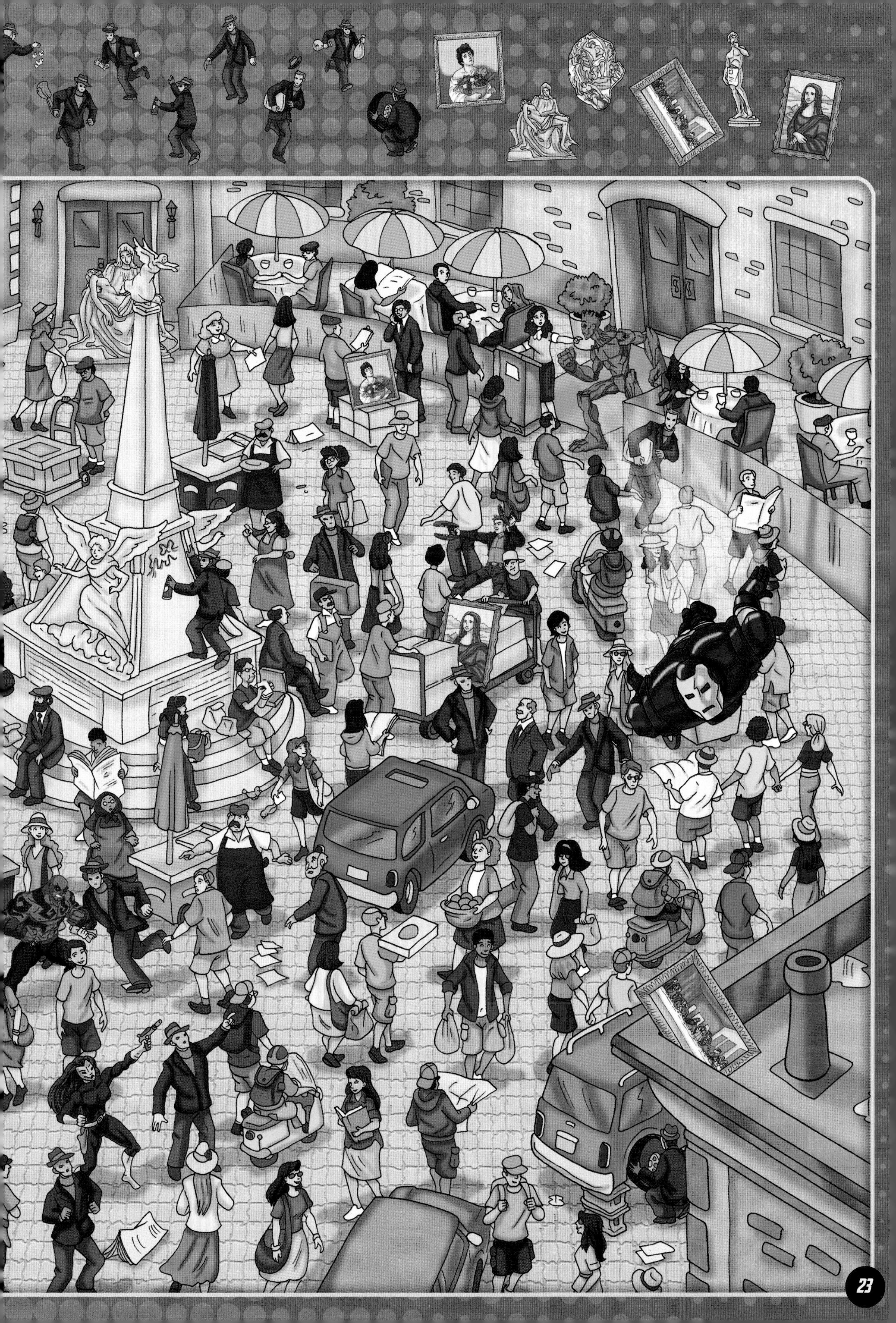

PICTURE PUZZLE

IRON MAN LOVES HIS FANS AS MUCH AS HE LOVES VANQUISHING EVIL.

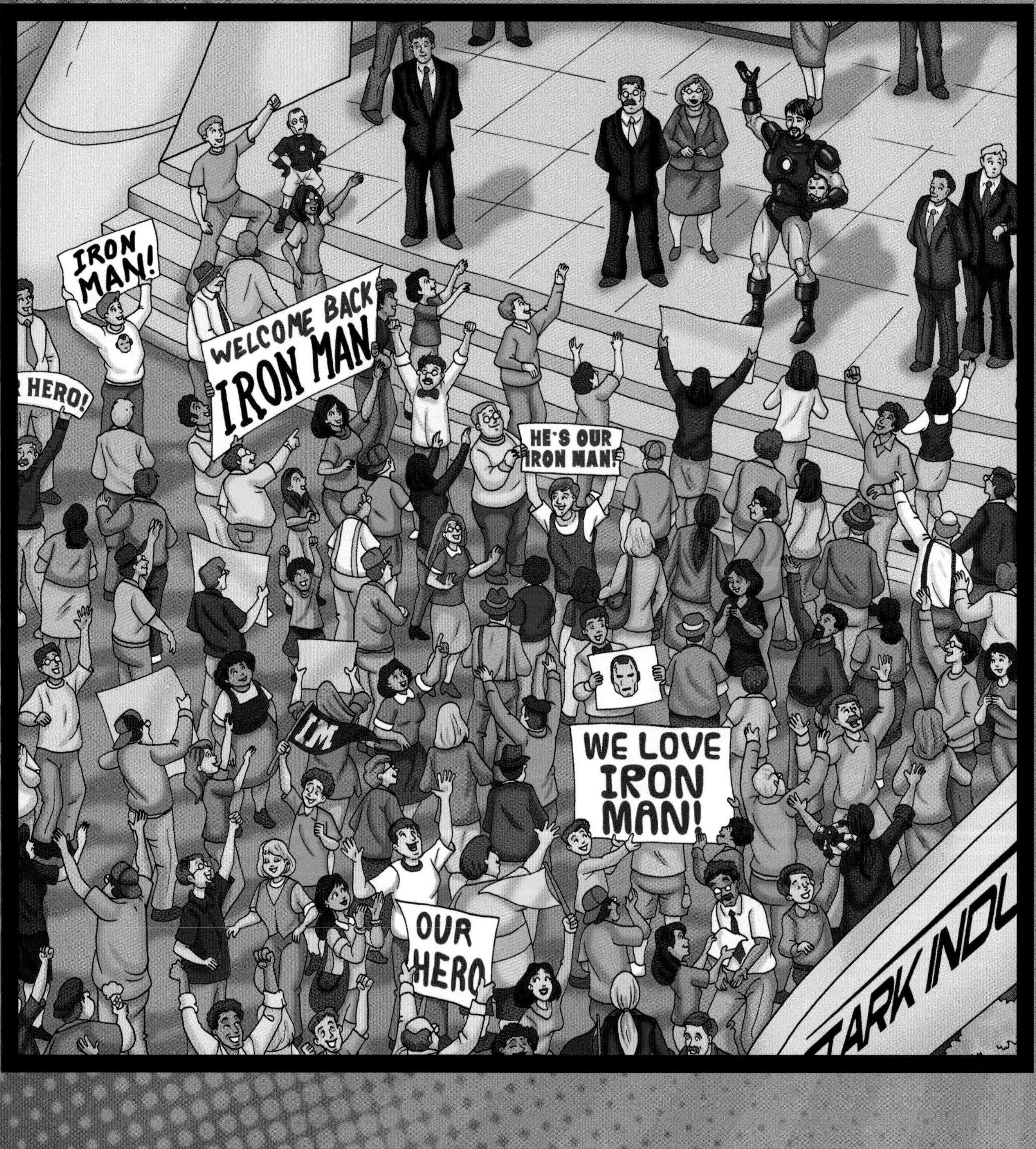

IRON MAN!
WELCOME BACK IRON MAN
R HERO!
HE'S OUR IRON MAN!
I.M
WE LOVE IRON MAN!
OUR HERO
STARK INDU

HELP CELEBRATE BY SEARCHING FOR 10 DIFFERENCES BETWEEN THESE SCENES.

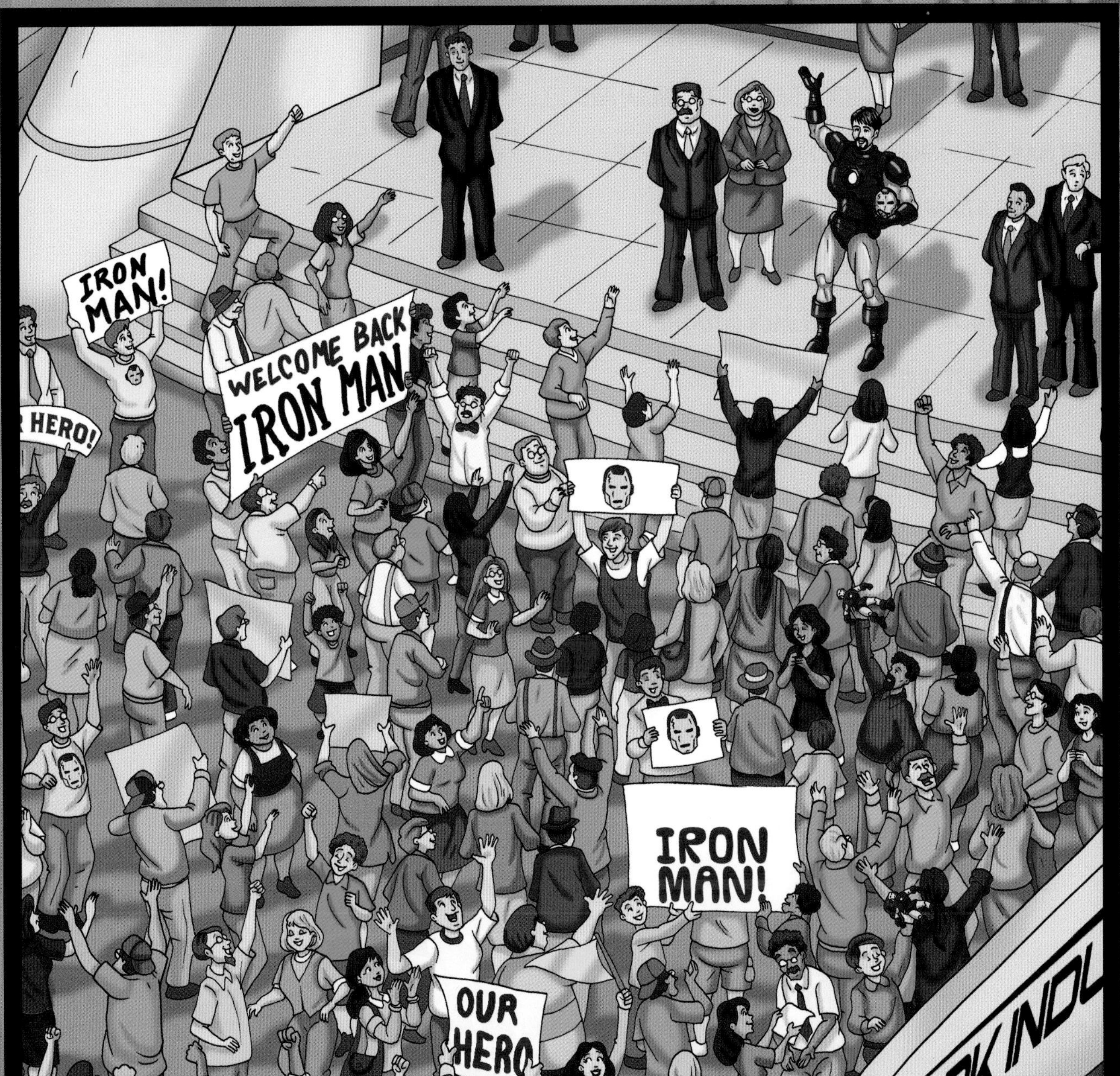
IRON MAN!
WELCOME BACK IRON MAN
R HERO!
IRON MAN!
OUR HERO
TARK INDU

Answer key: color of Iron Man sweater, kid in costume, color of middle suit, He's Our Iron Man sign, Iron Man face on T-shirt, IM flag, color of polo shirt in bottom left, color of Our Hero sign, We Love Iron Man sign, upraised action figure

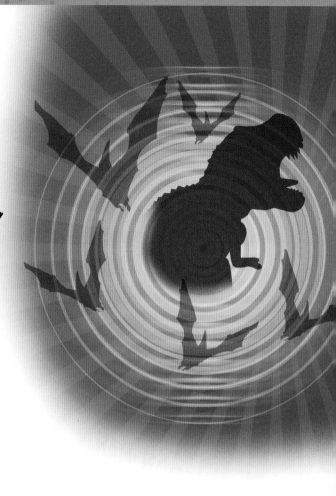

DINO DANGER

"HULK SMASH!"

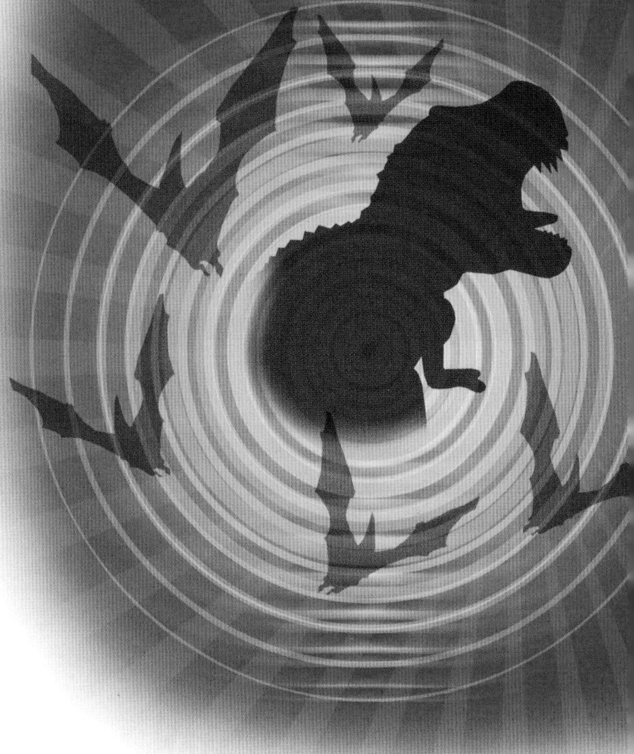

NICK FURY RACES INTO THE AVENGERS' LAB.

"A STRANGE PORTAL HAS OPENED IN CENTRAL PARK!" HE TELLS DR. BRUCE BANNER AND TONY STARK.

BANNER AND STARK QUICKLY BECOME THE HULK AND IRON MAN. THEY RACE TO THE PARK AND DISCOVER... DINOSAURS STOMPING THROUGH THE PORTAL!

IRON MAN SETS HIS BLAST RAYS TO STUN.

"WE HAVE TO GET THE DINOS BACK INTO THE PORTAL WITHOUT HURTING THEM," HE SAYS.

"HULK GENTLE!" SAYS HULK.

IRON MAN BATTLES A PTERODACTYL WHILE HULK WRESTLES A T. REX. JUST IN TIME, THE QUINJET LANDS. THE REST OF THE AVENGERS HAVE ARRIVED!

THE AVENGERS FIGHT THE DINOSAURS BACK, BUT MORE AND MORE KEEP COMING THROUGH THE PORTAL.

IN A MIGHTY FEAT OF STRENGTH, HULK HURLS AN ENORMOUS CHUNK OF EARTH AT THE DINOSAURS, BOWLING THE BEASTS BACK INTO THE PORTAL. THEN THE PORTAL CLOSES BEHIND THEM.

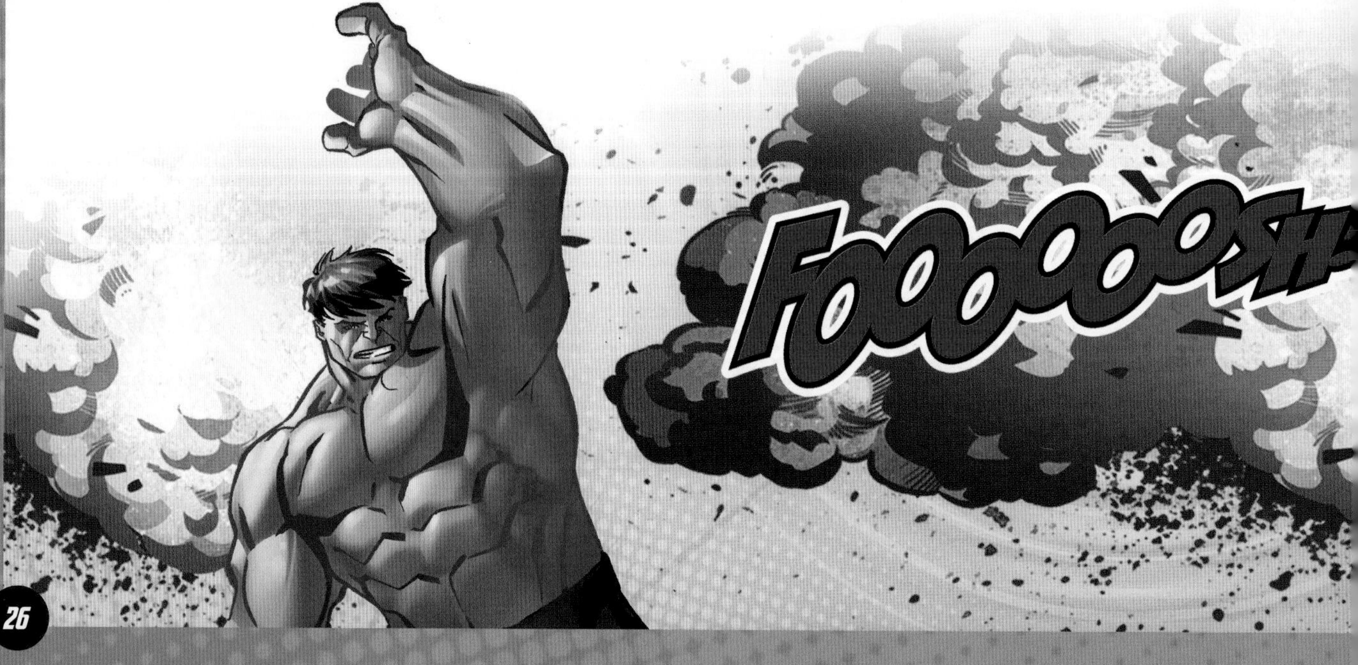
FOOOOOOSH

JUST AS THE HEROES THINK THE DANGER IS DONE, LOKI APPEARS.

"NOW THAT MY DINOSAURS HAVE TIRED YOU OUT," LOKI SAYS, "THE REAL FUN CAN BEGIN!"

WITH A WAVE OF HIS STAFF, LOKI UNLEASHES AN ARMY OF EVIL ASGARDIANS!

THE AVENGERS BATTLE LOKI'S ARMY WITH ALL THEIR MIGHT.

"NO NEED TO BE GENTLE THIS TIME, HULK!" SAYS IRON MAN.

AFTER A FEROCIOUS FIGHT, THE EXHAUSTED AVENGERS MANAGE TO DEFEAT LOKI AND HIS ARMY.

"NICE TRY, LOKI," SAYS CAPTAIN AMERICA WITH A YAWN. "BUT THE AVENGERS WILL ALWAYS BE UP FOR SAVING THE WORLD!"

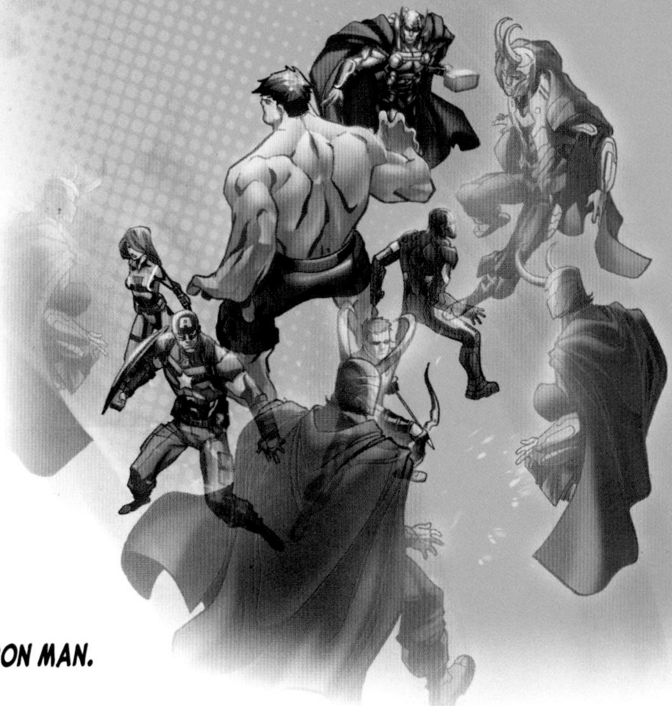

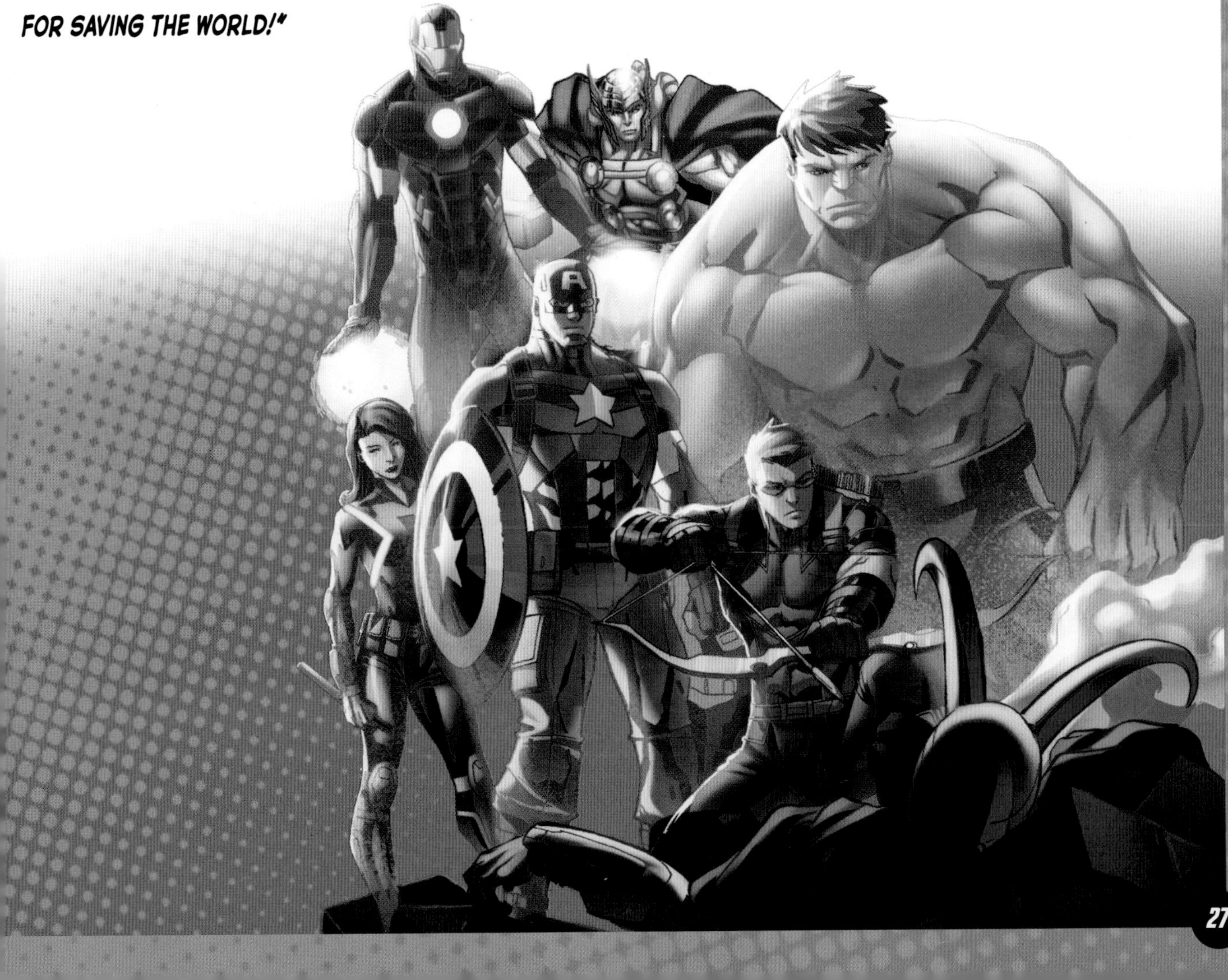

THE AVENGERS HAVE HIDDEN THE INFINITY GEMS DEEP INSIDE A DESERT WASTELAND, BUT THANOS HAS UNCOVERED THEIR PLOT! IF HE GETS HIS HANDS ON THE GEMS, HE WILL HAVE MORE POWER THAN THEY CAN POSSIBLY IMAGINE. HULK PROVIDES A DISTRACTION WHILE THE REST OF THE AVENGERS STRIKE! FIND HULK'S FELLOW FIGHTERS AND THESE INFINITY GEMS BEFORE THANOS DOES:

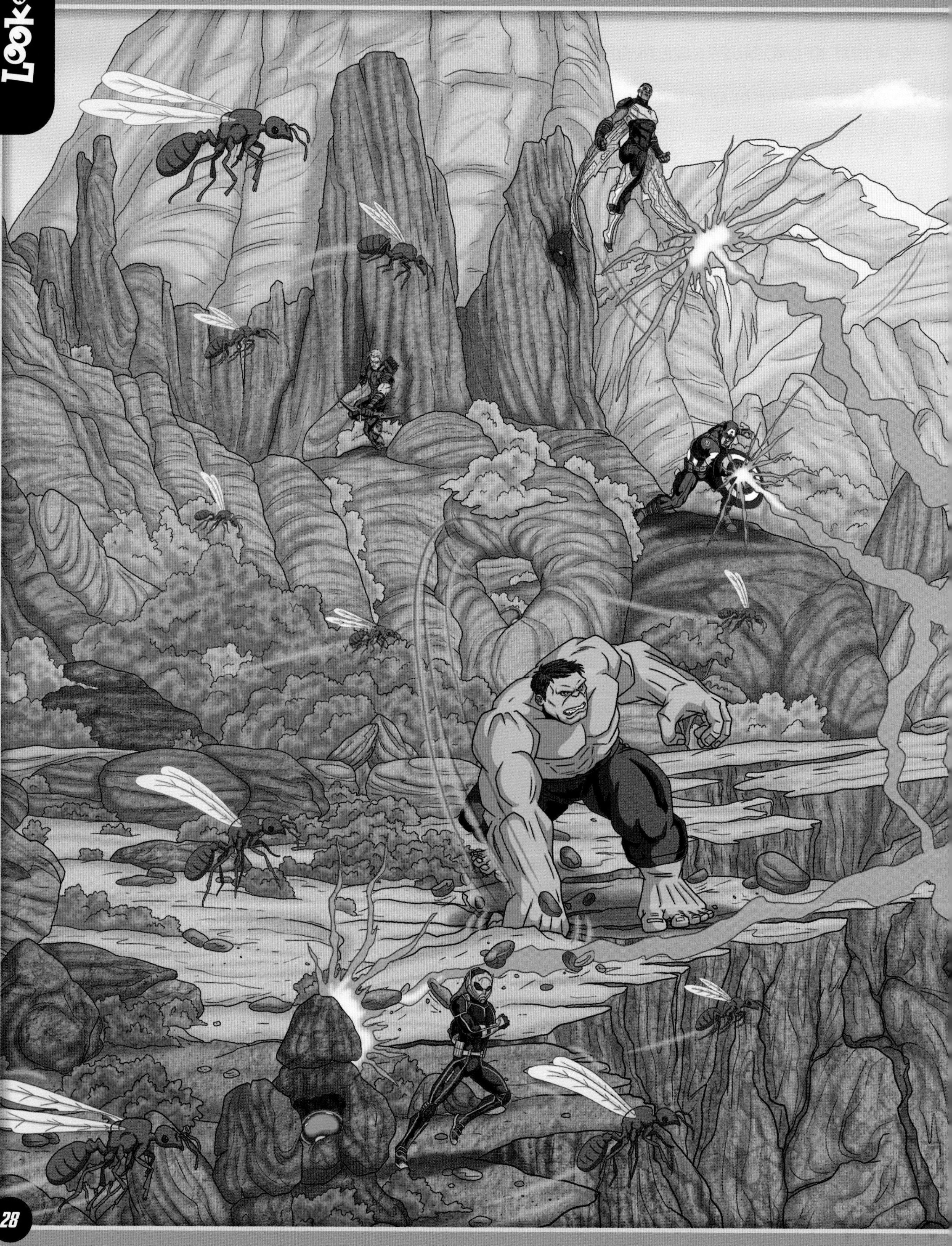

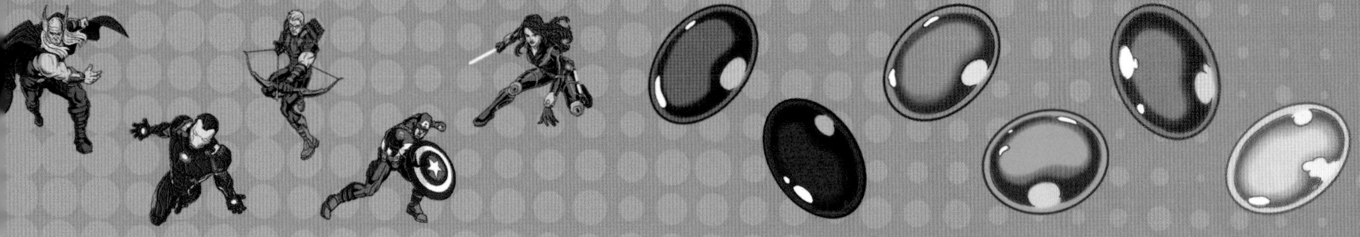

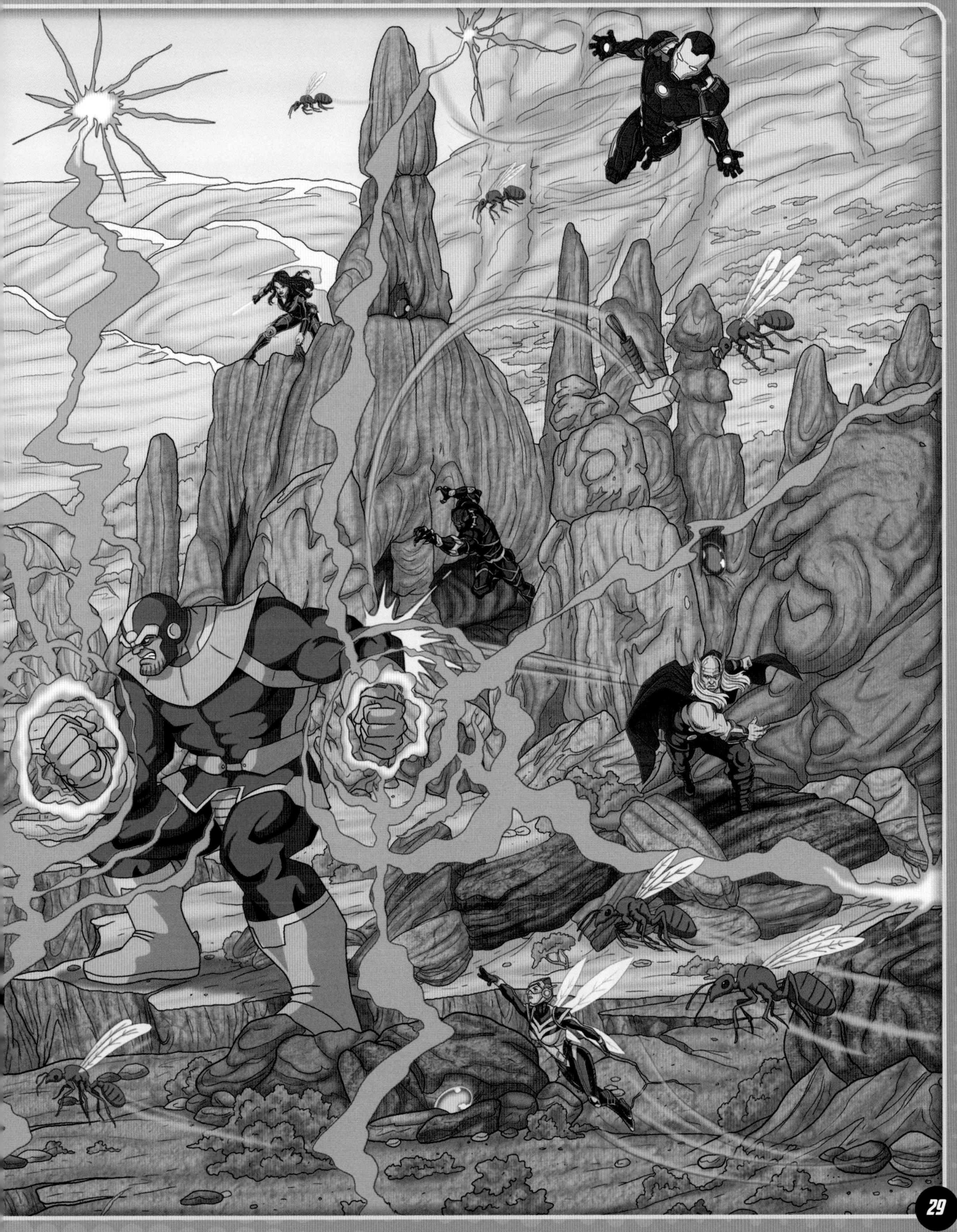

PICTURE PUZZLE

THE ABOMINATION SURE CASTS A CLOUD OVER A BEAUTIFUL DAY!

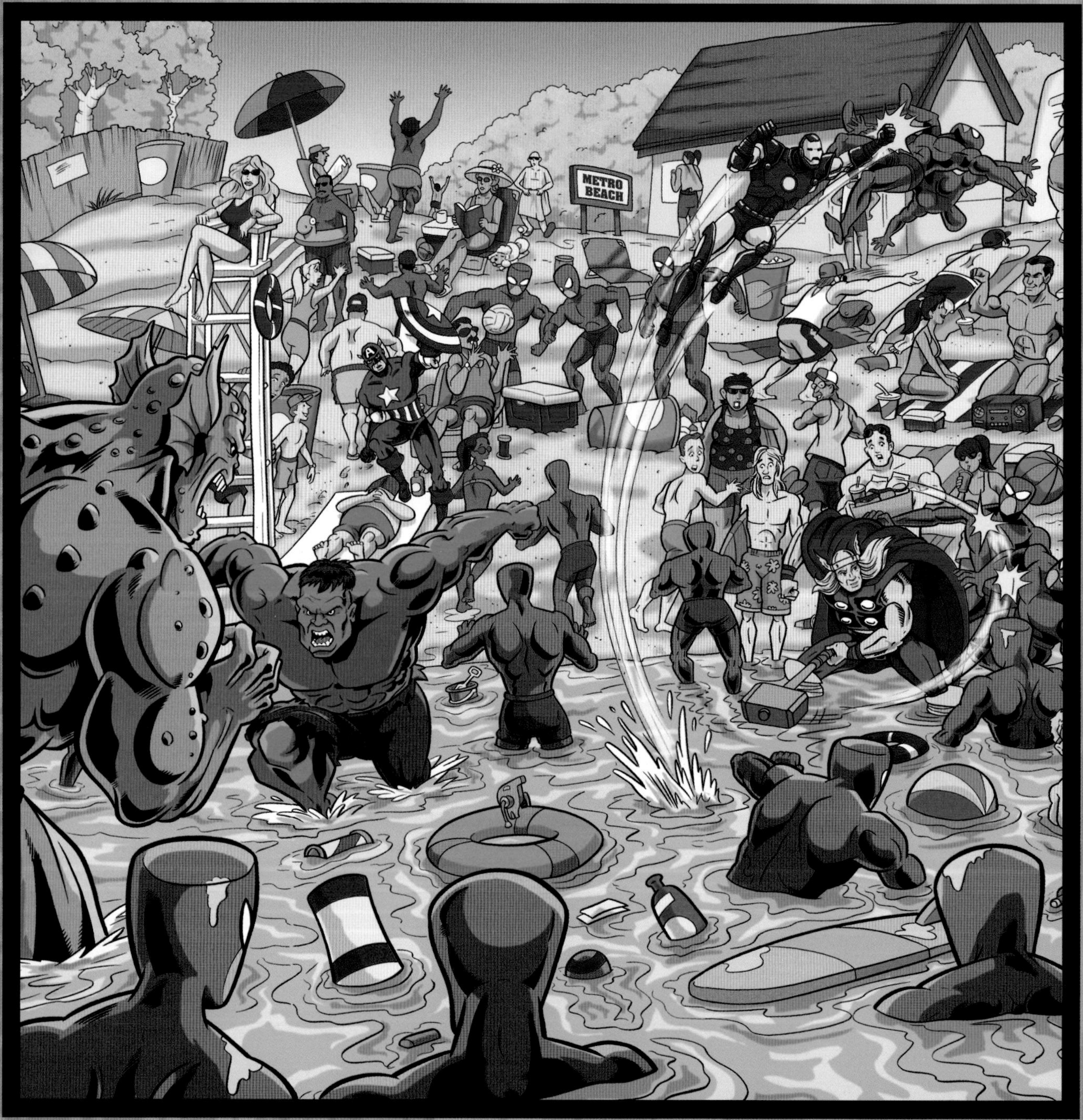
METRO BEACH

FIND 10 DIFFERENCES BETWEEN THESE SUNNY SCENES.

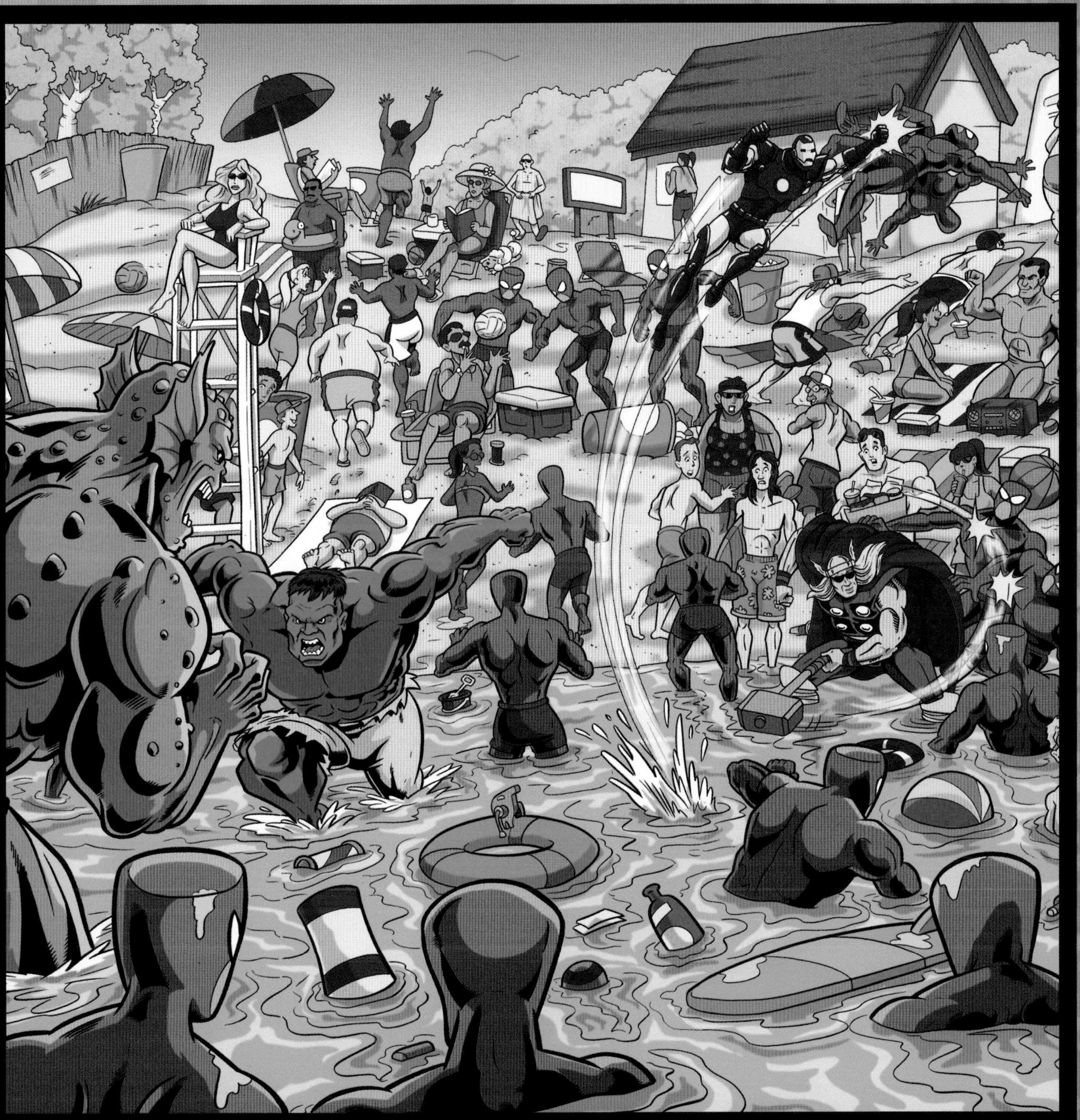

Answer key: trash can by the fence, blue volleyball, Captain America, Metro Beach sign, cooler color, surfer's hair color, Hulk's shorts color, Thor's sunglasses, floating surf board color, pail color

OUT OF THE RED ROOM

"THE COVERT AVENGER!"

NATASHA ROMANOFF IS THE RED ROOM'S PERFECT AGENT: AN EXPERT FIGHTER AND A CUNNING SPY, WHO IS CONDITIONED WITH ABSOLUTE LOYALTY.

THE RED ROOM GIVES HER THE TITLE OF BLACK WIDOW AND A DANGEROUS WEAPON: THE WIDOW'S BITE, BRACELETS THAT FIRE POWERFUL BOLTS OF ELECTRICITY.

NATASHA SLOWLY REALIZES THAT HER MISSIONS ARE HURTING INNOCENT PEOPLE, BUT SHE DOESN'T SEE ANY WAY OUT...UNTIL SHE MEETS A HERO NAMED HAWKEYE.

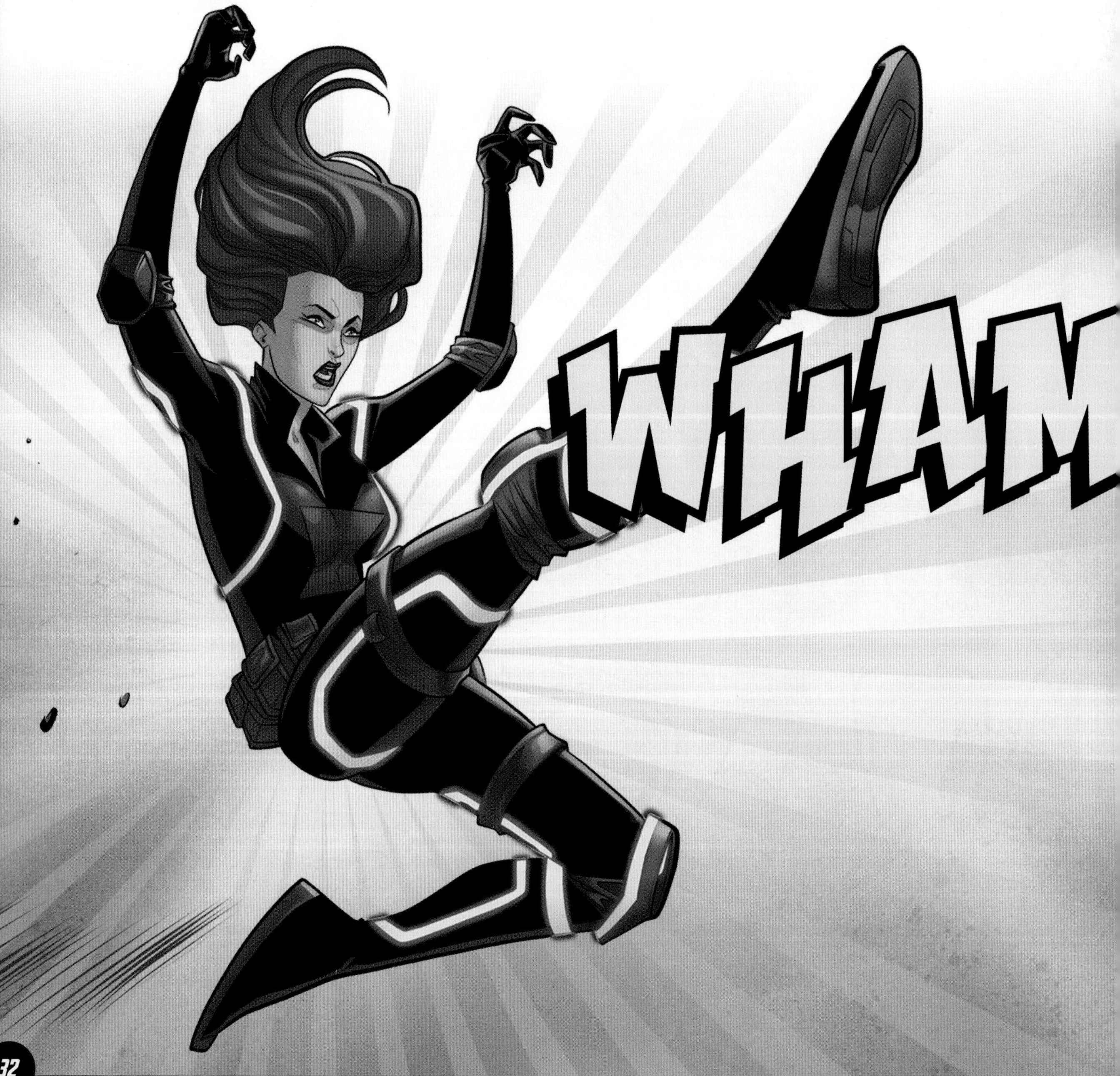
WHAM

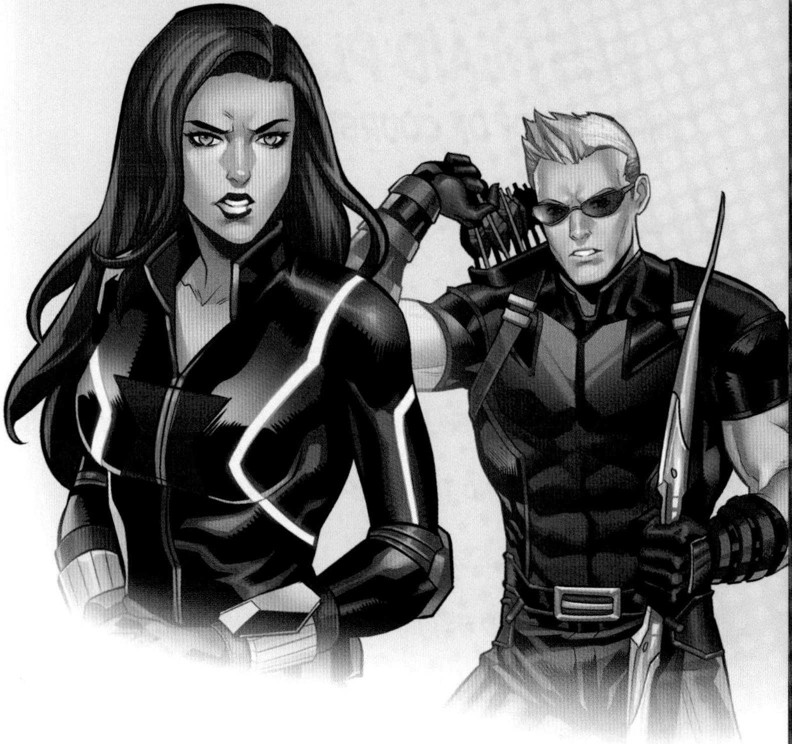

"I'M SO TIRED," NATASHA TELLS HIM. "I JUST WISH I COULD HELP PEOPLE INSTEAD."

"YOU CAN," HAWKEYE SAYS. "COME WITH ME. I KNOW A GUY."

HAWKEYE INTRODUCES NATASHA TO NICK FURY, WHO GIVES HER A JOB WITH HAWKEYE AT S.H.I.E.L.D.

ONE DAY, FURY CALLS THEM WITH THEIR BIGGEST MISSION YET. "WE'RE GOING TO NEED ALL HANDS ON DECK FOR THIS ONE," NICK FURY SAYS. "IT'S TIME TO MEET THE REST OF THE TEAM."

BLACK WIDOW AND HAWKEYE JOIN A SUPER HERO TEAM DEDICATED TO PROTECTING THE EARTH. FROM THAT DAY ON, BLACK WIDOW IS AN AVENGER.

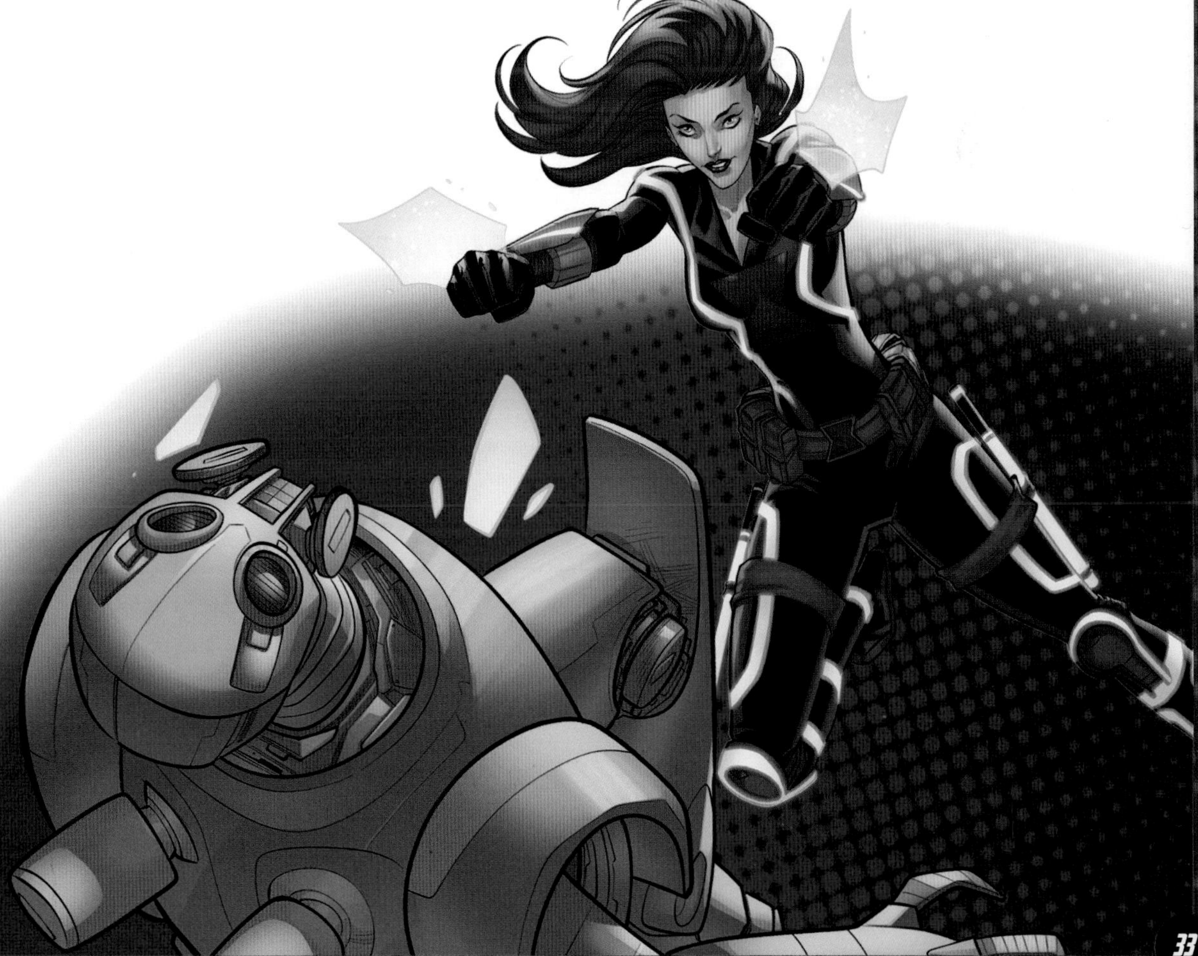

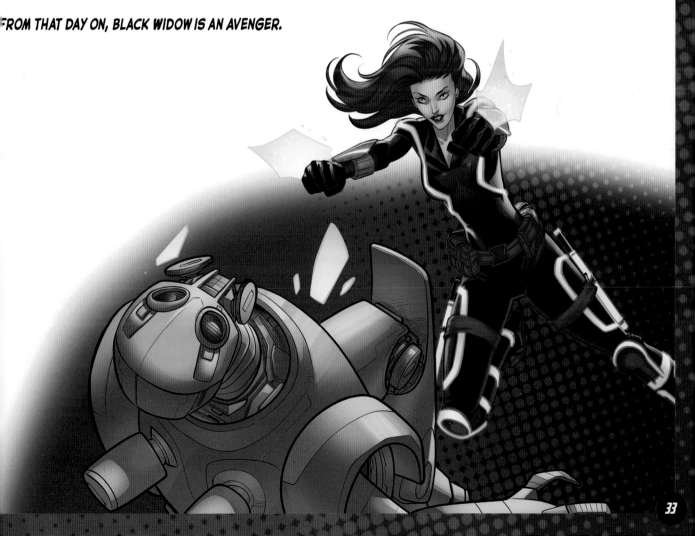

BEST-LAID PLANS
"IMPRESSED? OF COURSE YOU ARE!"

BLACK WIDOW AND HAWKEYE SNEAK THROUGH A SECRET HYDRA BASE.

ON HER LAST MISSION, BLACK WIDOW FOUND OUT THAT HYDRA IS BUILDING A NEW SUPERWEAPON. NOW, SHE AND HAWKEYE HAVE TO FIND THE WEAPON PLANS AND BRING THEM BACK TO S.H.I.E.L.D.

"WE JUST NEED TO GET IN, GET THE PLANS, AND GET OUT," BLACK WIDOW SAYS.

THE PLANS ARE IN A LOCKED VAULT DEEP INSIDE THE BASE.

"THEY COULDN'T MAKE THIS EASY ON US, HUH?" HAWKEYE JOKES.

"I CAN OPEN THE VAULT," BLACK WIDOW SAYS, "BUT THEY'LL HAVE ROBOTS PATROLLING."

"MY HAWK EYES ARE ON IT," HAWKEYE SAYS, HEADING INTO THE HALL TO KEEP WATCH.

BLACK WIDOW NEEDS TO HACK THE SYSTEM—WITHOUT TRIGGERING ANY ALARMS!

"WE'VE GOT THE PLANS!" BLACK WIDOW TELLS HAWKEYE.

"WE'VE ALSO GOT COMPANY," HAWKEYE CALLS BACK. A HYDRA PATROL JUST SPOTTED HIM, AND ROBOTS ARE POURING IN!

"WE NEED TO GET TO THE ROOF," BLACK WIDOW SAYS, TOSSING HAWKEYE A DRIVE WITH THE PLANS. "FOLLOW ME!"

ON THE ROOF, THE HEROES FIND THEIR

JUMP SHIP...AND A LOT MORE HYDRA ROBOTS!

AS THE HEROES RACE TOWARD THE SHIP, A ROBOT

SLAMS INTO HAWKEYE, AND THE DRIVE GOES FLYING.

"I'LL GET IT," BLACK WIDOW SAYS. "YOU DISTRACT

THE METAL-HEADS!"

WHILE HAWKEYE RAINS DOWN ARROWS, BLACK

WIDOW RACES TOWARD THE SHIP, GRABBING

THE DRIVE ON THE WAY.

AS THE SHIP LEAVES THE ROOF, HAWKEYE SAYS,

"SORRY I DROPPED THE DRIVE."

"YOUR SHARPSHOOTING HELPED GET IT BACK," BLACK WIDOW SAYS. "THAT'S WHY WE'RE A GREAT TEAM."

"YOU'RE RIGHT," HAWKEYE SAYS. JUST THEN, HIS STOMACH RUMBLES. "CLOSE CALLS MAKE ME HUNGRY."

"WANT TO STOP FOR TACOS?" BLACK WIDOW ASKS.

HAWKEYE GRINS. "*THIS* IS WHY WE'RE A GREAT TEAM."

PICTURE PUZZLE

HELP PROTECT S.H.I.E.L.D.'S OFFICES FROM HYDRA!

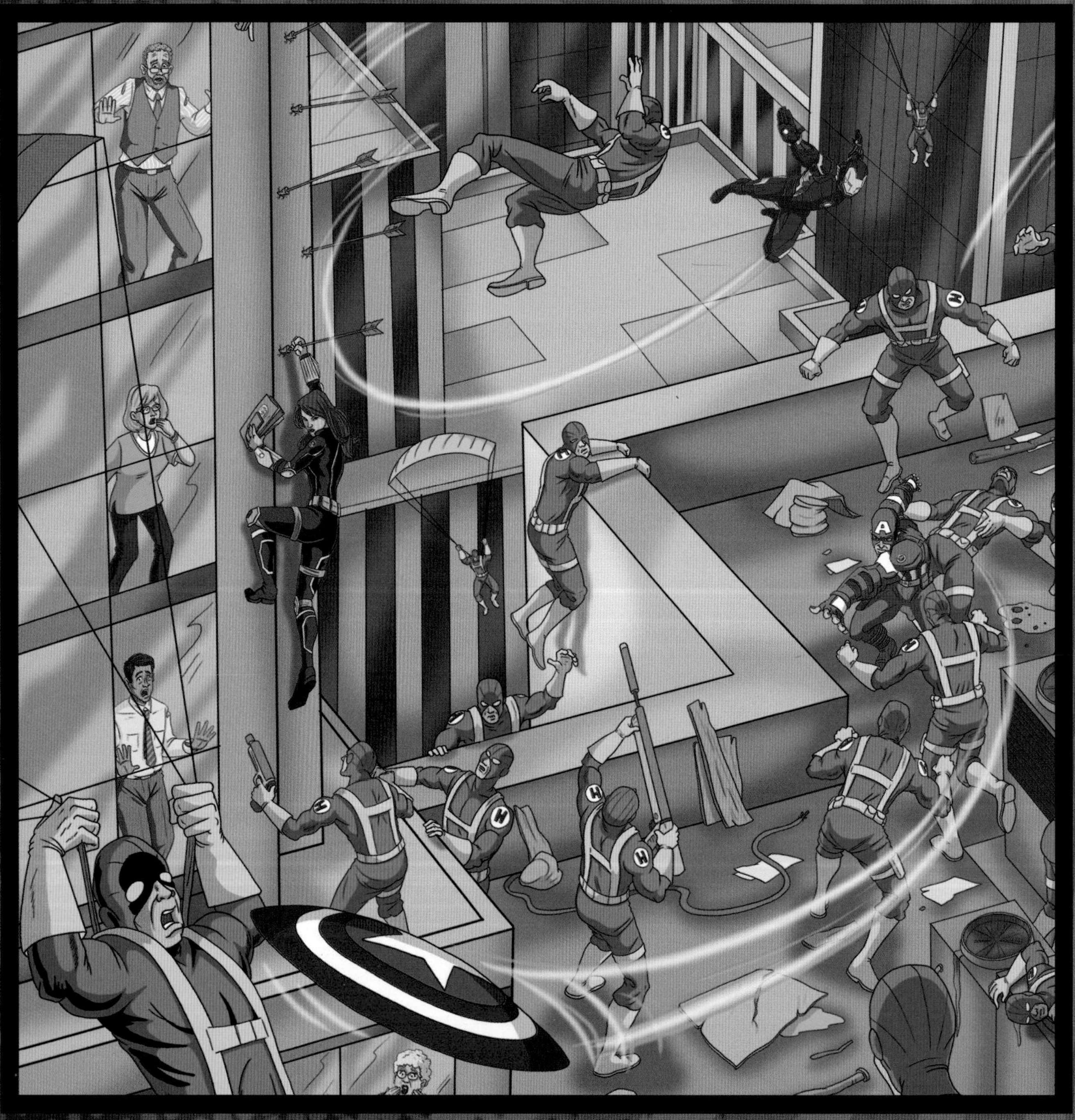

HOME IN ON 10 DIFFERENCES BETWEEN THE SCENES.

Answer key: bystander in window, missing arrow, parachuting Hydra agent, reaching hand on right, Cap's shield, planks of wood, Hawkeye, Iron Man, Hydra uniform color, missing Hydra logo

THOR

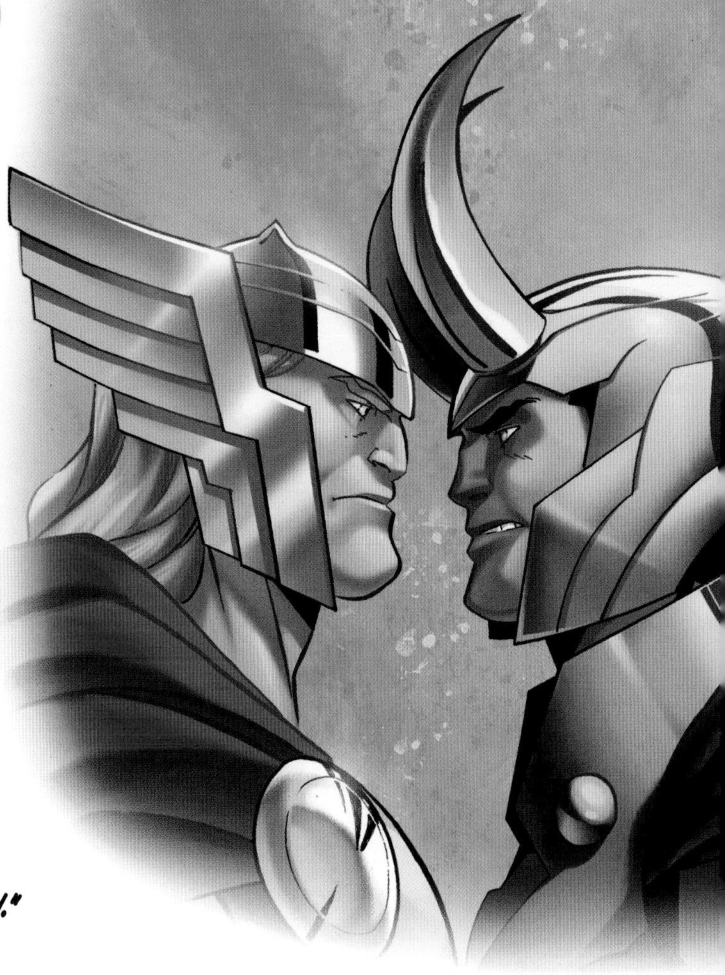

THOR, PRINCE OF ASGARD

"FOR ASGARD!"

THOR AND HIS YOUNGER BROTHER, LOKI, ARE THE PRINCES OF ASGARD. THOR IS A GREAT WARRIOR, WHILE LOKI IS KNOWN FOR HIS CUNNING AND MISCHIEF.

ONE DAY, THOR'S FATHER ODIN HAS A MIGHTY HAMMER, MJOLNIR, MADE JUST FOR THOR.

"BUT YOU WILL BE UNABLE TO LIFT IT," ODIN SAYS, "UNTIL YOU PROVE YOURSELF WORTHY."

ONLY WHEN HE STOPS THINKING OF GLORY AND STARTS CONSIDERING THE GOOD OF ASGARD IS THOR ABLE TO LIFT THE MIGHTY HAMMER.

"I AM STRONG AND POWERFUL," THOR SAYS PROUDLY. "NO ONE AND NOTHING CAN STOP ME!"

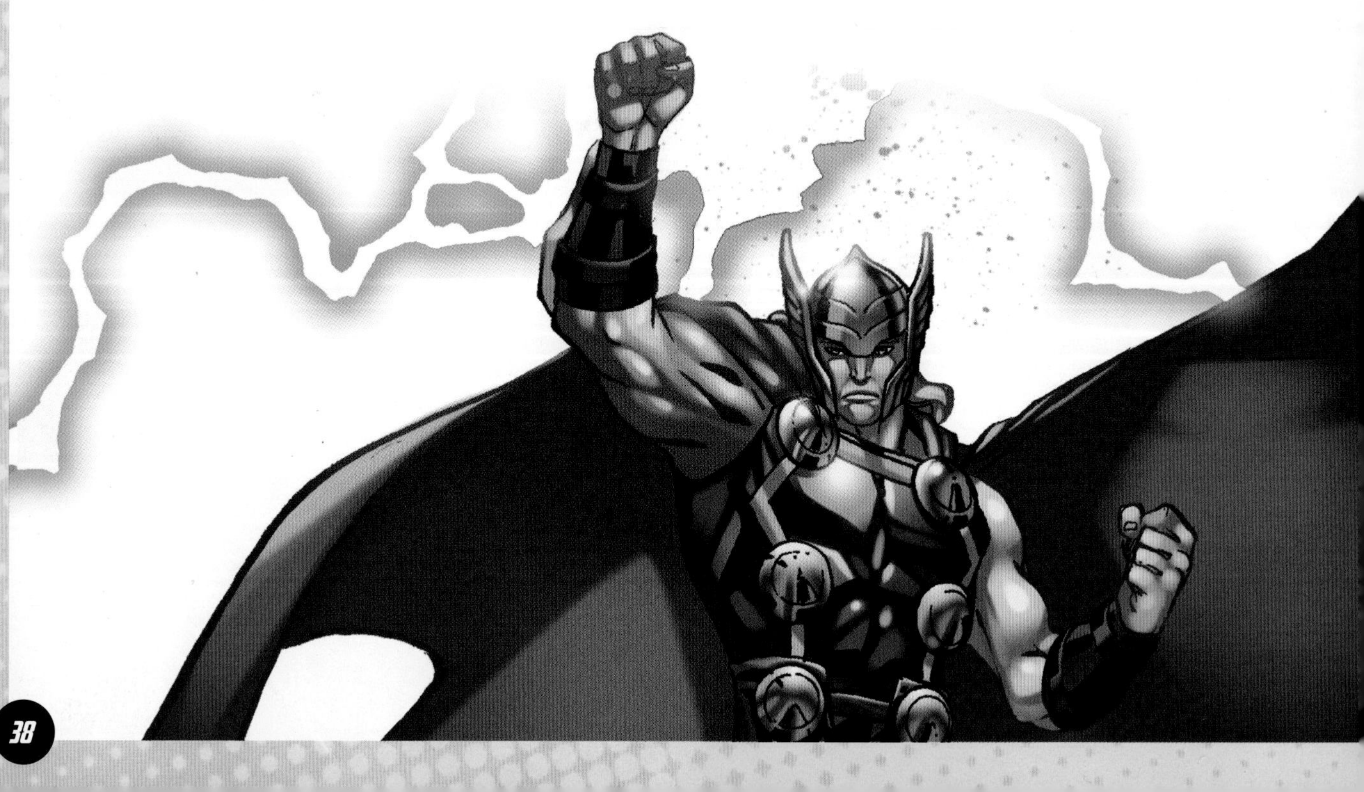

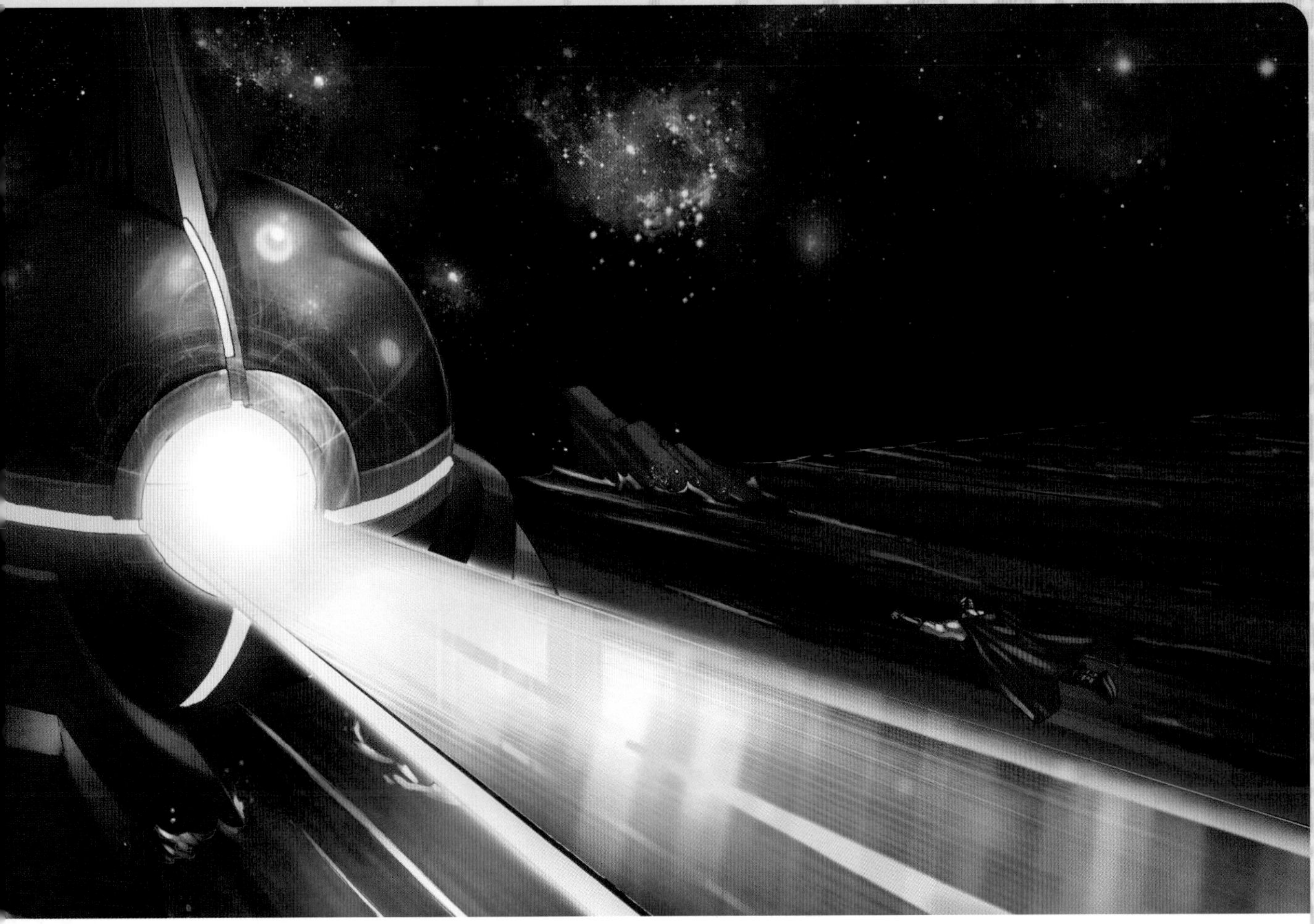

ODIN, ANGERED BY HIS SON'S ARROGANCE, WIPES THOR'S MEMORY AND SENDS HIM TO EARTH IN THE BODY OF DR. DONALD BLAKE.

AS BLAKE, THOR HELPS MANY PEOPLE AND LEARNS COMPASSION. ONLY THEN IS HIS IDENTITY AS A PRINCE OF ASGARD REVEALED.

ODIN WELCOMES THOR HOME WITH OPEN ARMS...BUT LOKI, HAVING LOST HIS CHANCE AT THE THRONE, PROMISES MORE MISCHIEF TO COME...

IT'S A GOOD THING THE AVENGERS ARE ALWAYS READY FOR A CHALLENGE!

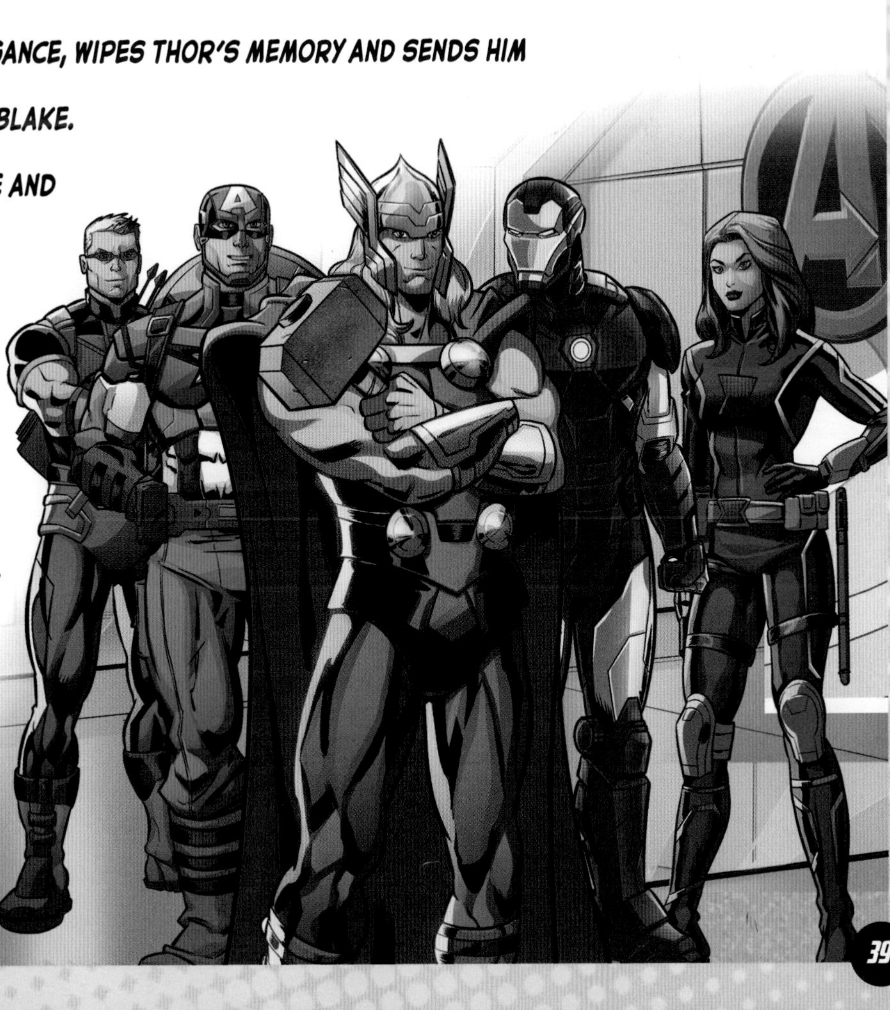

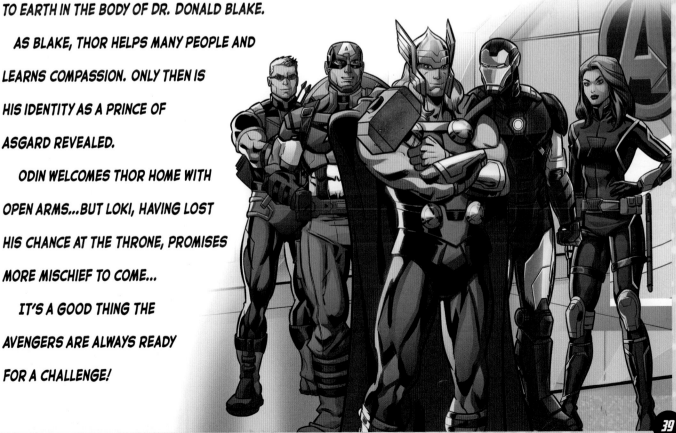

ABSORBING MAN HAS CORNERED THOR AT A CONSTRUCTION SITE! BEFORE THOR CAN ESCAPE, ABSORBING MAN TOUCHES THE STEEL GIRDERS...AND TRANSFORMS INTO A TOWERING TERROR! WHILE THOR OUTSMARTS HIS INDESTRUCTIBLE ADVERSARY, SPOT THESE OBJECTS HE CAN USE FOR COVER, AND THESE HARD-WORKING ONLOOKERS:

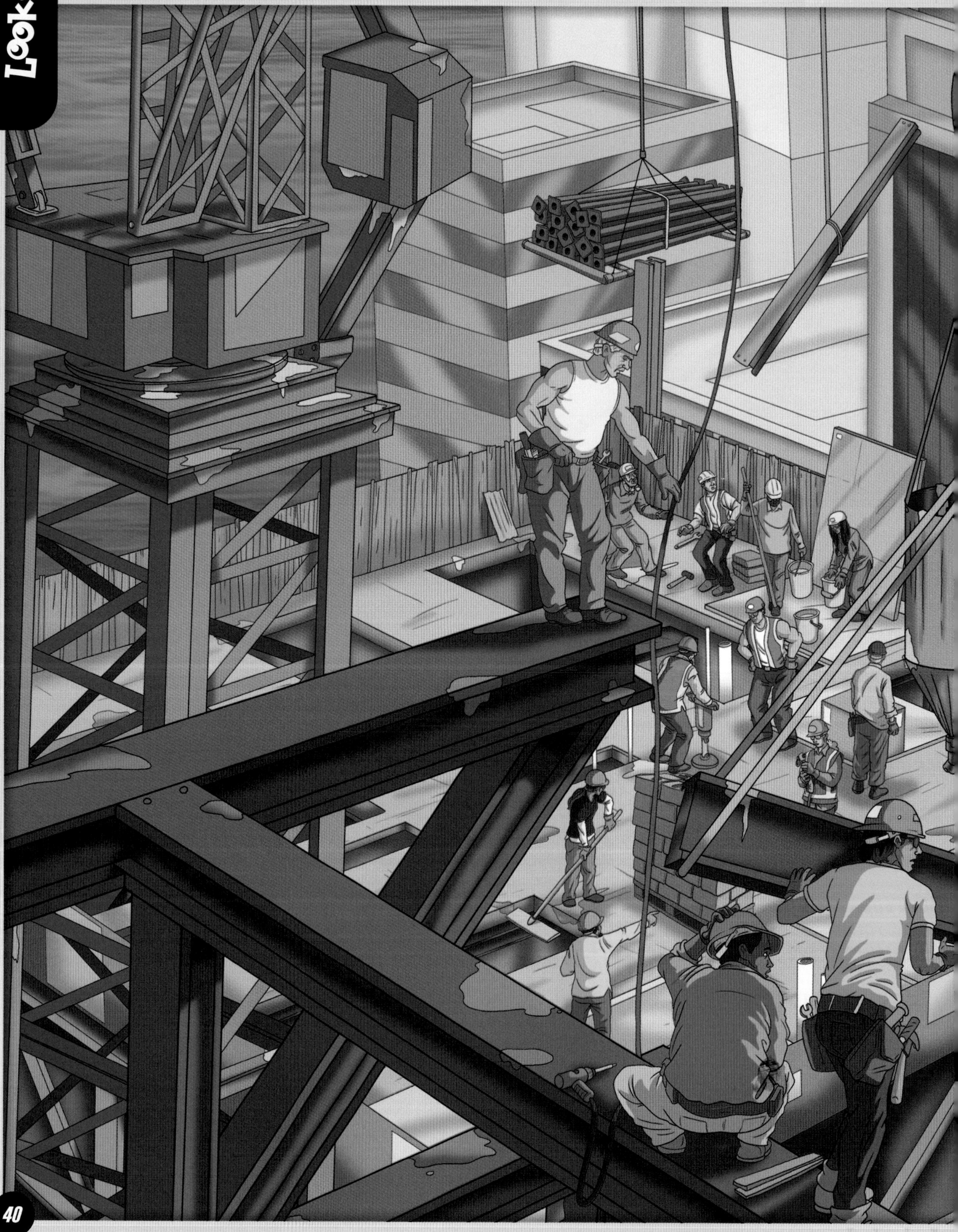

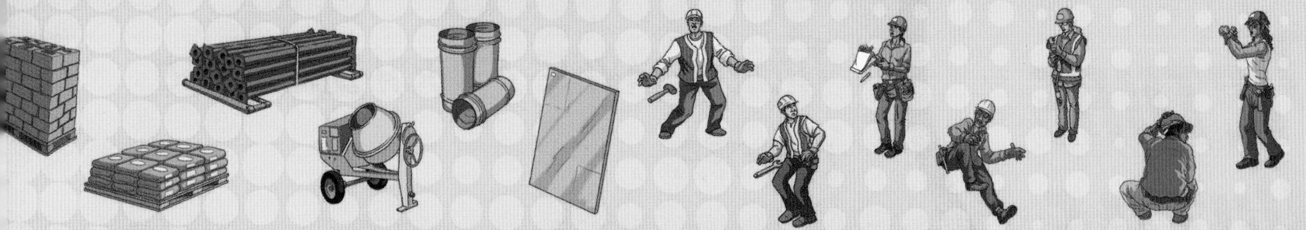

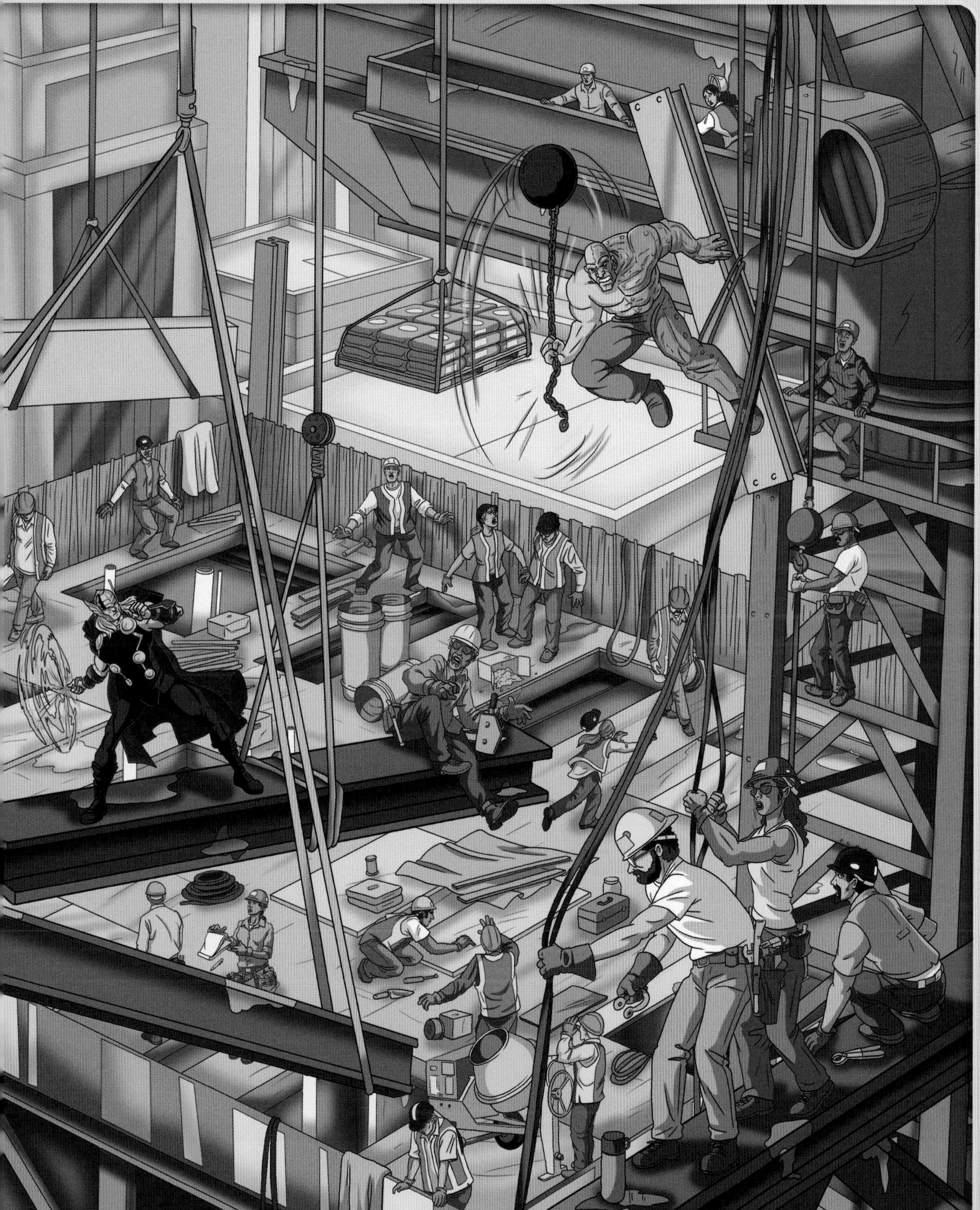

Picture Puzzle

Thor is taking a much-deserved day off.

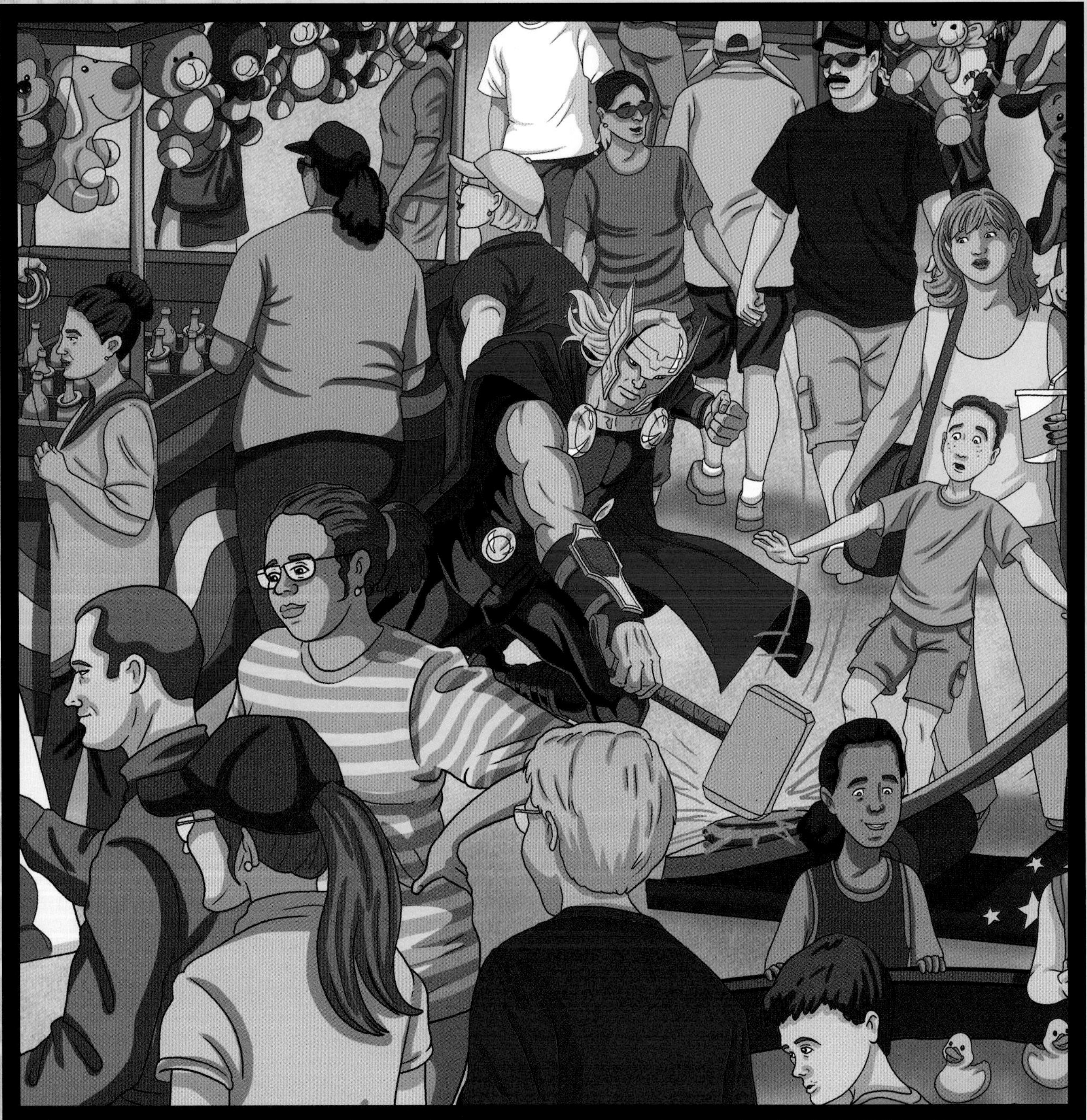

Can you find 10 things that are different between these scenes?

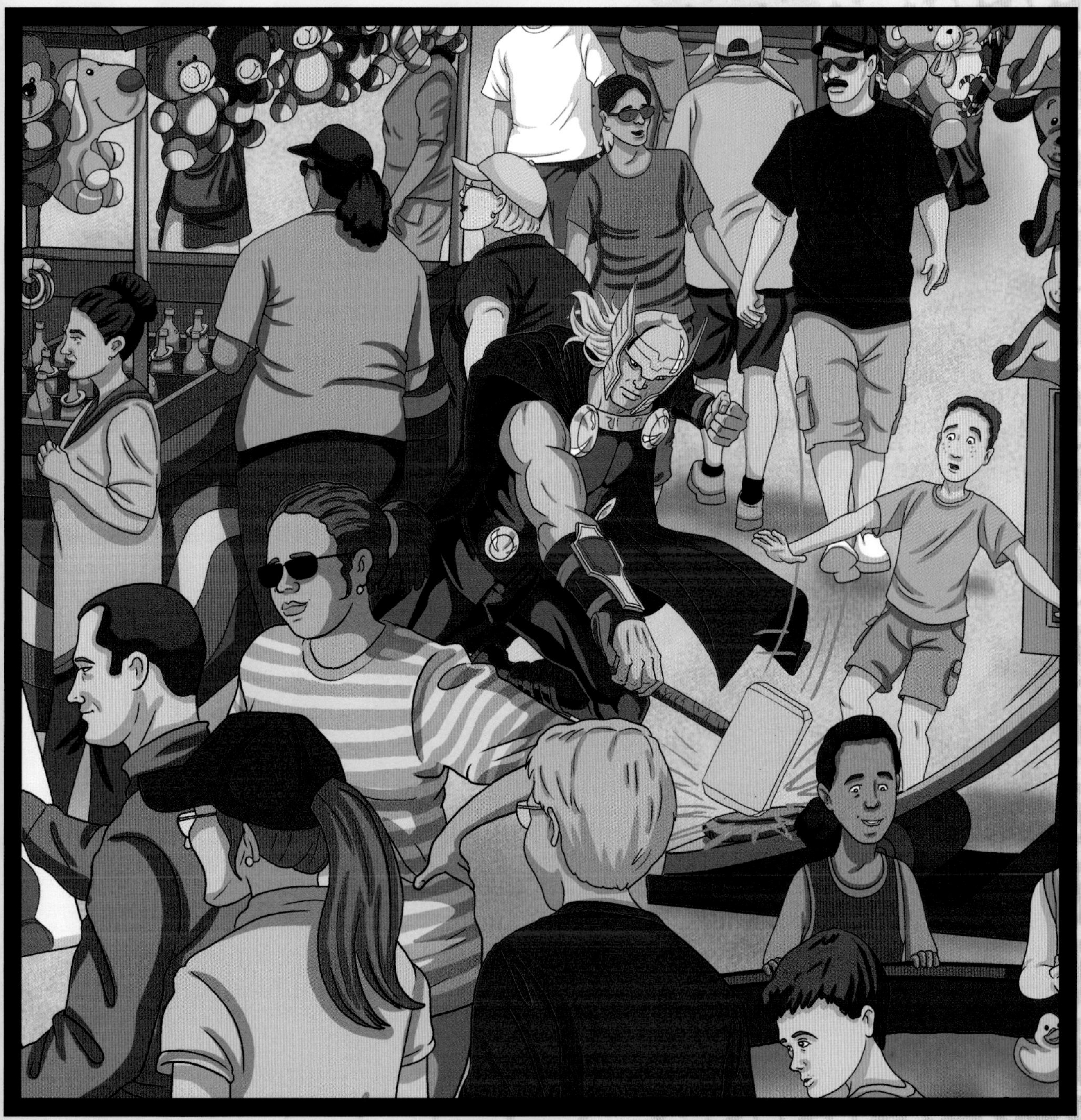

Answer key: prize bear color, baseball cap color, hair color of man in lower left, color of socks, Avengers logo on T-shirt, Thor's hammer, woman's glasses, second duck, missing stars, woman holding a drink

BLACK PANTHER

BECOMING BLACK PANTHER

"WAKANDA FOREVER!"

THE KINGDOM OF WAKANDA HAS ALWAYS RELIED ON A STRONG RULER TO PROTECT ITS PEOPLE. BLACK PANTHER IS THE NAME GIVEN TO THOSE WORTHY OF THIS HEREDITARY HONOR.

IN THE DISTANT PAST, A METEORITE MADE OF VIBRANIUM CRASHED INTO WAKANDA. FOR MANY GENERATIONS, EACH BLAC PANTHER HAS PROTECTED THIS RARE AND VALUABLE MINERAL FROM GREEDY VILLAINS LIKE ULYSSES KLAW.

YOUNG T'CHALLA HOPES TO ONE DAY BECOME THE BLACK PANTHER LIKE HIS FATHER BEFORE HIM. *WAKANDA DESERVES A WISE AND KIND LEADER,* T'CHALLA THINKS.

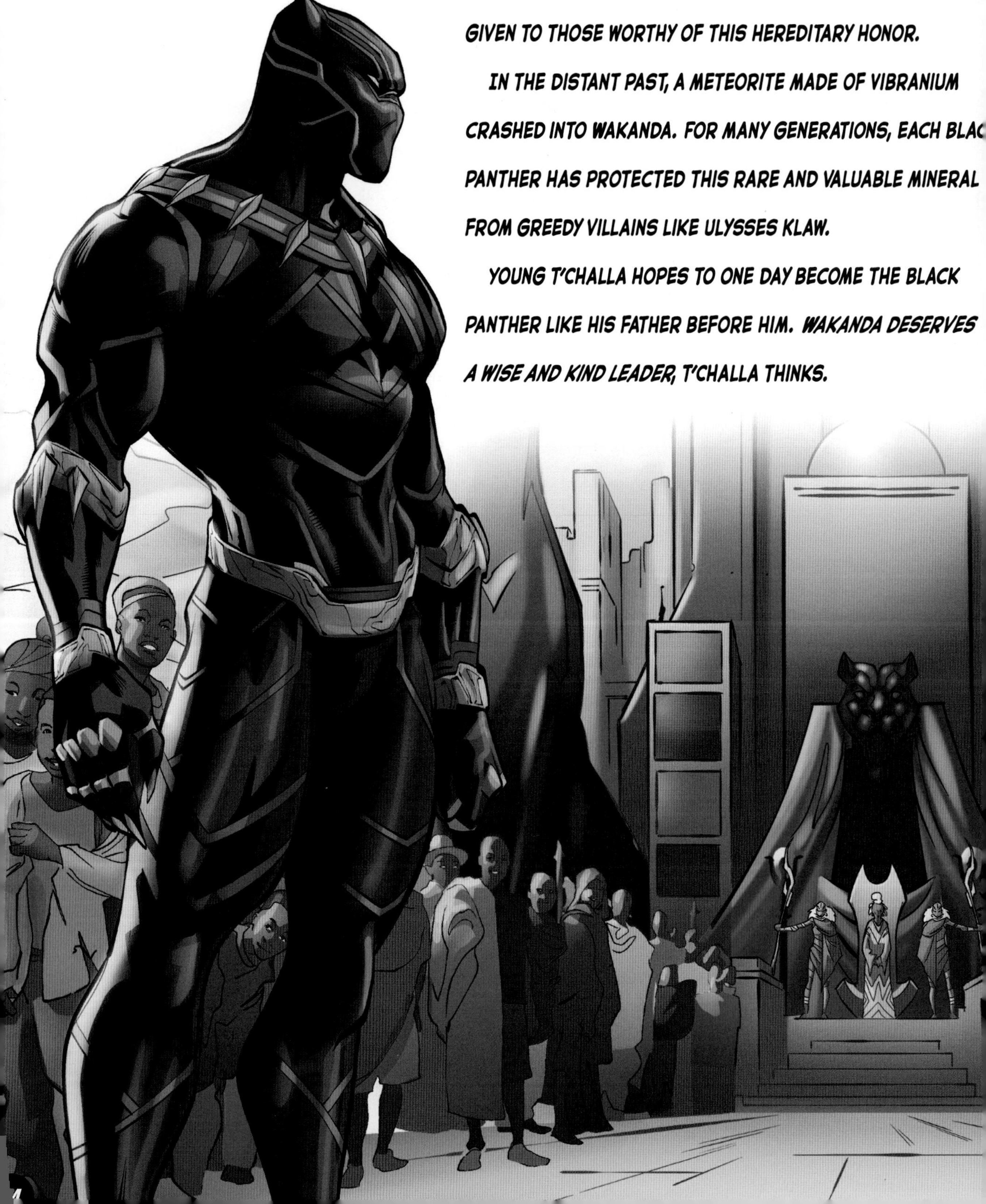

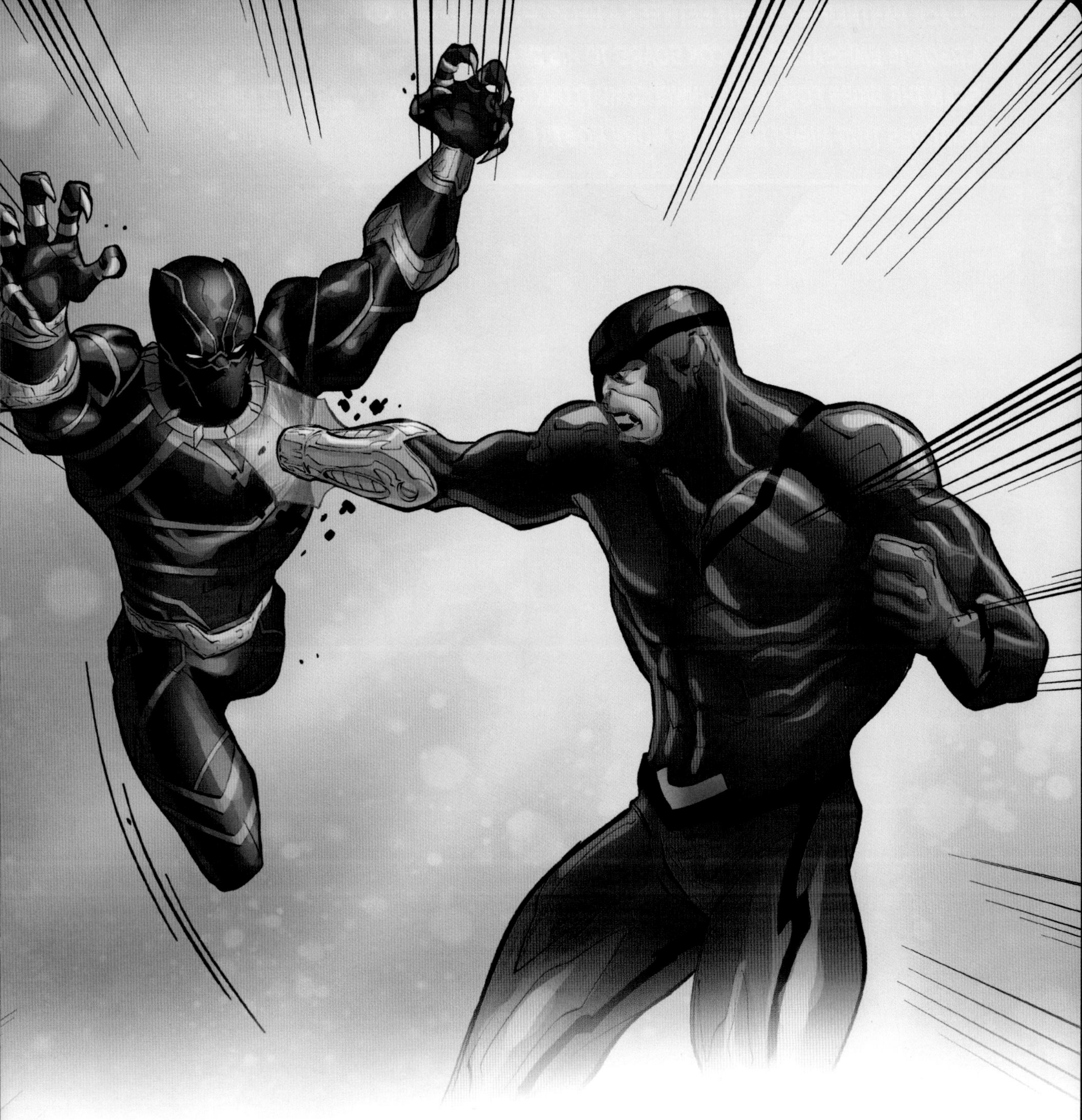

FIRST, T'CHALLA MUST EMBARK ON A WAKANDAN RITE OF PASSAGE. HE VISITS EUROPE AND THE UNITED STATES, ATTENDS SCHOOL, AND LEARNS ABOUT THE WORLD. THEN HE RETURNS HOME TO FACE A GRUELING SERIES OF TESTS.

T'CHALLA OVERCOMES EACH CHALLENGE AND EARNS HIS PLACE AS THE BLACK PANTHER. THANKS TO HIS NIGHT-VISION MASK, FIERCE CLAWS, AND VIBRANIUM SUIT, BLACK PANTHER CAN GO TOE-TO-TOE WITH ANY VILLAIN.

WITH THE AVENGERS BY HIS SIDE, THE BLACK PANTHER WILL ALWAYS FIGHT FOR GOOD!

BLACK PANTHER IS CAUGHT BETWEEN A HELICOPTER AND A HARD PLACE! AS HE TAKES ON KLAW'S AIRBORNE EMISSARIES, FALCON SOARS TO HIS RESCUE. WHILE THE DAUNTLESS DUO DEFENDS WAKANDA, SCAN THE SKIES FOR THESE UNWELCOME FLUNKIES—AND DON'T FORGET TO CHECK THE GROUND FOR FEATURES THAT MIGHT BE HIDING MORE HOSTILE HENCHMEN:

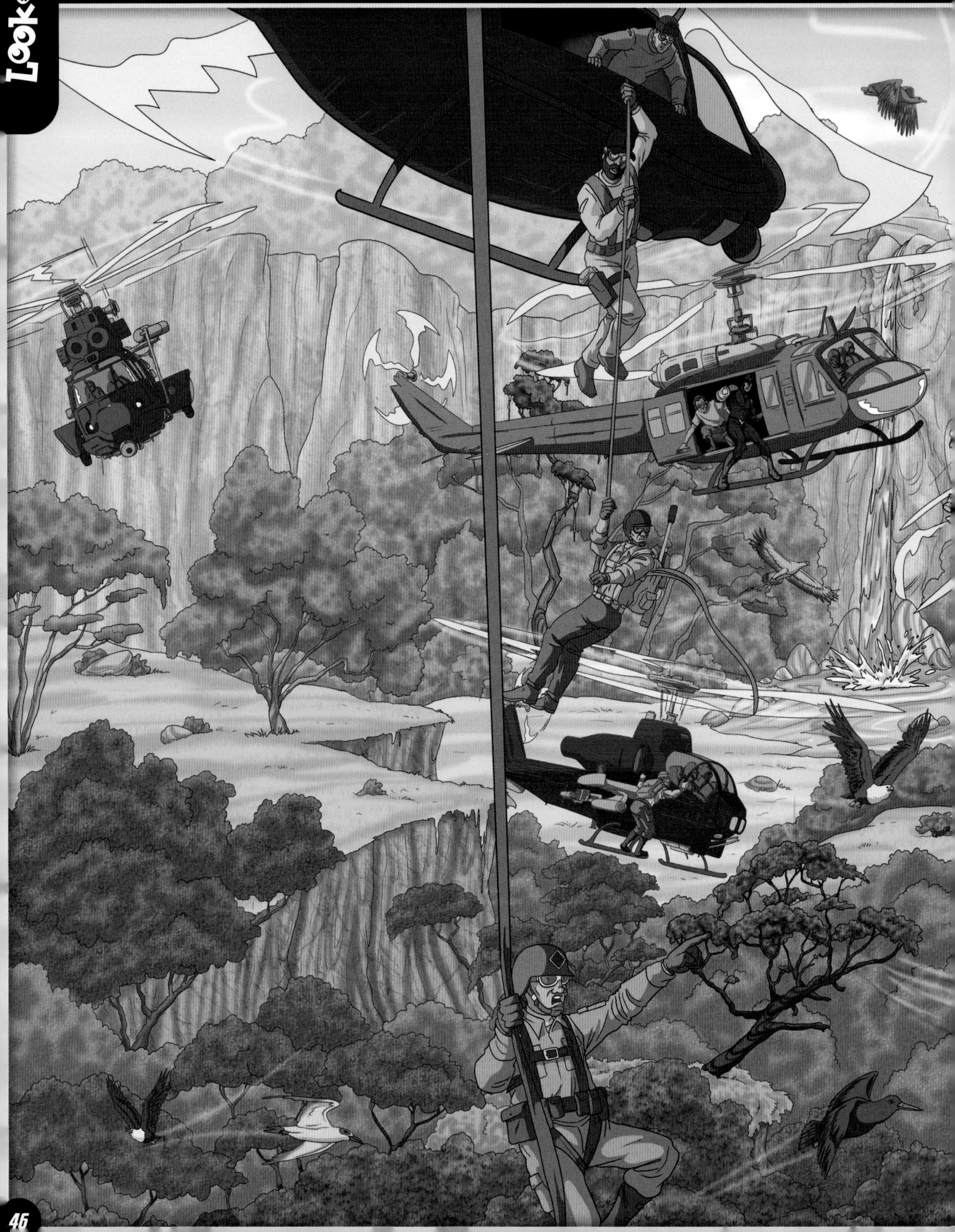

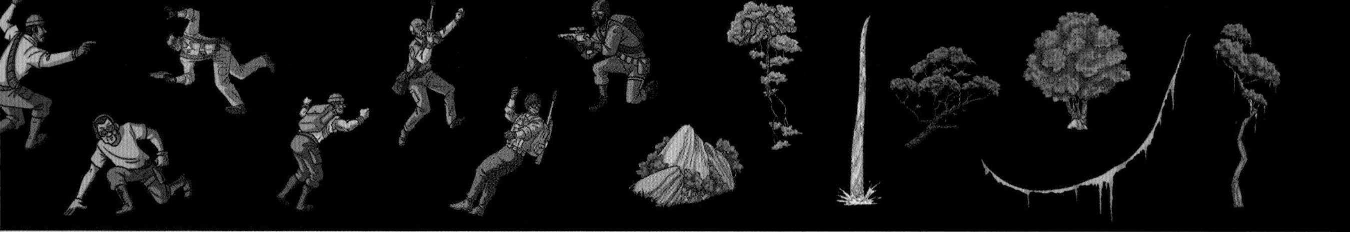

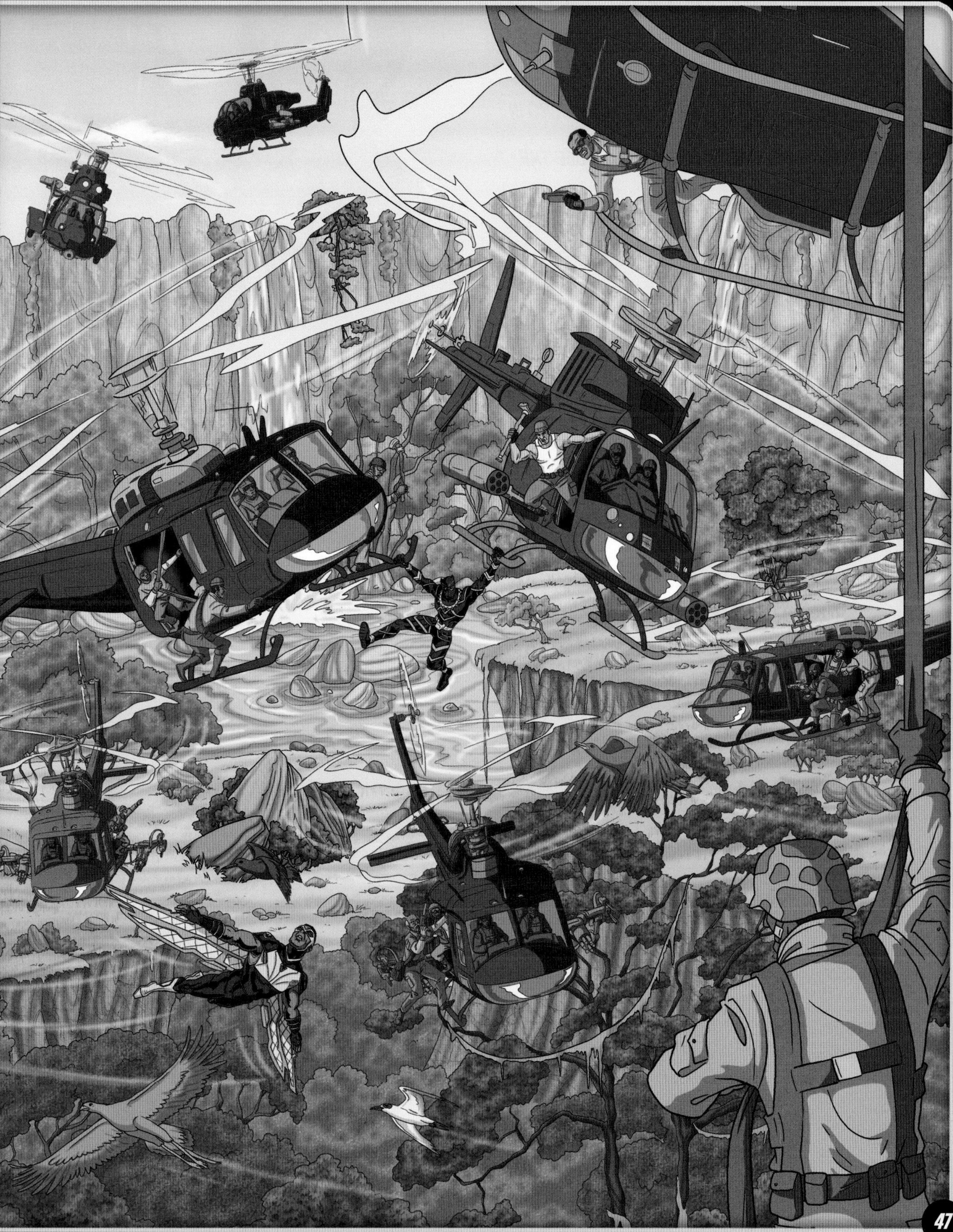

ON THE HUNT

"KING OF WAKANDA!"

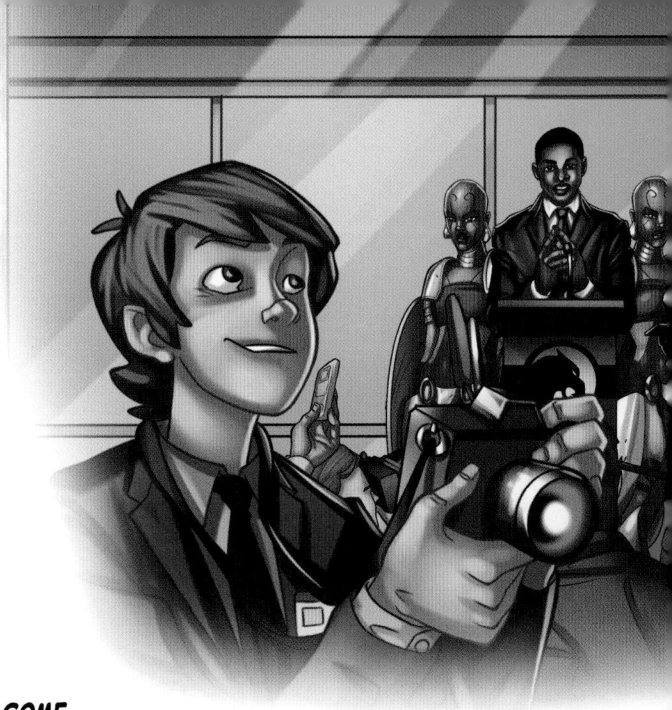

THE KING OF WAKANDA, T'CHALLA, IS SPEAKING IN MANHATTAN TODAY! CROWDS GATHER TO SEE THE FAMOUS BLACK PANTHER.

NO ONE IS MORE EXCITED FOR T'CHALLA'S SPEECH THAN PETER PARKER.

MEANWHILE, KRAVEN IS ON THE HUNT. HE CAPTURES SOME CHEETAHS, BUT THAT DOESN'T FEEL LIKE ENOUGH. KRAVEN WANTS MORE CHALLENGING PREY, AND HE KNOWS THE PERFECT PLACE TO FIND IT...

HALFWAY THROUGH T'CHALLA'S SPEECH, KRAVEN BURSTS INTO THE ROOM AND RELEASES HIS CHEETAHS ON THE CROWD! PETER'S SPIDER-SENSE GOES CRAZY. HE HAS TO HELP, AND FAST!

SPIDER-MAN LEAPS TOWARD THE CHEETAHS AND SPRAYS WEBBING AT THEM. BUT THE CHEETAHS TURN ON HIM. NOW SPIDEY NEEDS HELP!

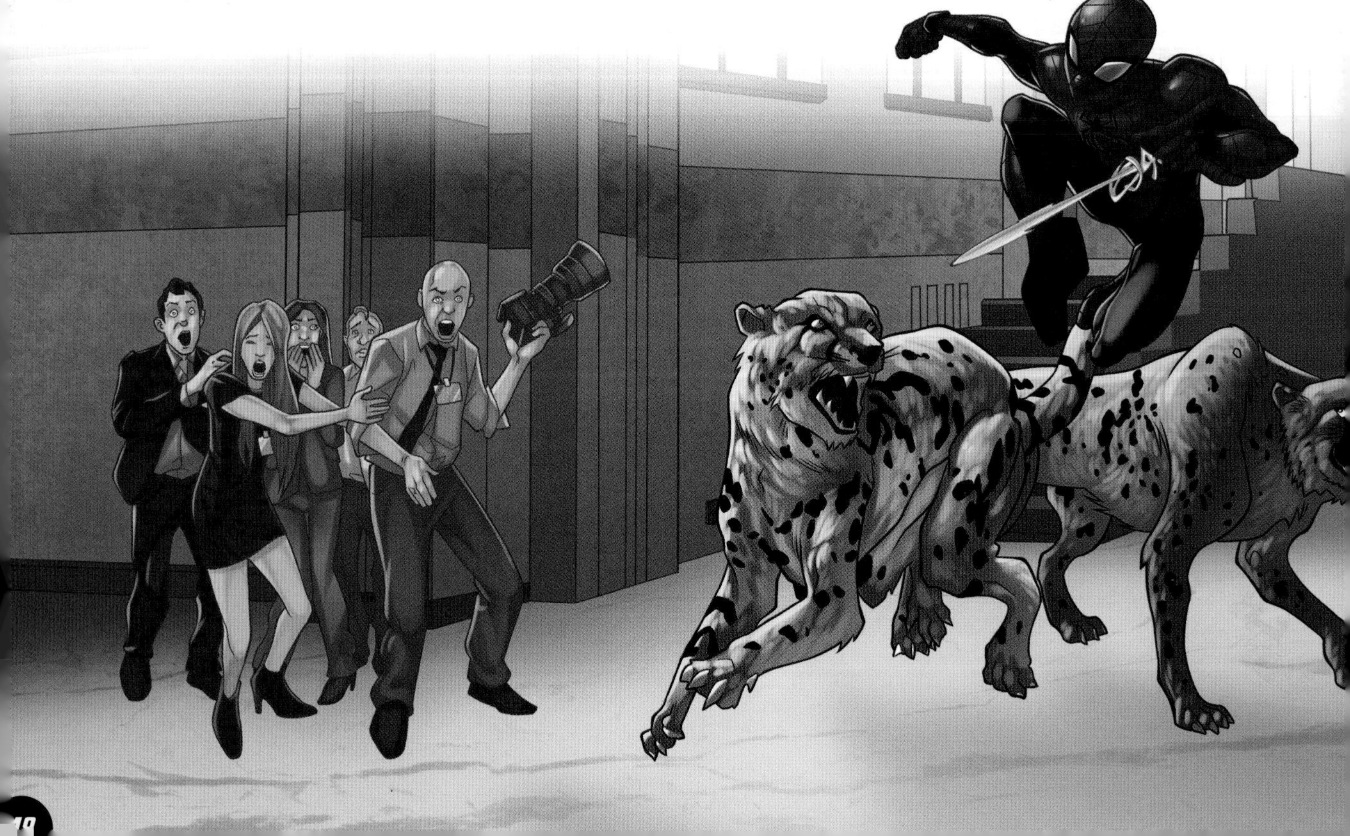

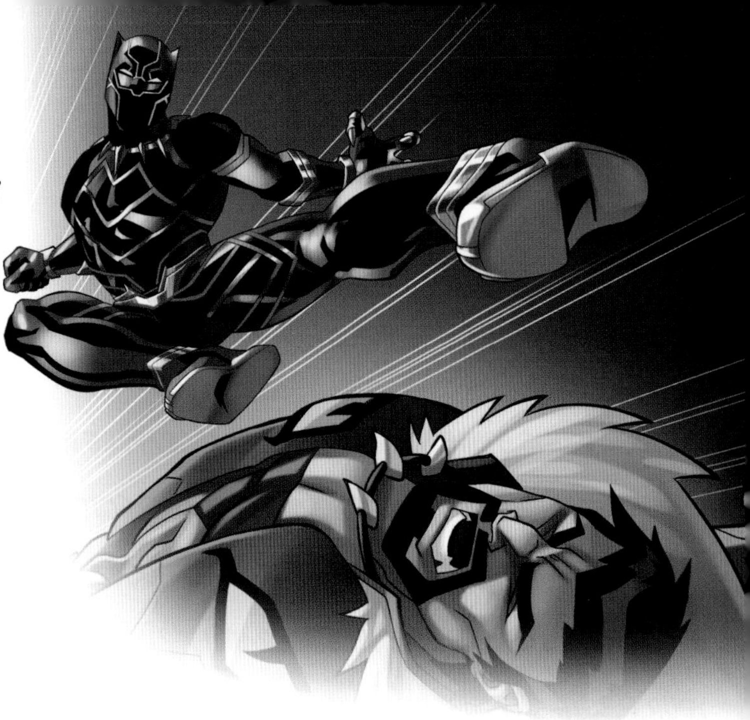

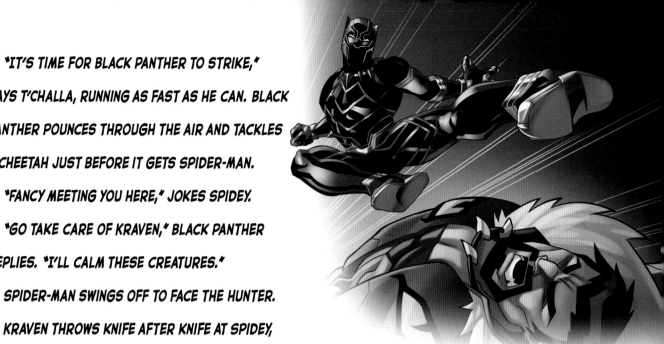

"IT'S TIME FOR BLACK PANTHER TO STRIKE," SAYS T'CHALLA, RUNNING AS FAST AS HE CAN. BLACK PANTHER POUNCES THROUGH THE AIR AND TACKLES A CHEETAH JUST BEFORE IT GETS SPIDER-MAN.

"FANCY MEETING YOU HERE," JOKES SPIDEY.

"GO TAKE CARE OF KRAVEN," BLACK PANTHER REPLIES. "I'LL CALM THESE CREATURES."

SPIDER-MAN SWINGS OFF TO FACE THE HUNTER.

KRAVEN THROWS KNIFE AFTER KNIFE AT SPIDEY, BUT THE HERO DODGES THEM ALL.

WITH A POWERFUL BLAST OF WEBBING, SPIDER-MAN DISARMS KRAVEN JUST AS BLACK PANTHER ARRIVES TO DELIVER THE FINAL BLOW.

KRAVEN IS DEFEATED! "HUNTED BY A SPIDER AND A CAT," HE COMPLAINS.

"SOMEONE DOESN'T LIKE BEING HELD IN CAPTIVITY," SAYS SPIDEY, SNAPPING A QUICK SELFIE TO COMMEMORATE THE DAY.

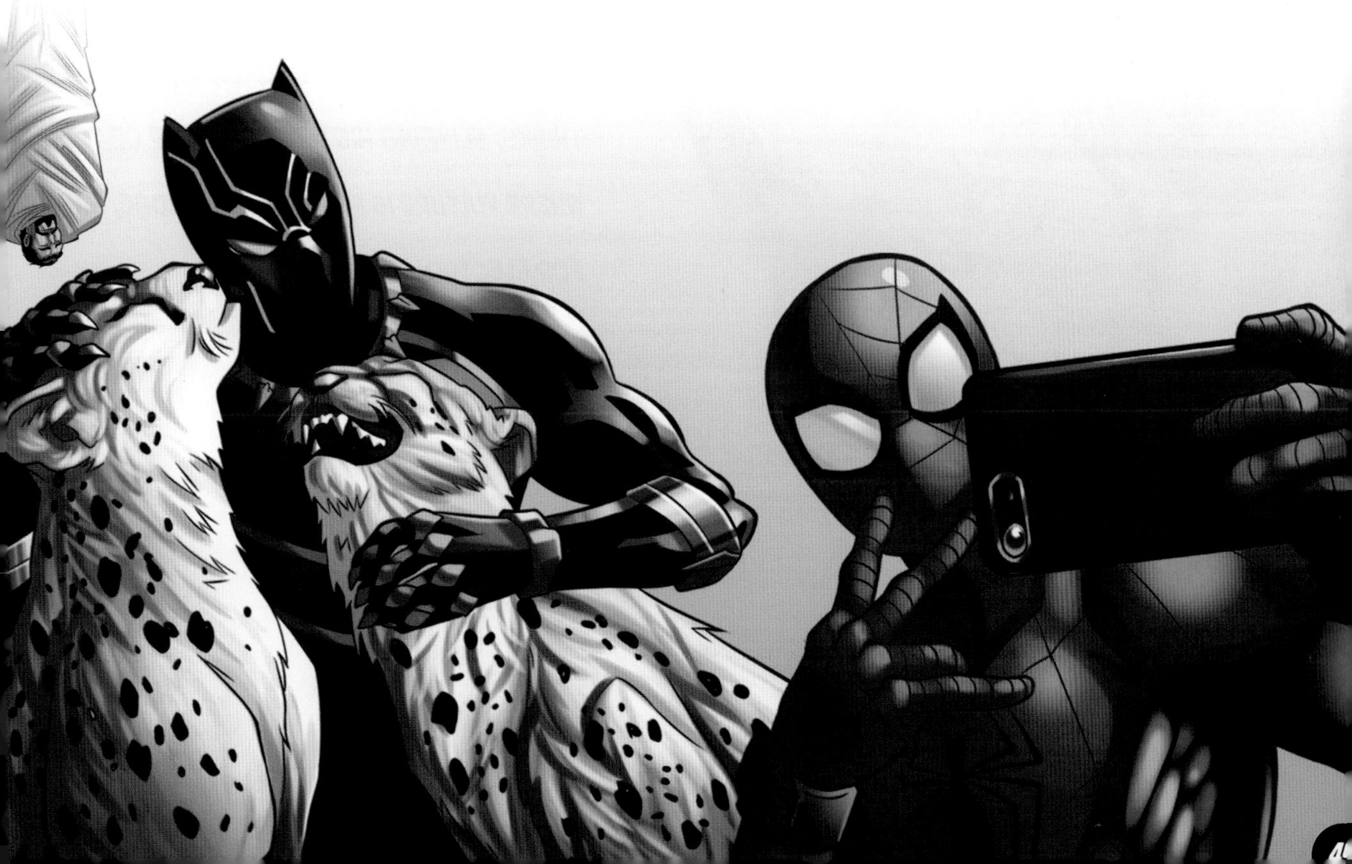

ONE FOR THE MONEY

"IT'S WEB-SLINGING TIME!"

SPIDER-MAN IS SWINGING AMONG THE SKYSCRAPERS WHEN HE SPOTS TROUBLE AT A NEARBY POWER PLANT: ELECTRO!

"I HAVE A TINGLY FEELING YOU'RE UP TO NO GOOD," SPIDER-MAN SAYS. "IS THAT MY SPIDER-SENSE? OR IS YOUR ELECTRICITY JUST RUBBING OFF ON ME?"

SPIDEY CAPTURES ELECTRO AND DEMANDS ANSWERS.

"WE'RE ROBBING A BANK, WEB-HEAD!" ELECTRO SAYS. "ONCE I KNOCK OUT THE POWER GRID, VULTURE WILL FLY TO THE TOP FLOOR OF THE BANK AND BREAK INTO THE ELECTRONIC SAFE. IT'S FOOLPROOF!"

THEN HE WARNS SPIDER-MAN: "DON'T EVEN THINK ABOUT STOPPING US. WE BROUGHT A BODYGUARD.

WONDER WHO THAT COULD BE, SPIDER-MAN THINKS, SLINGING HIS WAY TO THE TOP OF THE BANK WHERE VULTURE IS PERCHED ON A LEDGE, WAITING FOR ELECTRO'S CUE.

"WHAT ARE YOU DOING HERE?" VULTURE SNEERS.

"CUTTING THE POWER TO THIS PARTY!" SPIDEY

SAYS, AND HE TAKES OUT THE FLAPPING FIEND WITH

HIS DUAL WEBS.

DOWN BELOW, RHINO WAITS AT THE

BANK ENTRANCE.

"YOU MUST BE THE BODYGUARD," SPIDER-MAN SAYS,

SLAMMING INTO RHINO WITH A WELL-TIMED KICK. RHINO

IS TOUGH, BUT HE'S ALSO CLUMSY, SO SPIDER-MAN

EASILY WEARS HIM DOWN.

SOON, THE COPS ARRIVE TO HAUL THE VILLAINS AWAY.

"I'LL ALWAYS KEEP THIS CITY SAFE," SPIDEY SAYS. "AND YOU CAN TAKE THAT TO THE BANK!"

WHAT BETTER WAY TO OBTAIN PHOTOS FOR THE *DAILY BUGLE* THAN BY FIGHTING THE CRIME FRONT AND CENTER? DOC OCK IS ATTEMPTING TO ROB AN ART MUSEUM, BUT SPIDER-MAN INTENDS TO LEAVE A LASTING IMPRESSION. AS DOC OCK PURLOINS OLD PAINTINGS, FIND THESE INVALUABLE ARTIFACTS AND VILLAINOUS VISAGES:

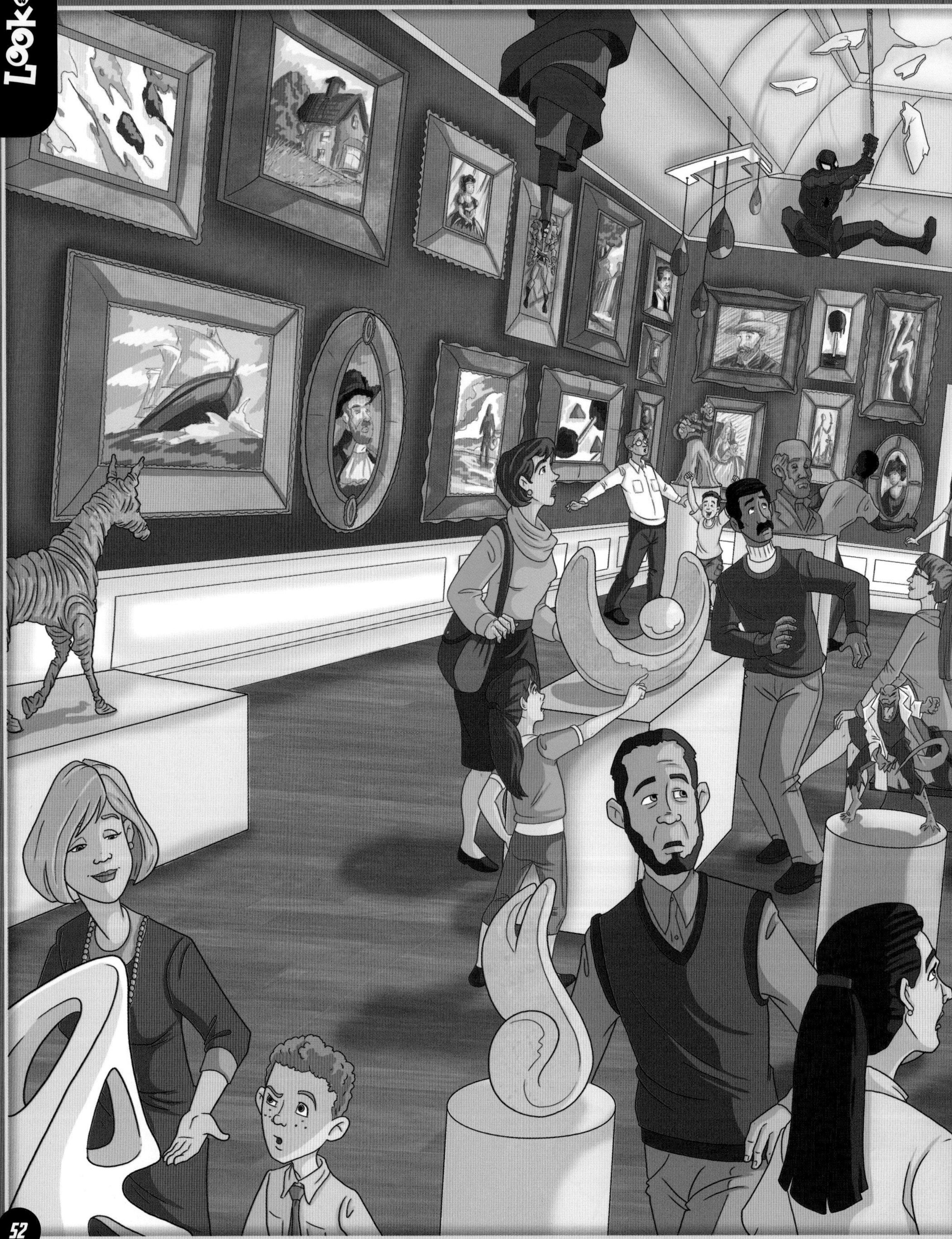

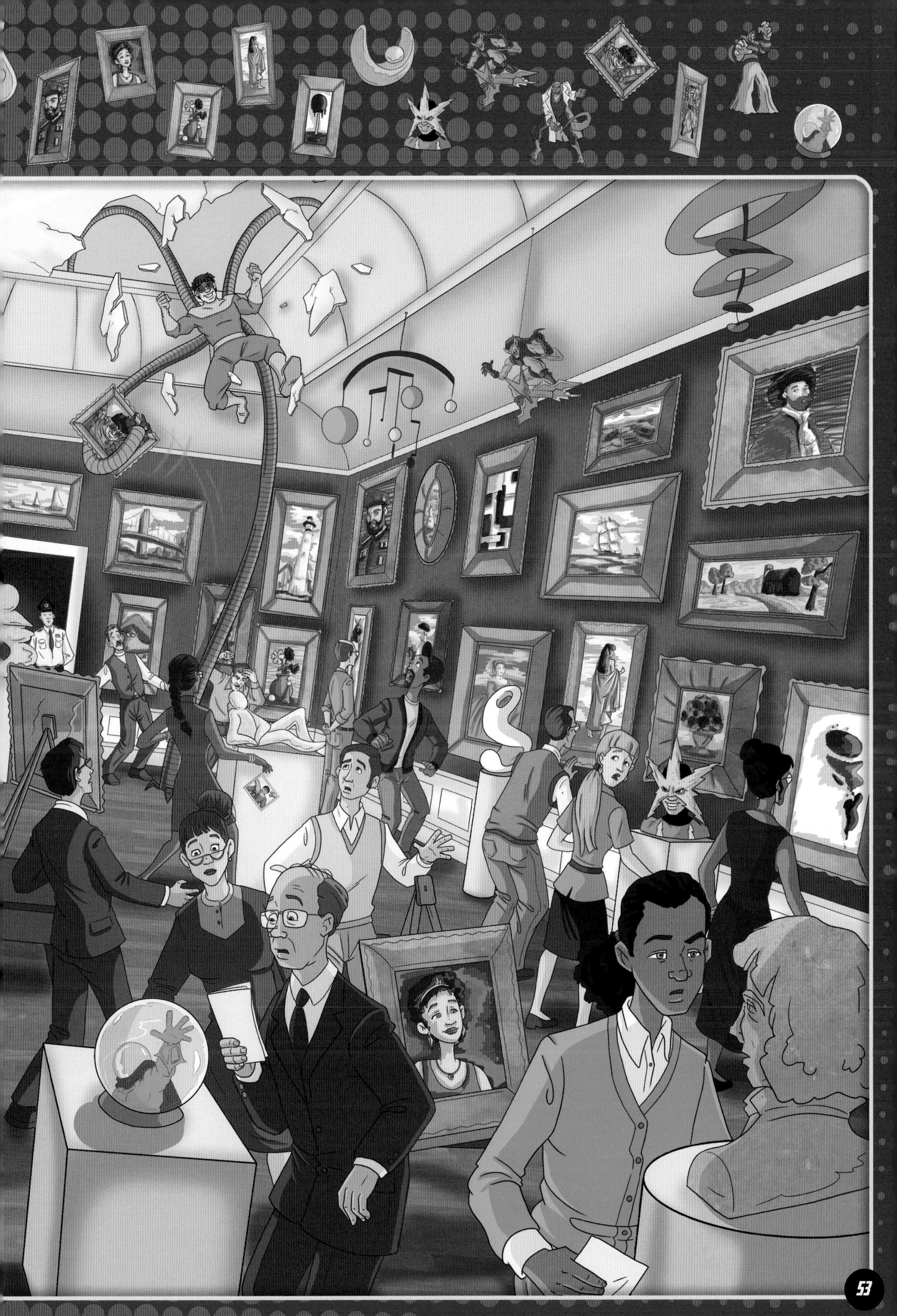

BENEATH THE CITY'S SURFACE, LIZARD UNLEASHES HIS ATTACK. CAN SPIDEY SUBDUE THE RAMBUNCTIOU REPTILE BEFORE THE SEWERS FLOOD? WHILE LIZARD TRIES TO FLUSH SPIDER-MAN FROM THE SEWER SYSTEM, LOOK FOR THESE DISCARDED OBJECTS AND INDUSTRIAL ITEMS:

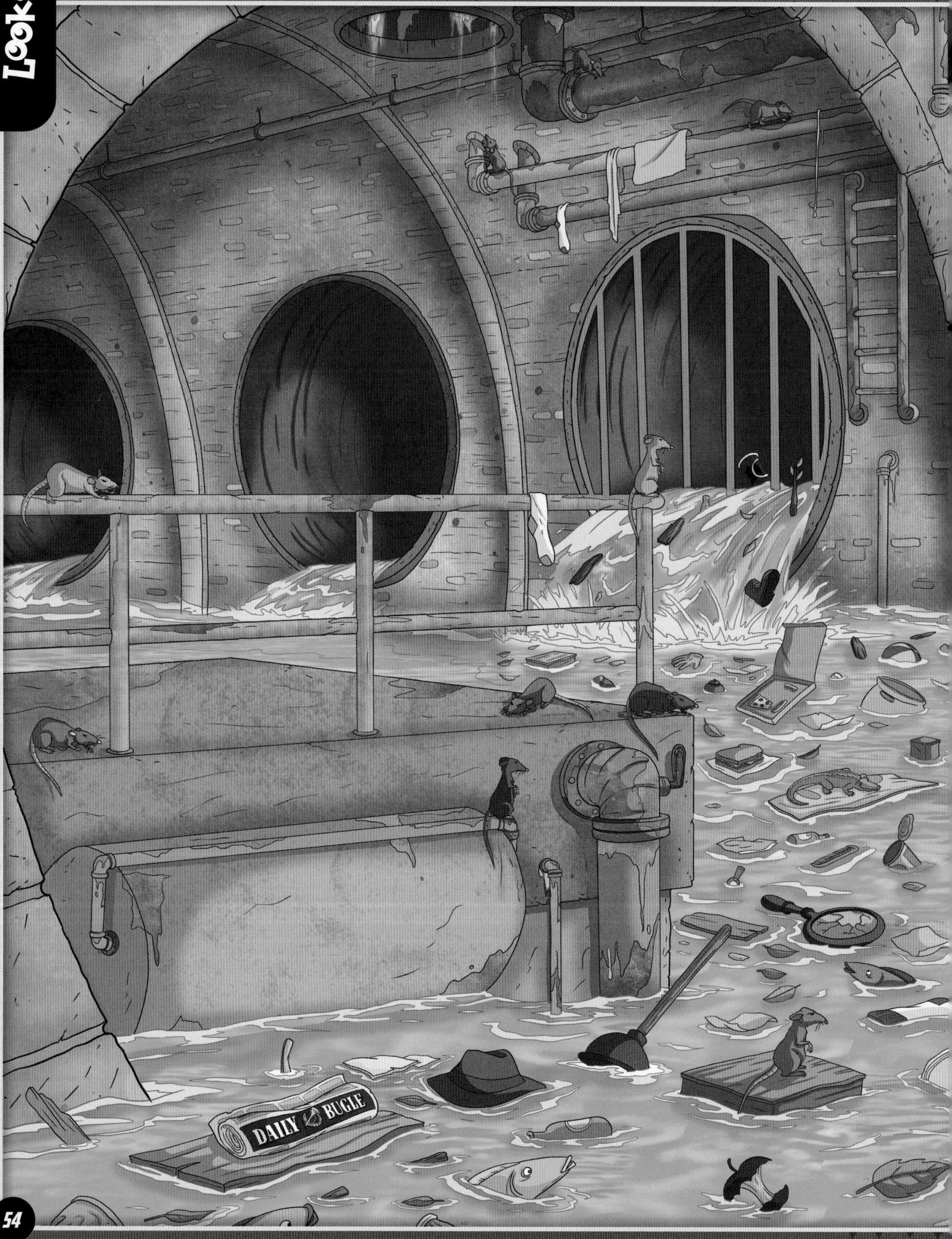
DAILY BUGLE

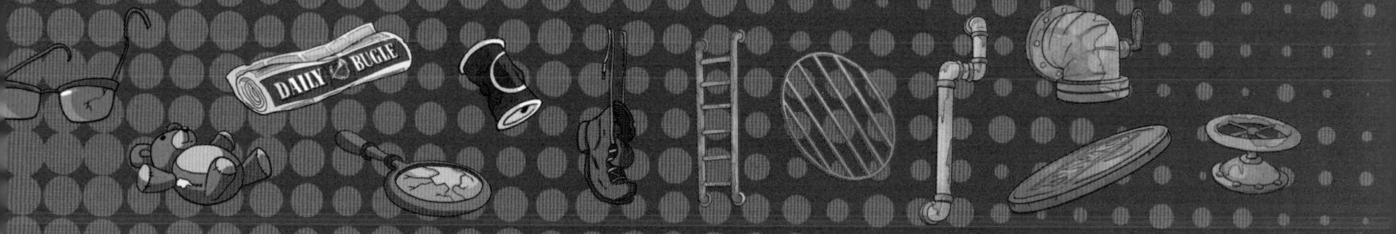
DAILY BUGLE

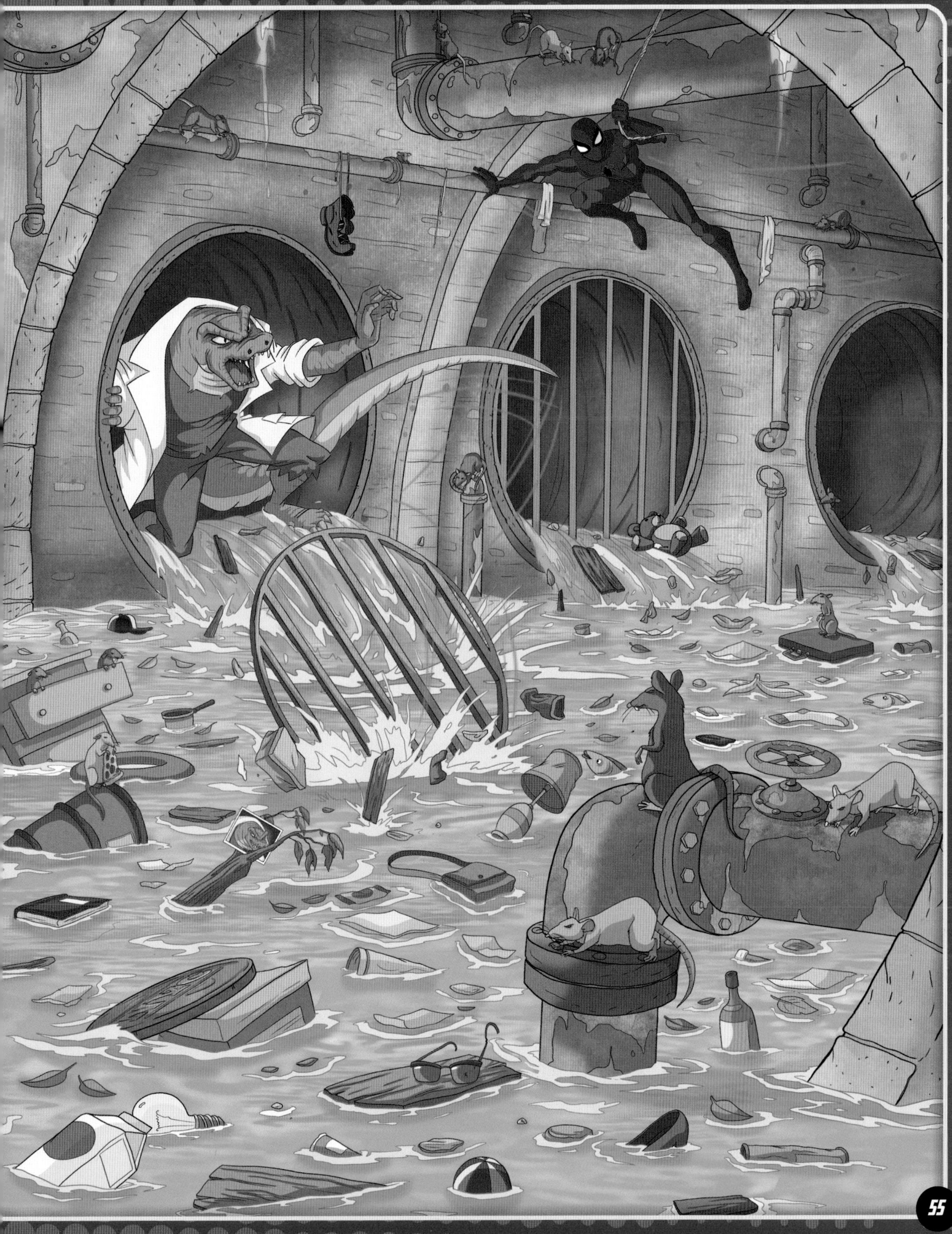

Picture Puzzle

Who can cut through the chaos and save the day?

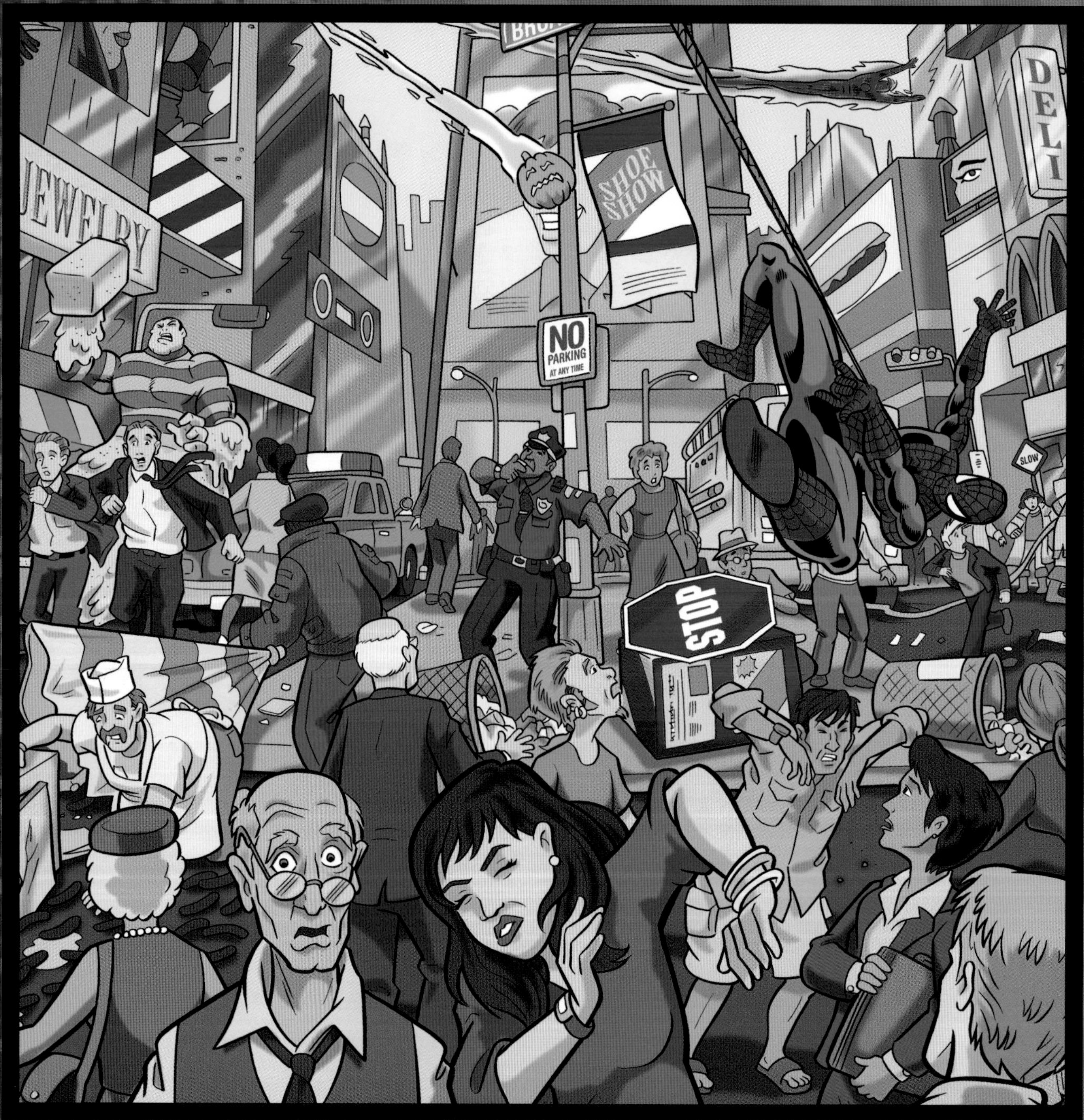

JEWELRY
SHOE SHOW
NO PARKING AT ANY TIME
DELI
STOP
SLOW

SPIDER-MAN! SEARCH FOR 10 DIFFERENCES BETWEEN THESE CITY SCENES.

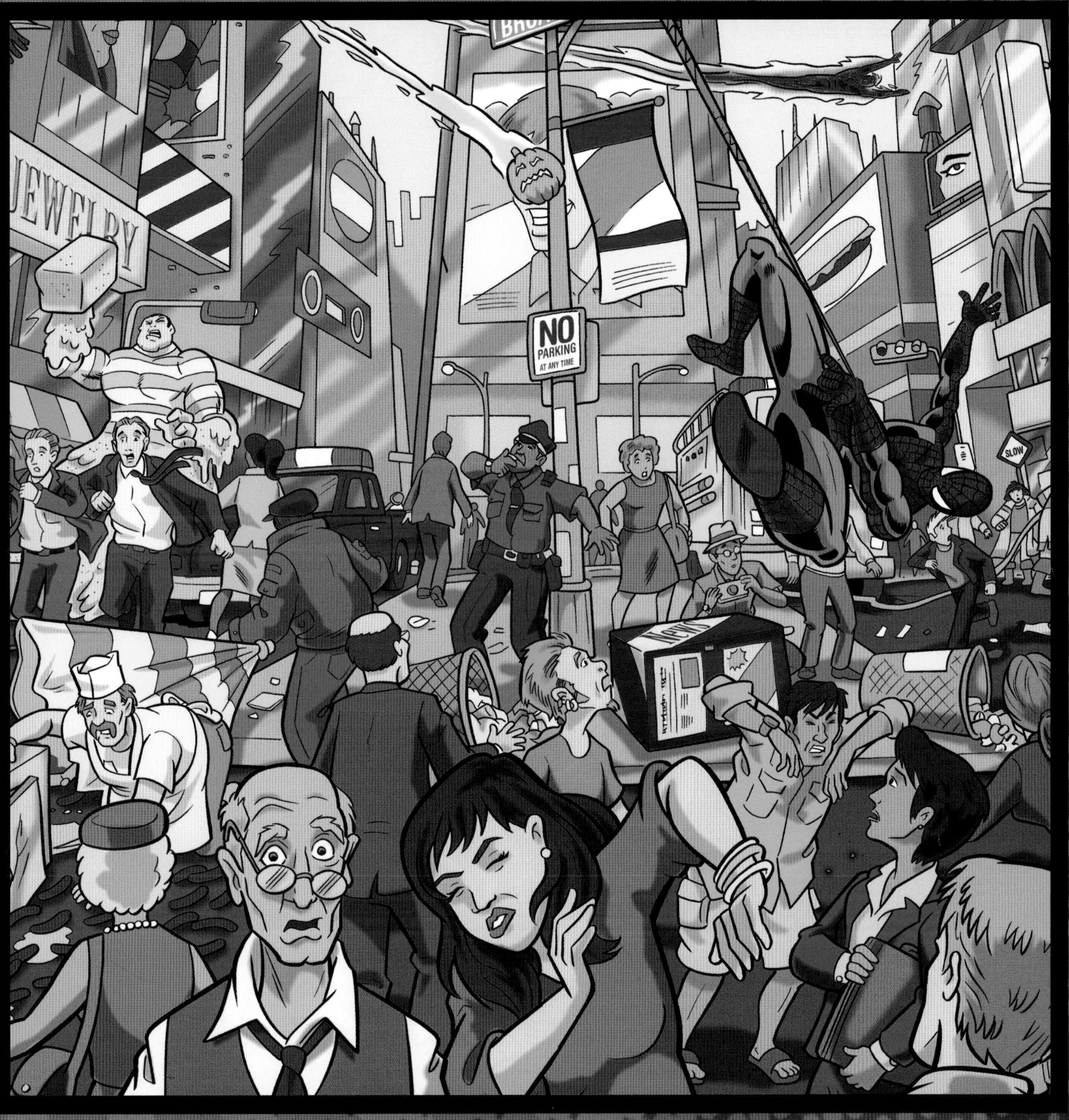
JEWELRY
NO PARKING AT ANY TIME
SLOW
NEWS

Answer key: Sandman's shirt color, shirt color under vest, woman's watch, man in purple suit's hair color, police officer's insignia, No Parking sign color, Shoe Show sign, Deli sign, stop sign, truck color

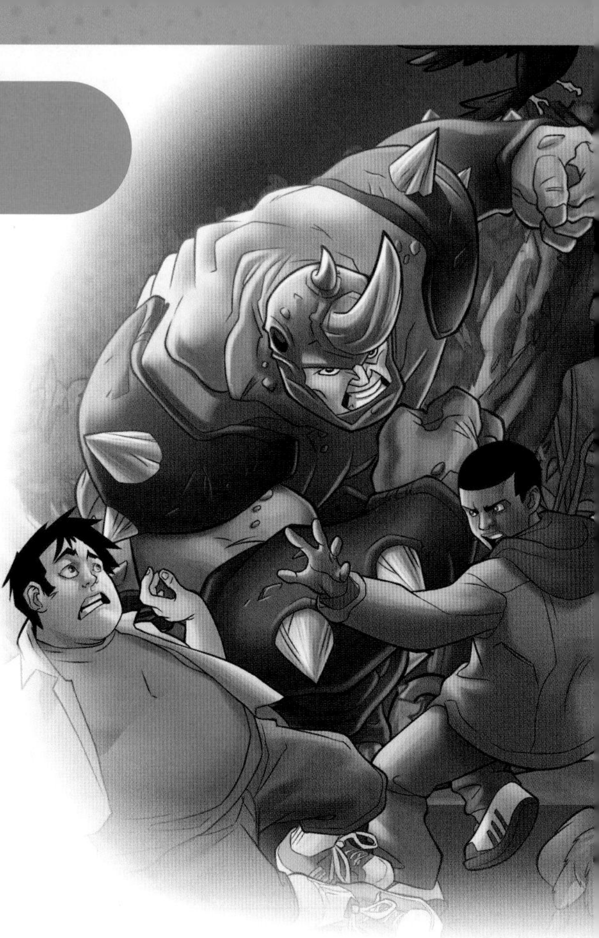

THE OTHER SPIDER-MAN

"YOUR FRIENDLY NEIGHBORHOOD SPIDER...MEN!"

MILES MORALES IS ENJOYING A DAY AT CENTRAL PARK ZOO WHEN, ALL OF A SUDDEN, THE ANIMALS START STAMPEDING!

ONE OF THE "ANIMALS" IS...RHINO!

LUCKILY, SPIDER-MAN SWINGS ONTO THE SCENE AND LASSOS RHINO JUST BEFORE THE BEAST TRAMPLES MILES.

BUT RHINO ANGRILY THROWS OFF SPIDER-MAN. SPIDEY GOES FLYING AND LANDS ON THE GROUND WITH A CRASH!

MILES RUSHES OVER TO CHECK ON SPIDER-MAN, AND REALIZES IT'S TIME TO HELP OUT...

...AS THE OTHER SPIDER-MAN!

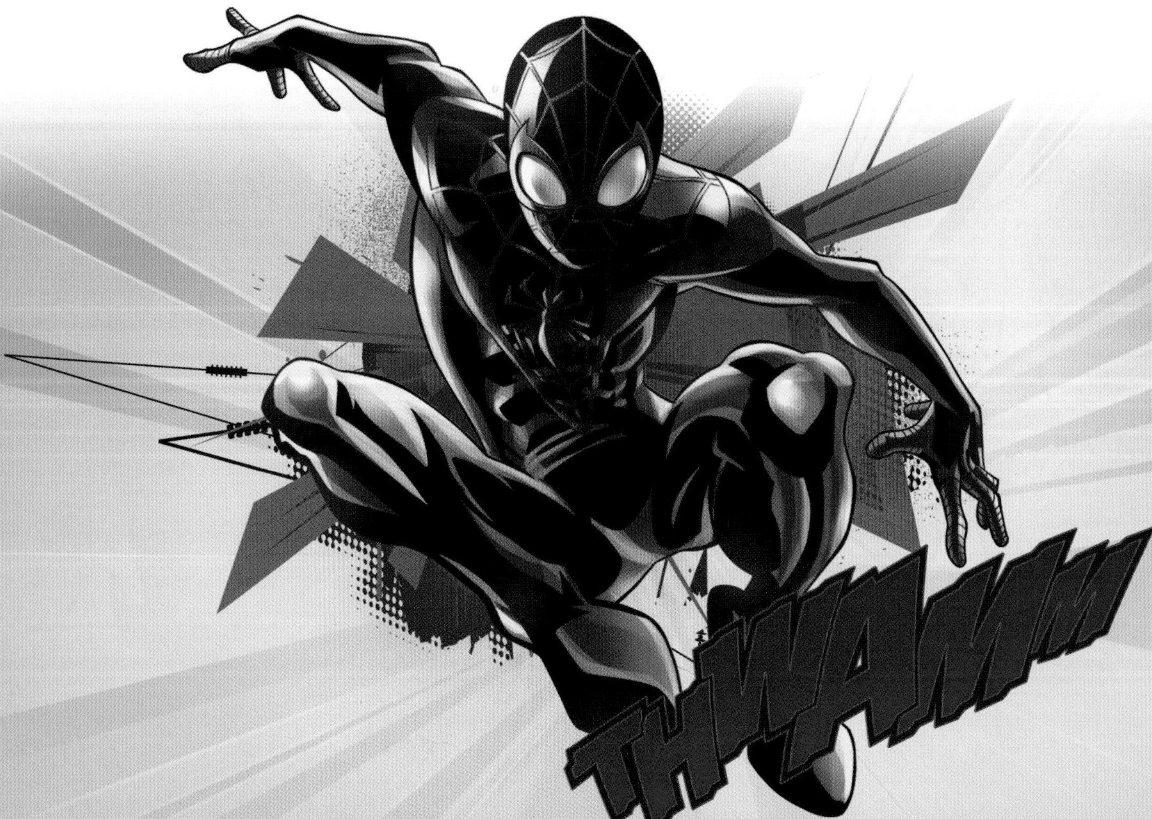
THWAMM

MILES LEAPS THROUGH THE AIR AND KICKS RHINO, GIVING SPIDER-MAN ENOUGH TIME TO RECOVER AND SWING BACK INTO ACTION.

"GO WRANGLE THE ZOO ANIMALS BEFORE THEY CAUSE MORE DAMAGE!" SPIDEY CALLS TO MILES.

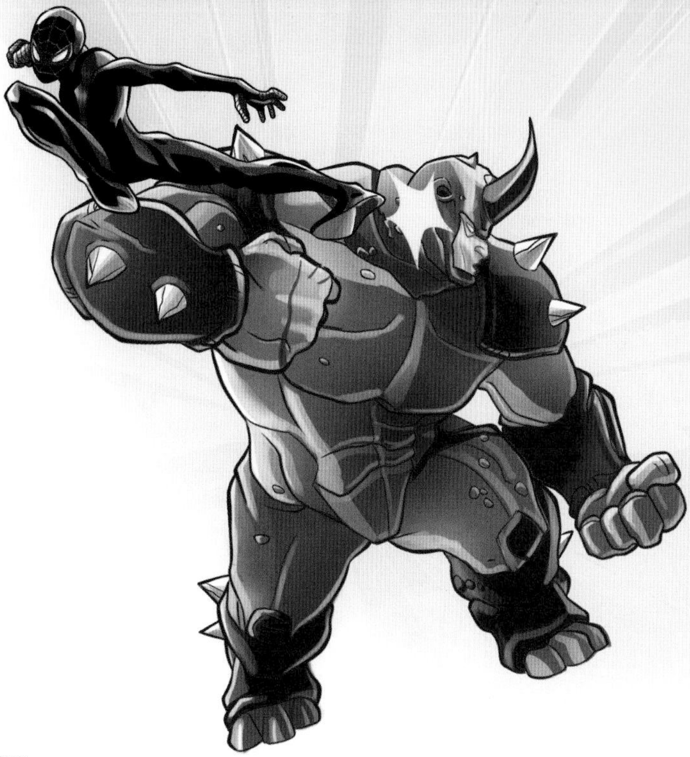

ONE BY ONE, MILES USES HIS SPECIAL SPIDER-POWERS TO GET THE ANIMALS BACK IN THEIR HABITATS.

JUST AS THE LAST ANIMAL IS CONTAINED, SPIDEY SMASHES INTO THE GROUND AT MILES'S FEET. SPIDER-MAN NEEDS THE OTHER SPIDER-MAN'S HELP BEATING RHINO! THE PAIR SWING INTO ACTION.

MILES BLASTS RHINO WITH HIS POWERFUL VENOM STRIKE WHILE SPIDER-MAN WEBS UP RHINO'S FEET. RHINO FALLS TO THE GROUND, DEFEATED.

"HAVE A NICE *TRIP!*" SPIDER-MAN JOKES.

THE OTHER SPIDER-MAN SMILES. "WE TOTALLY PUT THE *NO* IN RHINO!"

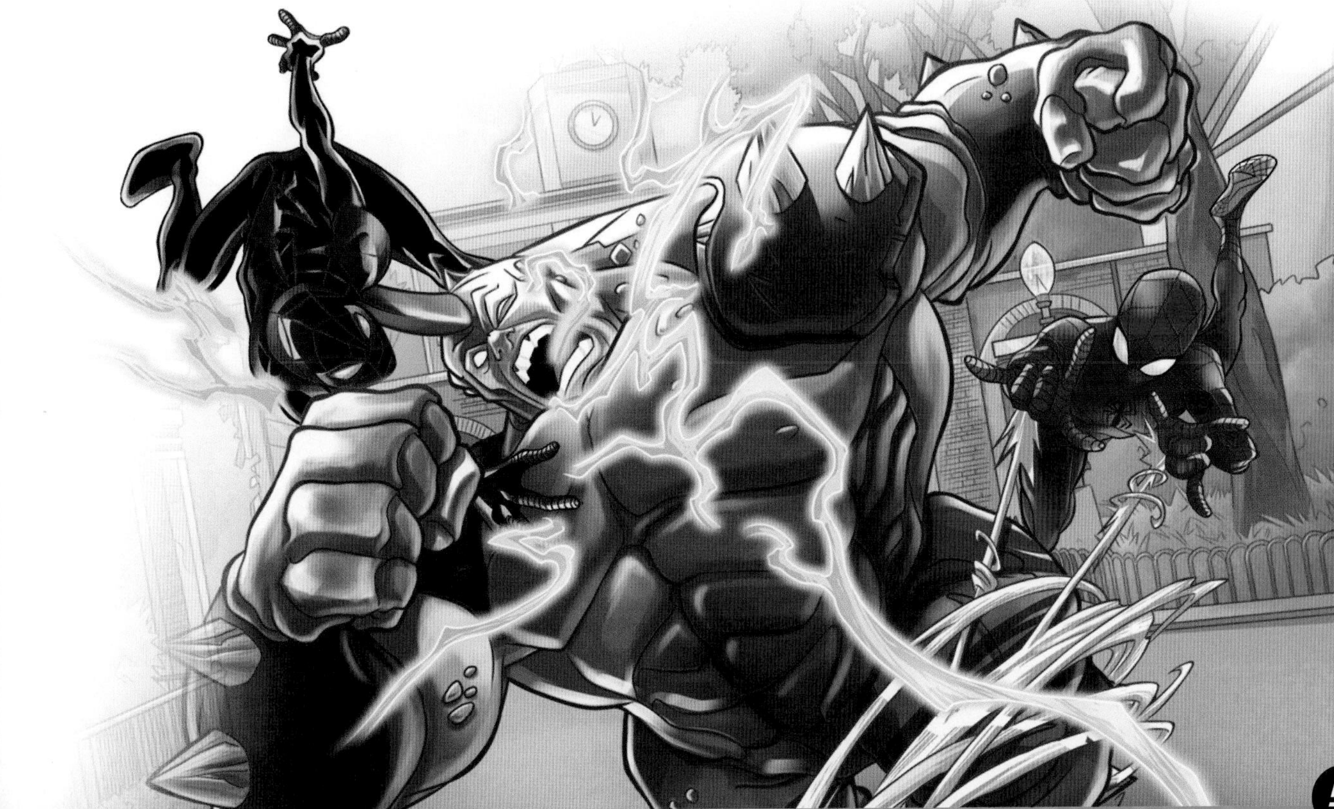

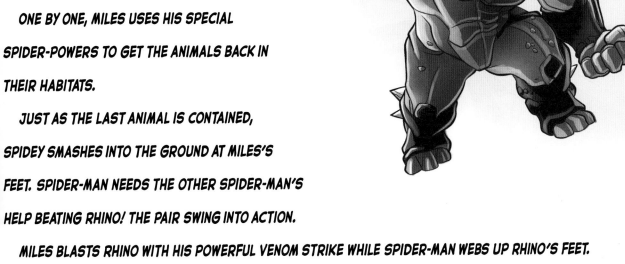

Look and Find®

UH-OH! DOC OCK IS TRYING TO KNOCK OUT THE CITY'S POWER IN ORDER TO LEAVE ITS CITIZENS HELPLESS AND TERRIFIED. AS SPIDEY JOINS IRON MAN IN BATTLING THE VILLAIN, SEARCH THE SCENE FOR THESE HANDY ELECTRICIANS AND THEIR TOOLS TO HELP FIX THE DAMAGE:

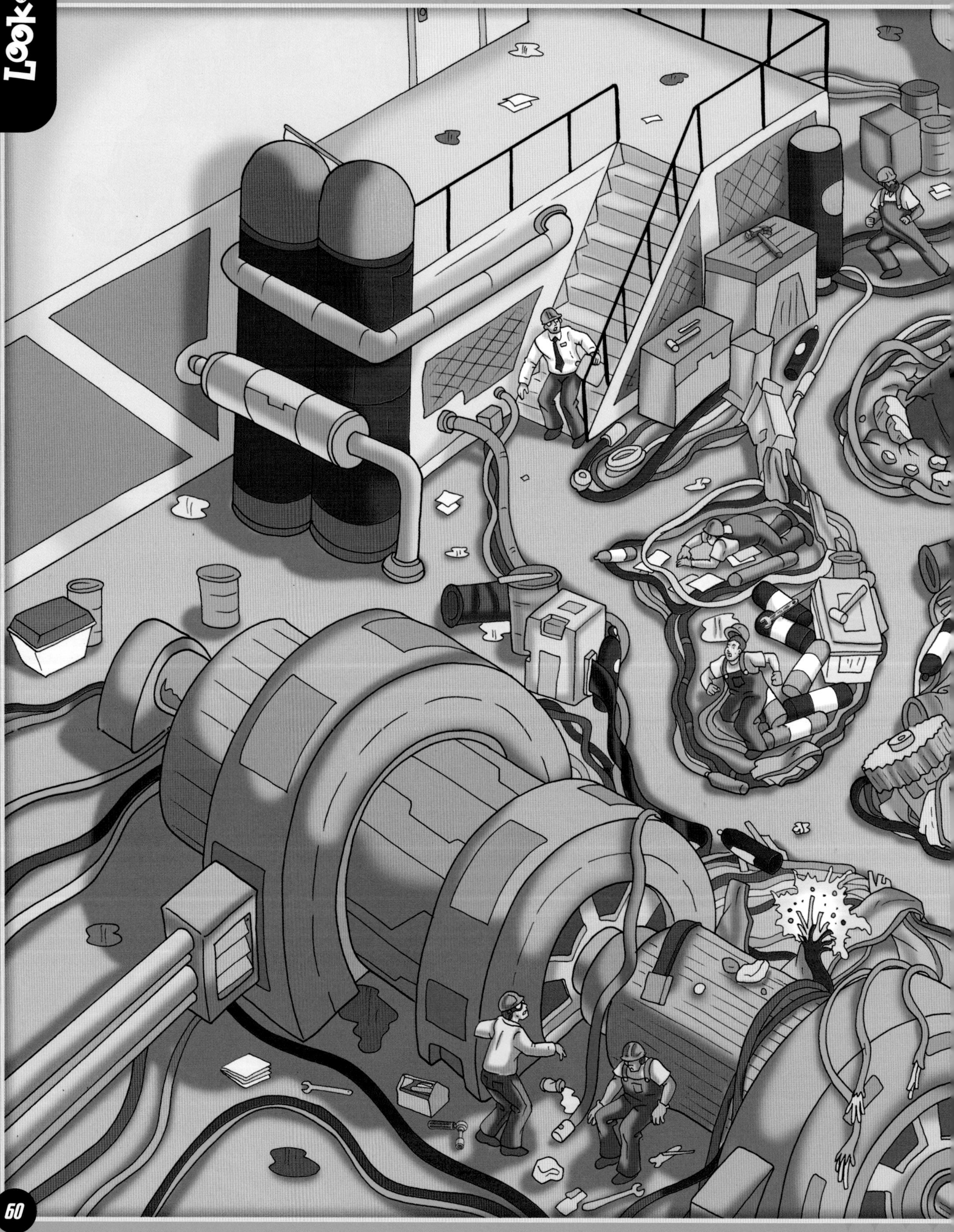

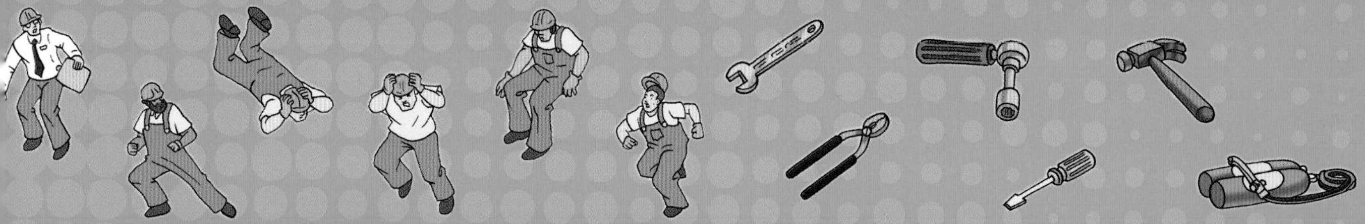

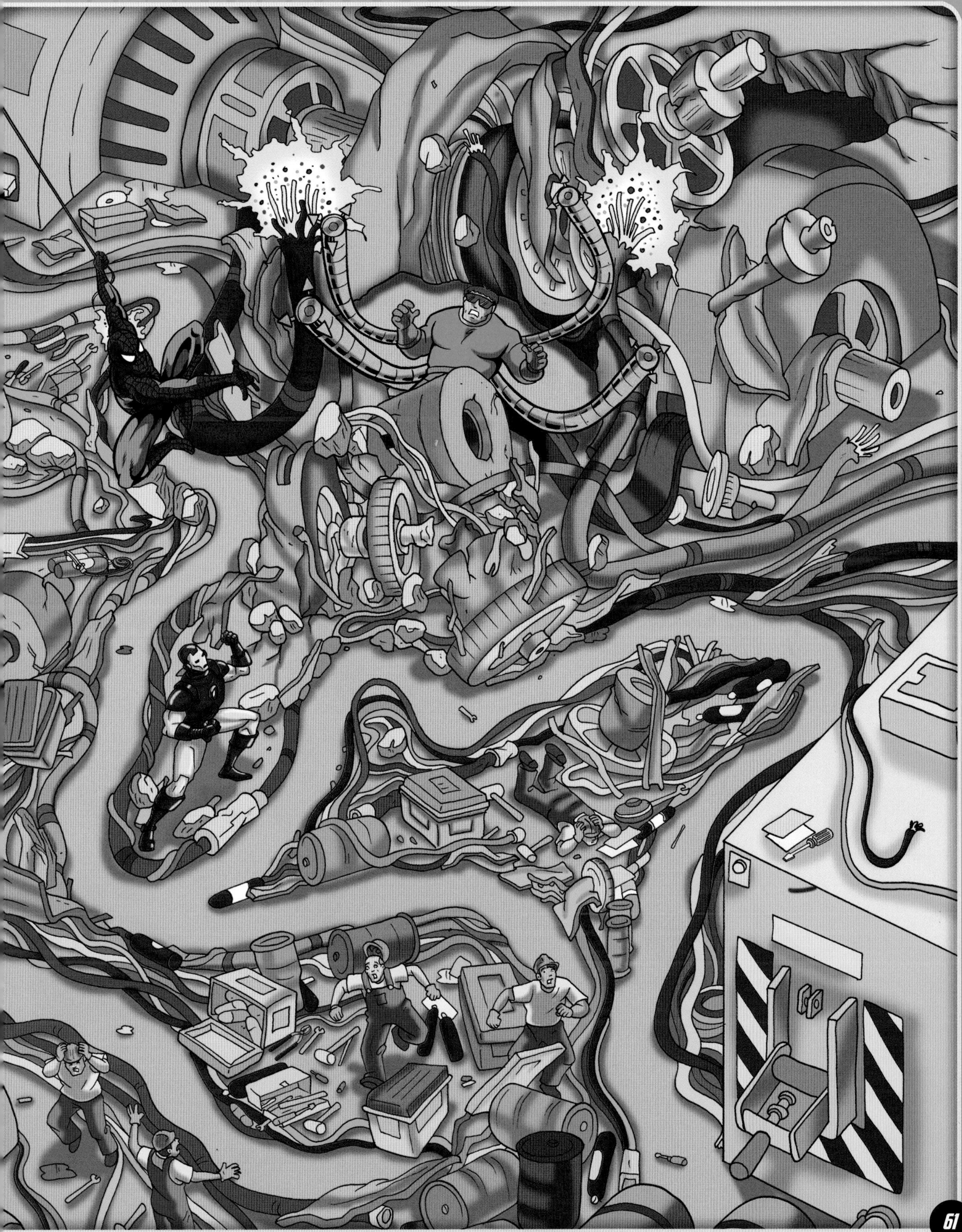

DEEP IN THE SWISS MOUNTAINS, ARNIM ZOLA CONSPIRES TO DEFEAT THE AVENGERS. ANT-MAN AND THE WASP SNEAK INTO ZOLA'S LIBRARY, SEEKING CLUES IN ORDER TO STOP HIM. WHILE ANT-MAN AND THE WASP STAY OUT OF SIGHT, SPOT THESE GLOBAL LANDMARKS AND EYE-OPENING BOOKS:

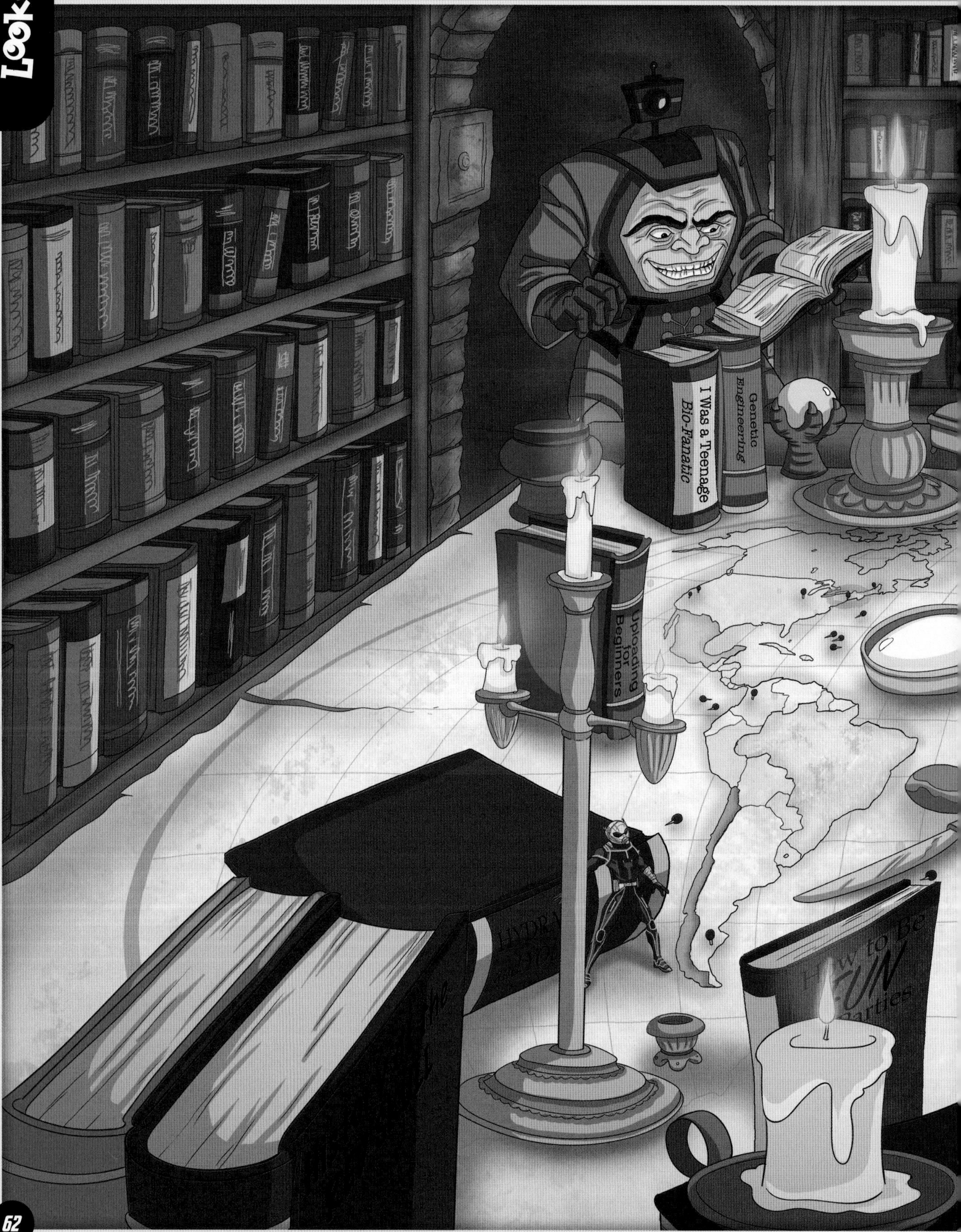

I Was a Teenage Bio-Fanatic
Genetic Engineering
Uploading for Beginners
HYDRA

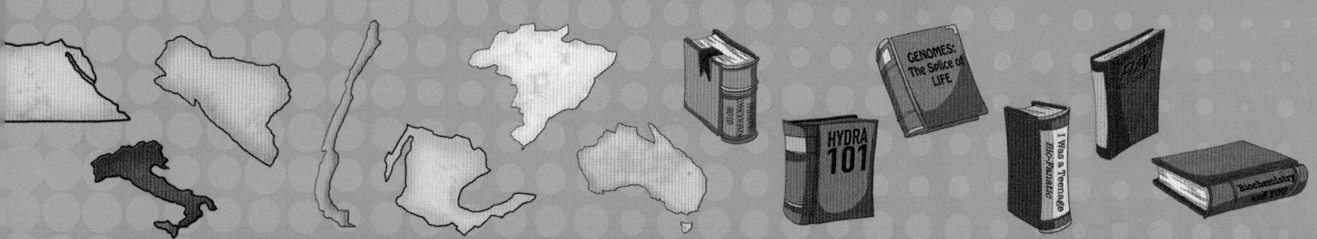
GENOMES: The Splice of LIFE
HYDRA 101
I Was a Teenage Bio-Fanatic
Biochemistry and YOU

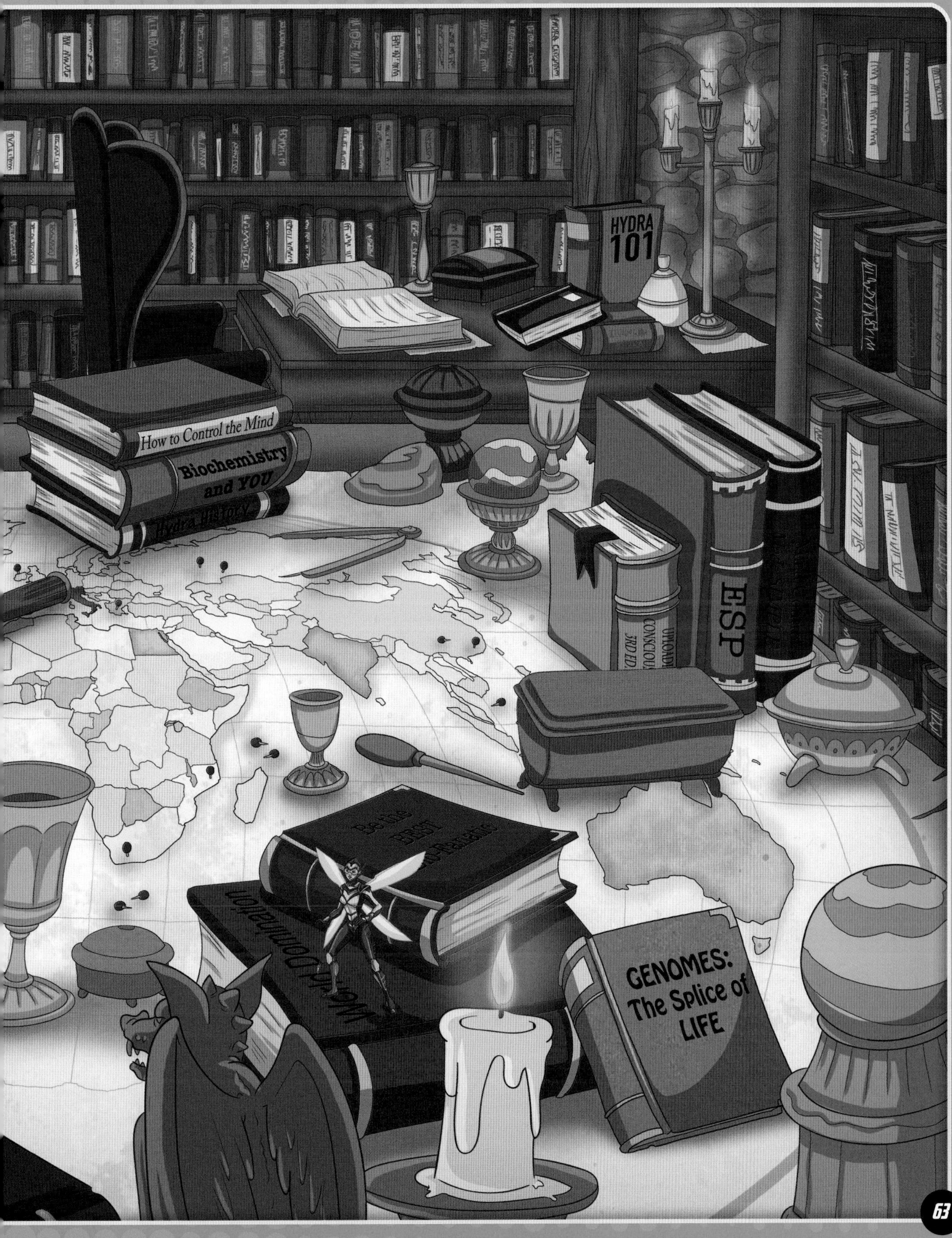
HYDRA 101
How to Control the Mind
Biochemistry and YOU
Hydra History
ESP
GENOMES: The Splice of LIFE

Picture Puzzle

Rocket and Groot have barely escaped

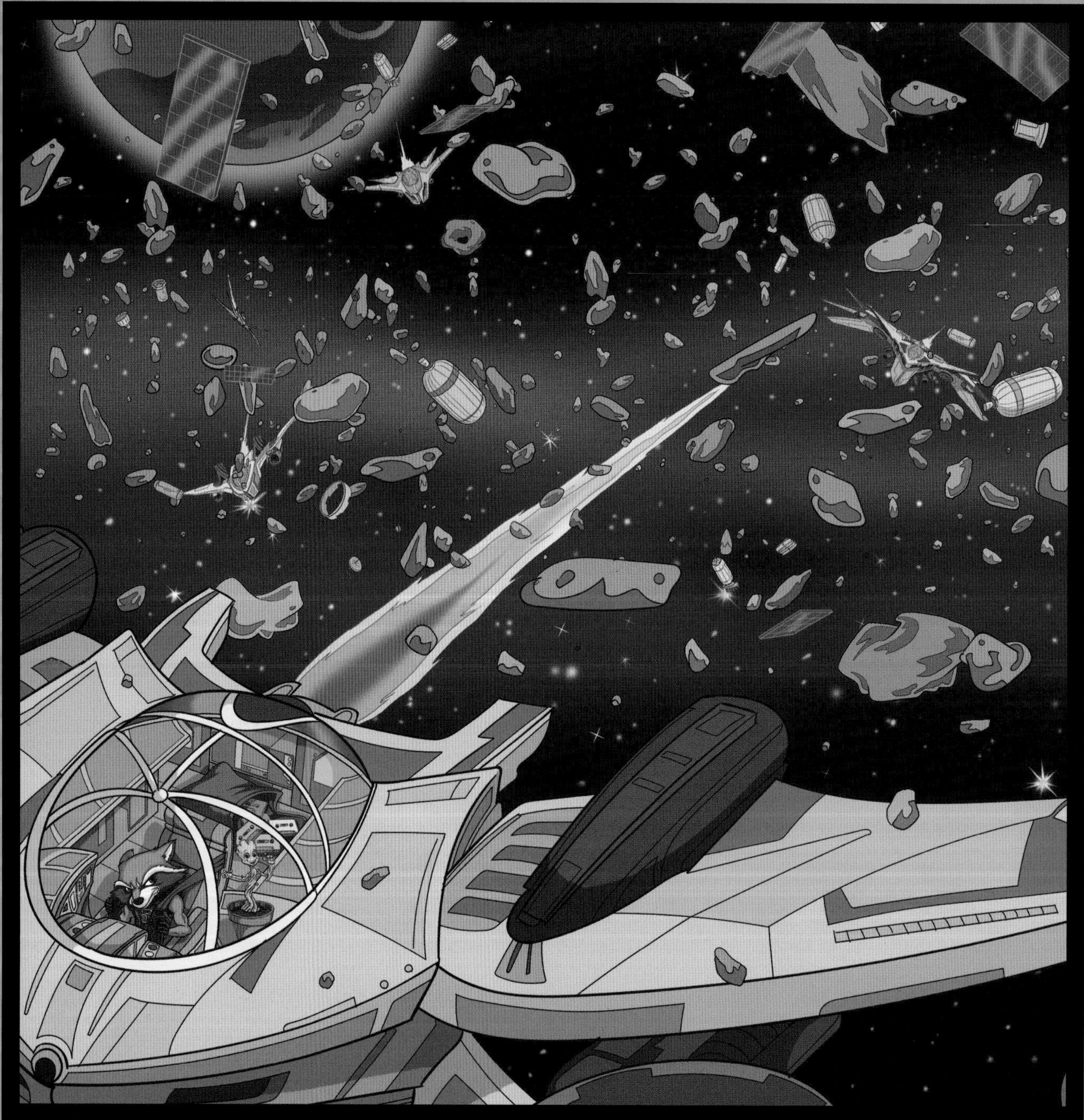

Look for 10 differences between these dramatic scenes.

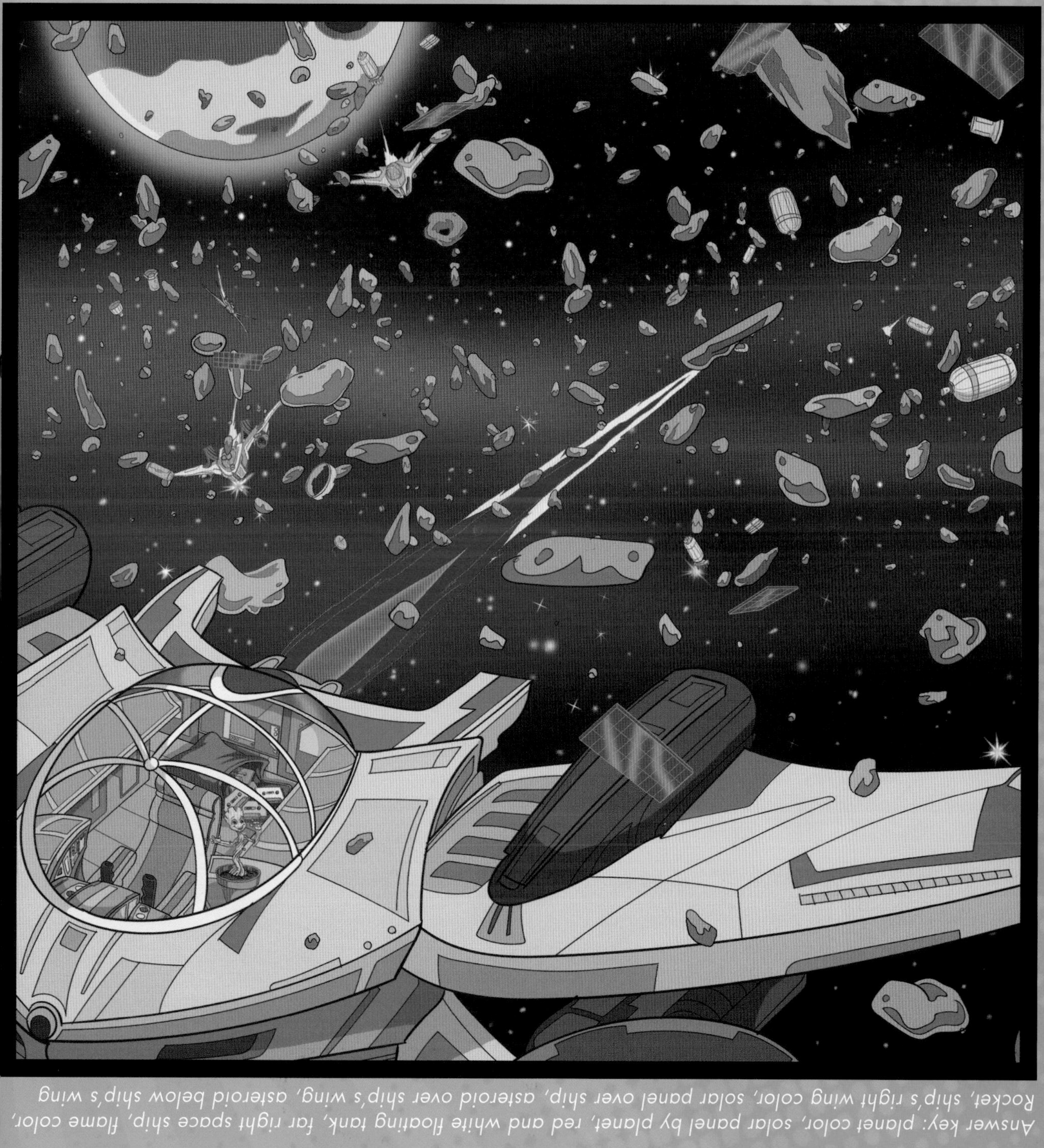

Answer key: planet color, solar panel by planet, red and white floating tank, far right space ship, flame color, Rocket, ship's right wing color, solar panel over ship, asteroid over ship's wing, asteroid below ship's wing

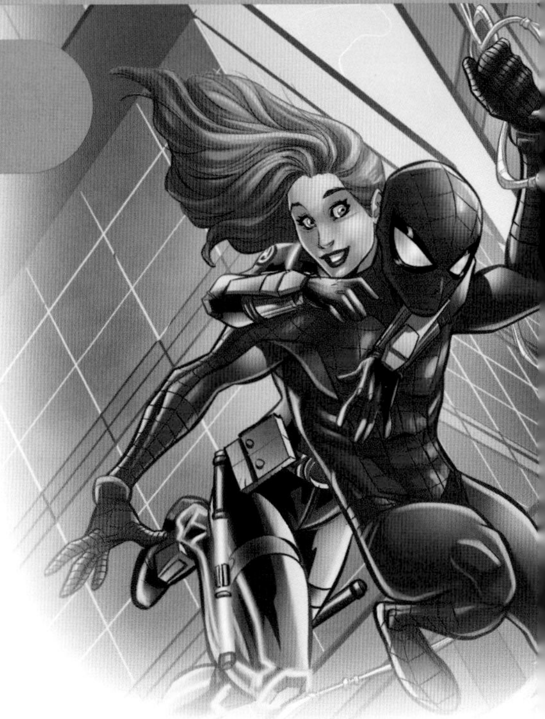

WIDOW'S STING

"WITH GREAT POWER COMES GREAT RESPONSIBILITY!"

SWINGING THROUGH THE CITY ONE SLOW DAY, SPIDER-MAN BUMPS INTO BLACK WIDOW.

THE FRIENDS HAVE A GREAT TIME SOARING THROUGH THE AIR TOGETHER. WHO KNEW BLACK WIDOW WAS SO MUCH FUN?

"WANT TO HANG OUT AT AVENGERS TOWER?" WIDOW ASKS. SPIDEY CAN'T SAY NO TO THAT!

AT THE TOWER, SPIDEY PLACES HIS HAND ON THE SECURITY SCANNER.

"AVENGERS GUEST, SPIDER-MAN. IDENTITY: CONFIRMED. WELCOME!" THE COMPUTER SAYS.

WHEN WIDOW PUTS HER HAND UP, AN ALARM GOES OFF!

THEN BLACK WIDOW DESTROYS THE SCANNER WITH HER WRIST BLASTER! SPIDER-MAN'S SPIDER-SENSE IS TINGLING. THIS CANNOT BE THE REAL BLACK WIDOW!

FAKE WIDOW ANGRILY BLASTS THE TOWER DOOR. IT DOESN'T BUD SO SHE SHOOTS HER BLASTER AT SPIDEY INSTEAD! BUT WIDOW'S BLASTS ARE BLOCKED BY...

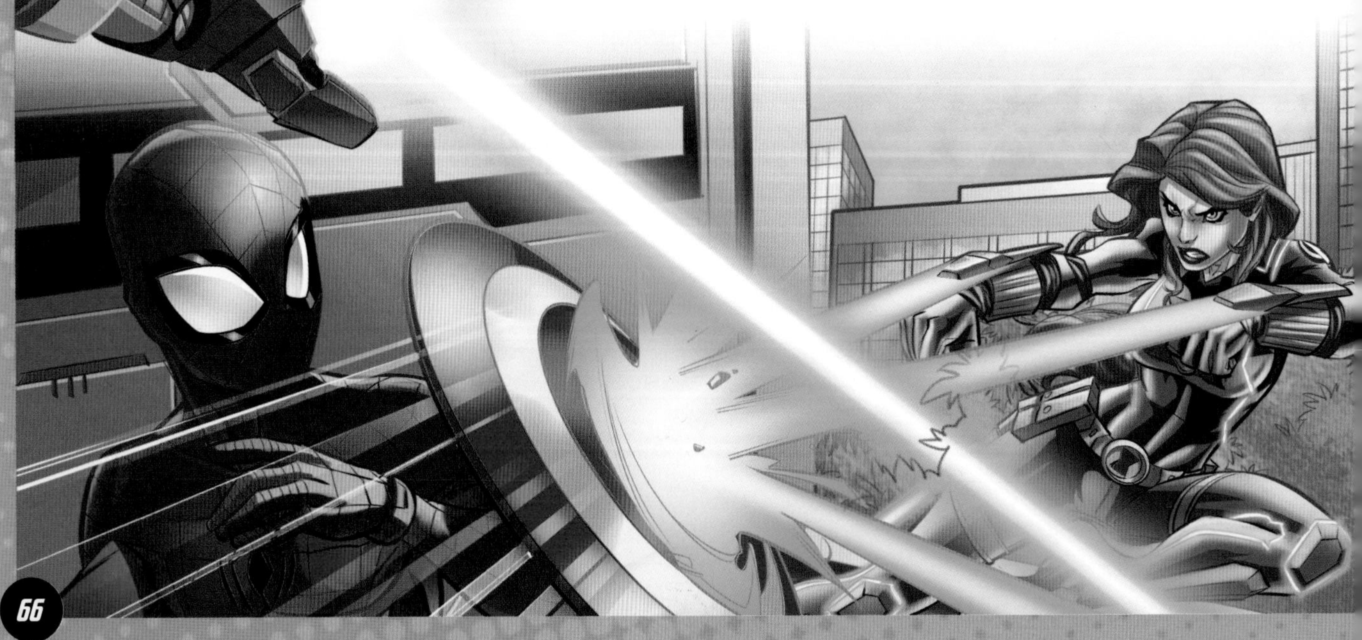

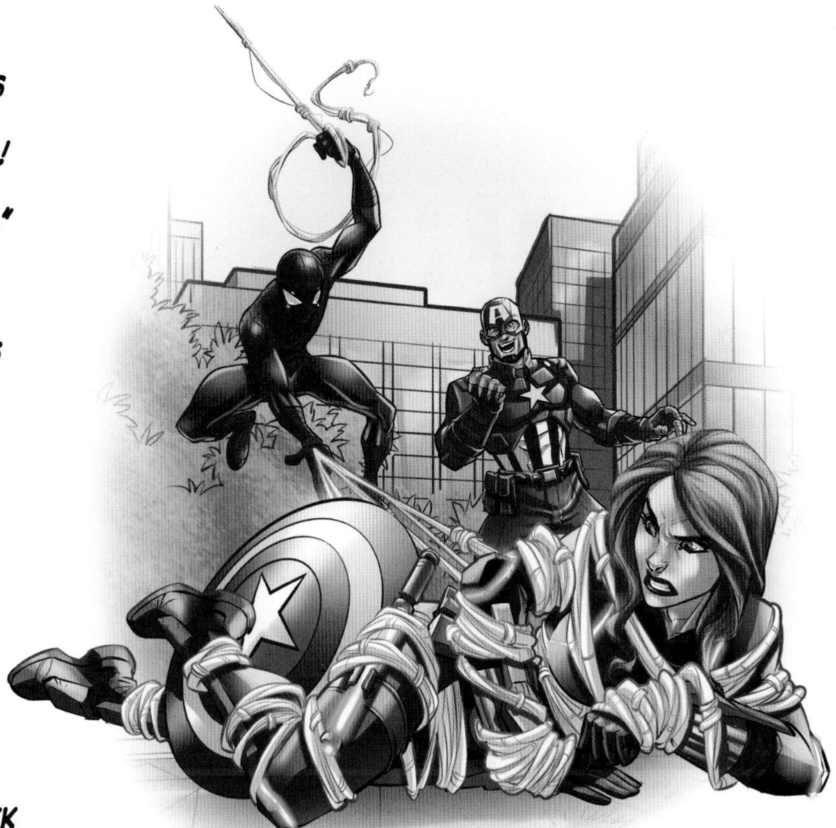

...TWO OF SPIDER-MAN'S *REAL* AVENGERS FRIENDS—IRON MAN AND CAPTAIN AMERICA!

"TOO BAD SPIDER-*FOOL* DIDN'T LET ME IN," BOGUS WIDOW SAYS, SHOOTING BLASTS AT IRON MAN. HE TRIES TO FLY AWAY, BUT SHE'S TOO FAST. WIDOW JUMPS ON IRON MAN'S BACK AND PULLS HIM DOWN.

SUDDENLY, CAPTAIN AMERICA'S SHIELD KNOCKS DOWN THE VILLAIN! SPIDER-MAN WEBS HER HANDS TOGETHER, JAMMING THE WRIST BLASTERS.

"NOW LET'S SEE WHO'S BEHIND THIS BLACK WIDOW MASK," SAYS SPIDEY.

WITH A TUG, PHONY WIDOW'S ENTIRE BODY CHANGES INTO THE MASTER OF DISGUISE, CHAMELEON! AS IRON MAN FLIES OFF WITH THE IMPOSTOR, SPIDER-MAN THANKS CAPTAIN AMERICA.

CAP LAUGHS. "SOMETIMES ALL IT TAKES IS A LITTLE HELP FROM YOUR *REAL* FRIENDS."

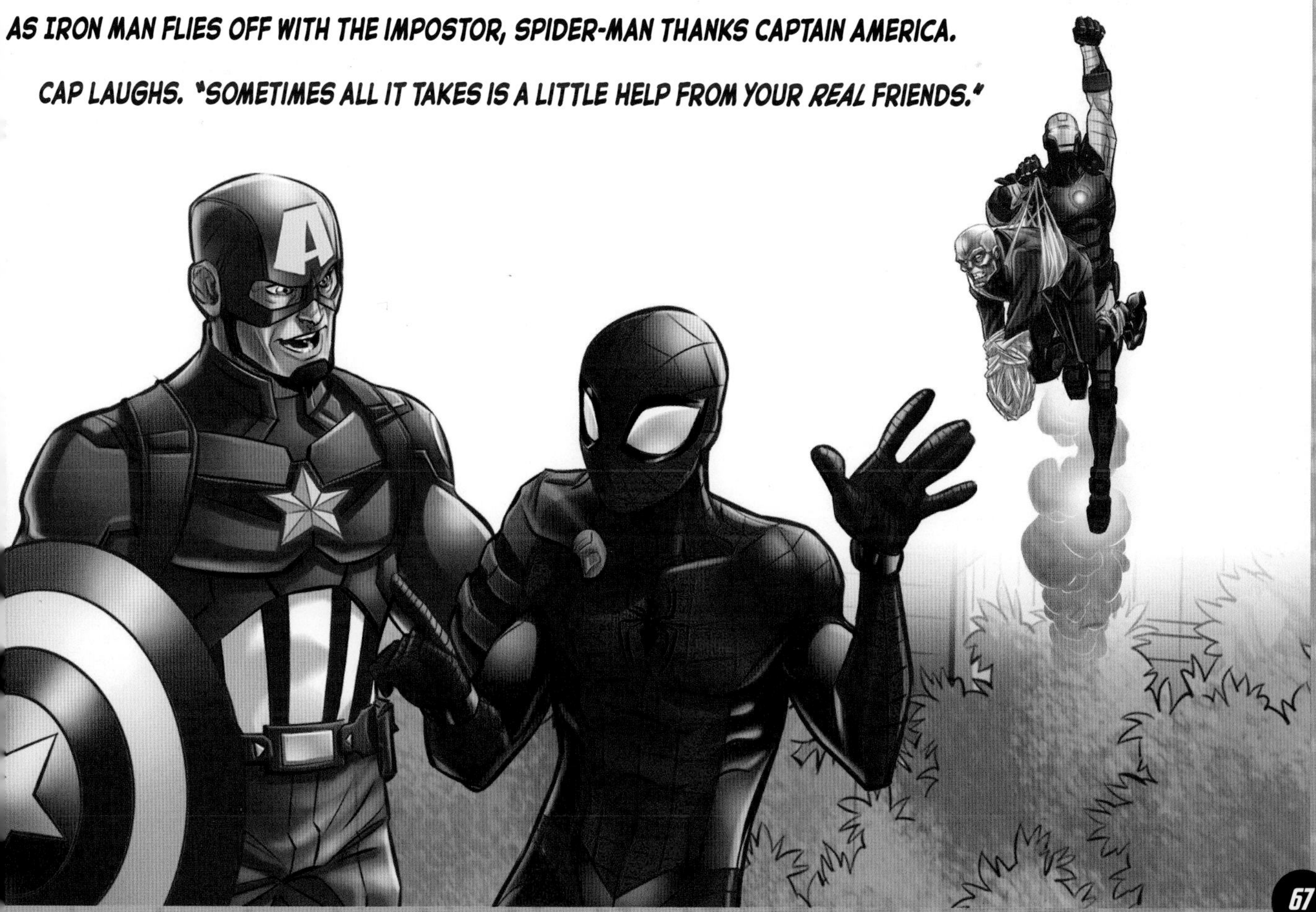

MYSTERIO, A MASTER OF ILLUSION, HAS SPIDER-MAN SEEING DOUBLE...AND TRIPLE! SPIDEY WILL HAVE TO GET TO MYSTERIO IF HE WANTS TO BREAK THE SPELL. WHILE SPIDER-MAN BATTLES HIS WAY PAST HIMSELF, SINGLE OUT THESE PETER PARKER IMPOSTORS FROM AMONG THESE ALLURING ADVERTISEMENTS:

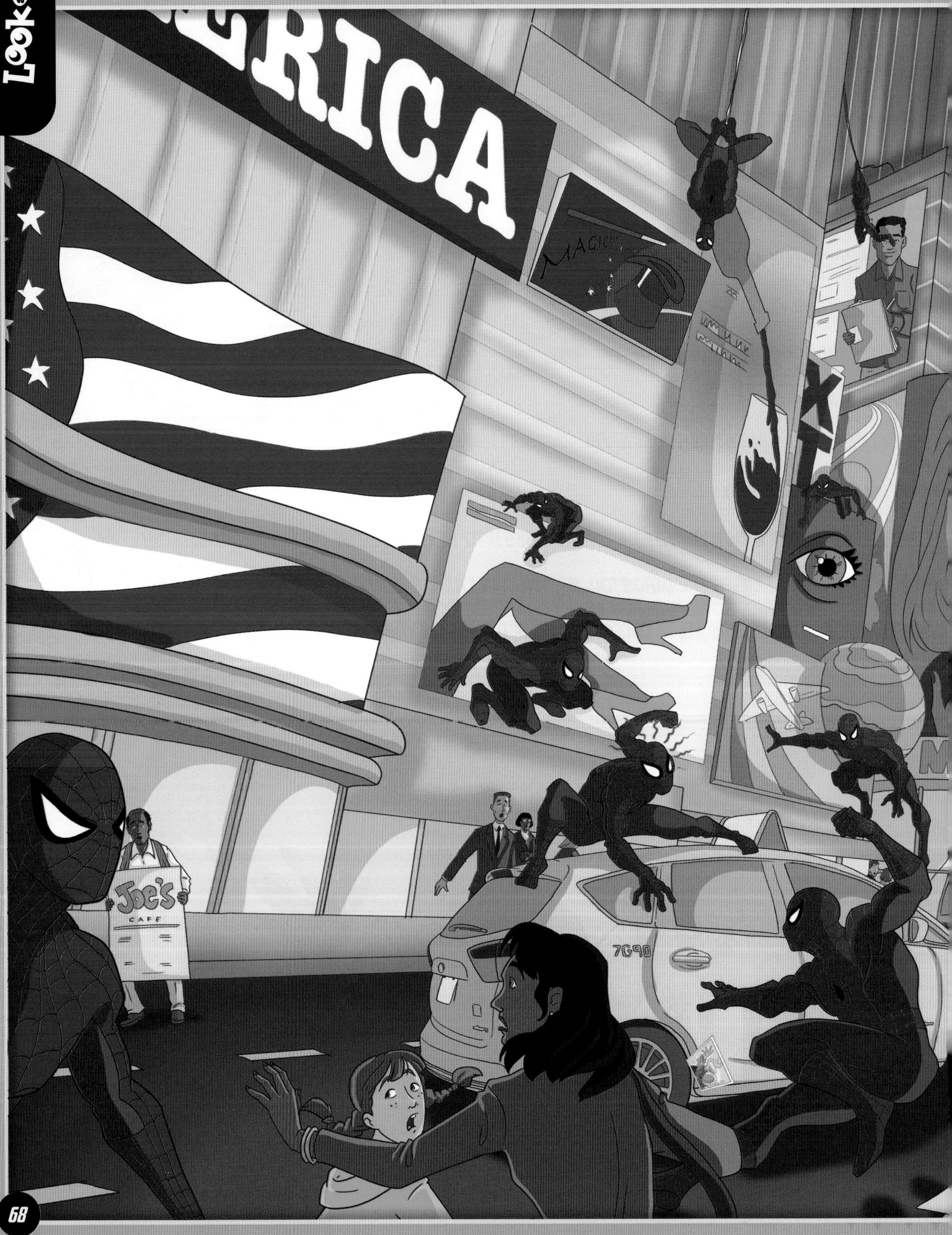
RICA
MAGIC!
JOE'S
CAFE
7G90

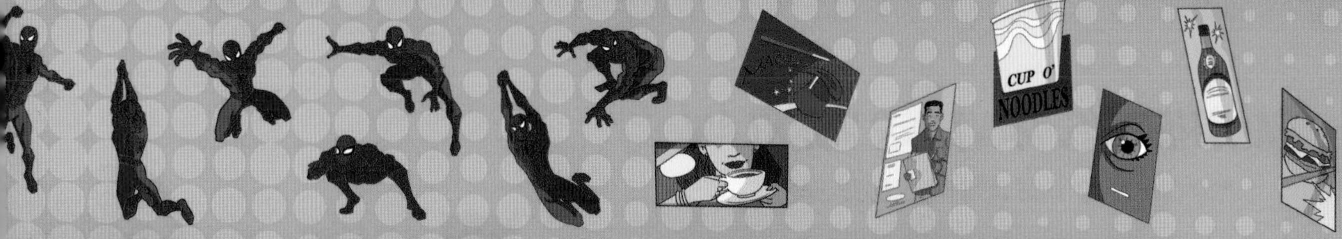
CUP O'
NOODLES

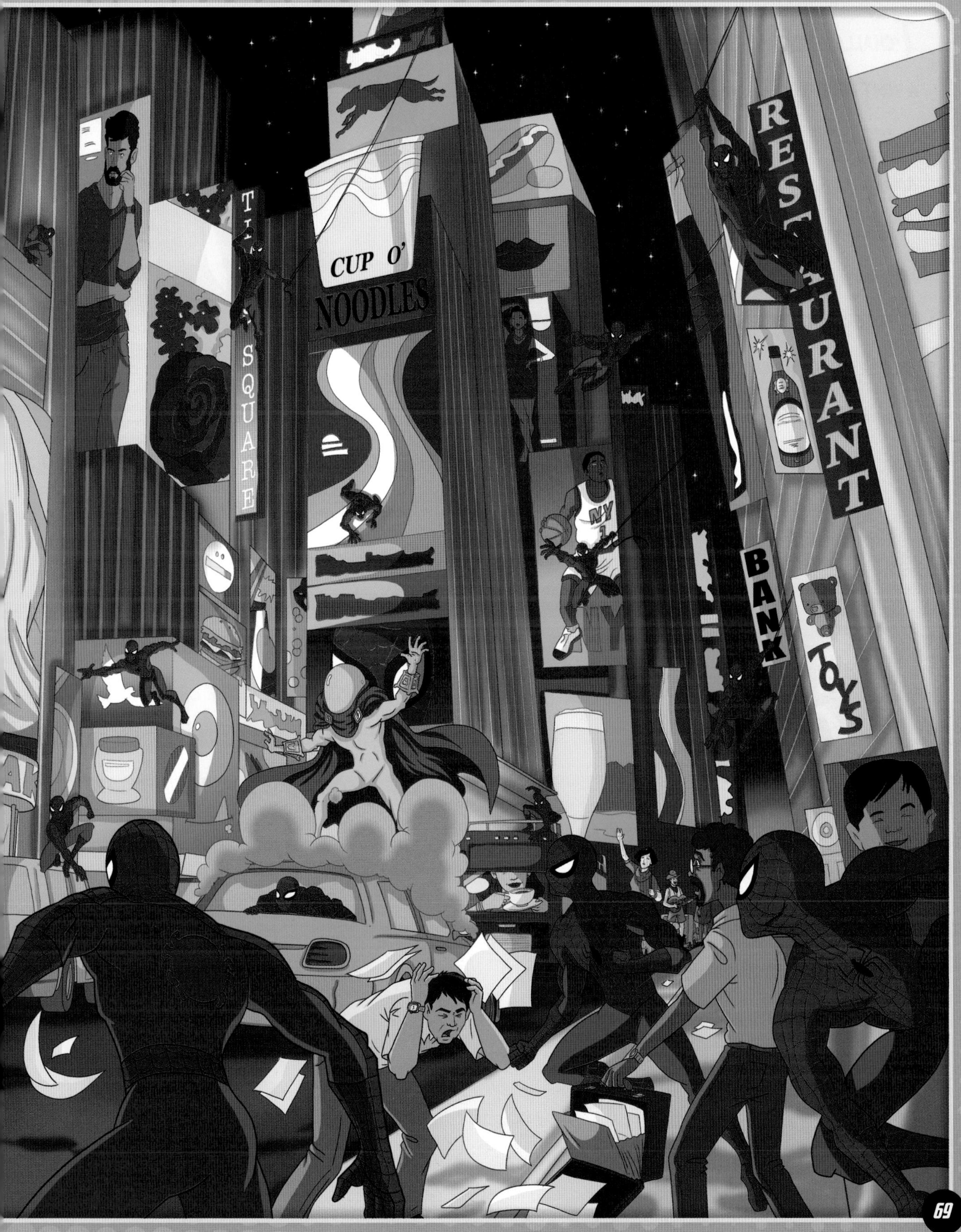
CUP O'
NOODLES
SQUARE
RES
URANT
NY
BANK
TOYS

PANTHER VS. PANTHER VS. KLAW

"NO ONE SAID THIS JOB WOULD BE EASY."

T'CHALLA, THE BLACK PANTHER, IS SURPRISED TO GET A VISIT FROM HIS FELLOW AVENGERS.

"SOMEONE ROBBED S.H.I.E.L.D. LAST NIGHT," CAPTAIN AMERICA SAYS, " ...DRESSED AS THE BLACK PANTHER."

WAR MACHINE SAYS, "SOMEONE'S TRYING TO FRAME YOU. WE THOUGHT YOU MIGHT WANT TO HELP CATCH HIM."

BLACK PANTHER GOES TO INVESTIGATE, LEAVING HIS SISTER SHURI TO WATCH OVER WAKANDA.

WHEN THE HEROES GET TO S.H.I.E.L.D. HEADQUARTERS, NICK FURY IS WAITING FOR THEM.

"THE GOOD NEWS IS, YOU WON'T HAVE TO GO FAR TO FIND THE IMPOSTOR," SAYS FURY. "THE BAD NEWS IS, THAT'S BECAUSE HE'S ALREADY HERE."

" JUST POINT THE WAY," BLACK PANTHER SAYS. HE FOLLOWS FURY'S DIRECTIONS AND FINDS THE IMPOSTOR SNEAKING AROUND THE CELL BLOCK.

T'CHALLA STOPS HIM, BUT HE HAS ALREADY FREED A S.H.I.E.L.D. PRISONER: THE SUPER VILLAIN KLAW!

"LIKE MY ANDROID COPY OF YOU?" KLAW ASKS. "IF YOU'RE HERE FIGHTING US...WHO'S PROTECTING YOUR PEOPLE?" LAUGHING, HE DISAPPEARS—HEADED FOR WAKANDA!

BLACK PANTHER RACES HOME, CALLING AHEAD TO WARN SHURI. "I HAVE AN IDEA," SHE SAYS. "JUST GIVE ME SOME TIME IN MY LAB."

WHEN BLACK PANTHER ARRIVES, KLAW IS USING SONIC ENERGY TO CREATE EARTHQUAKES!

"I MADE YOU A VIBRANIUM SPHERE," SHURI SAYS. "ONCE KLAW'S INSIDE, HE CAN'T ESCAPE, EVEN BY TURNING INTO SOUND."

"THEN WE HAVE A CHANCE," BLACK PANTHER SAYS. "THANK YOU, SHURI."

BLACK PANTHER MANAGES TO FIGHT KLAW INTO JUST THE RIGHT SPOT TO TRICK HIM INTO THE SPHERE.

WITH THE FAKE BLACK PANTHER DEFEATED AND KLAW LOCKED IN A VIBRANIUM SPHERE, BLACK PANTHER CAN FINALLY RETURN TO THE PALACE.

"AS SOON AS YOU CAUGHT HIM, THE QUAKES STOPPED," RAMONDA SAYS. "WELL DONE, MY SON!"

"I COULDN'T HAVE DONE IT WITHOUT SHURI," BLACK PANTHER SAYS. "TOGETHER, WE KEPT WAKANDA SAFE."

Look and Find®

TASKMASTER HAS THE UNCANNY ABILITY TO REPLICATE EVERY MOVEMENT HE SEES—INCLUDING ANT-MAN
SINCE ANT-MAN AND THE WASP CAN'T OUTFIGHT TASKMASTER, THEY WILL HAVE TO OUTNUMBER HIM INSTE
FIND THESE INSECTS HELPING THEM, AND HELP OUR HEROES AVOID TASKMASTER'S TRICK ARROWS:

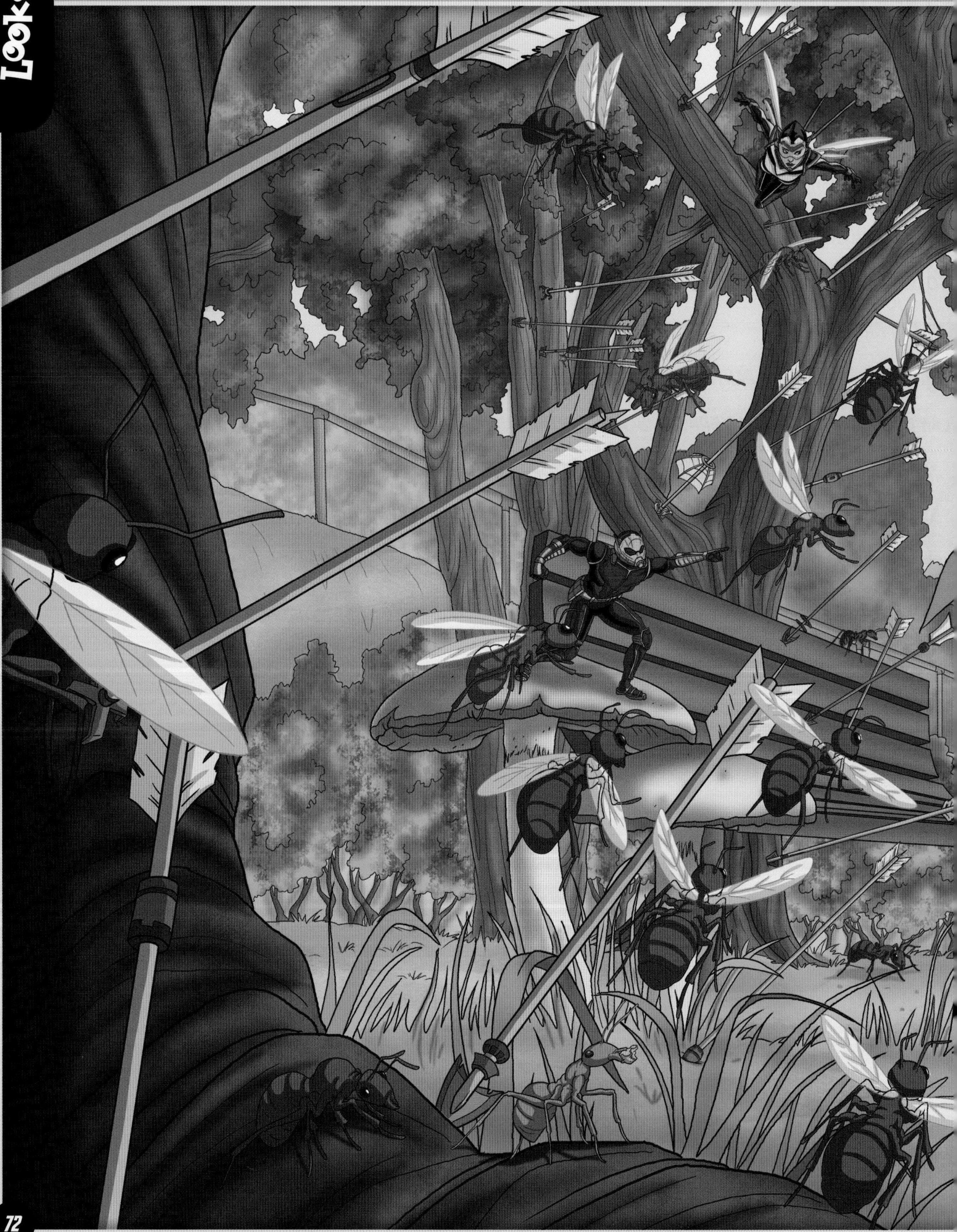

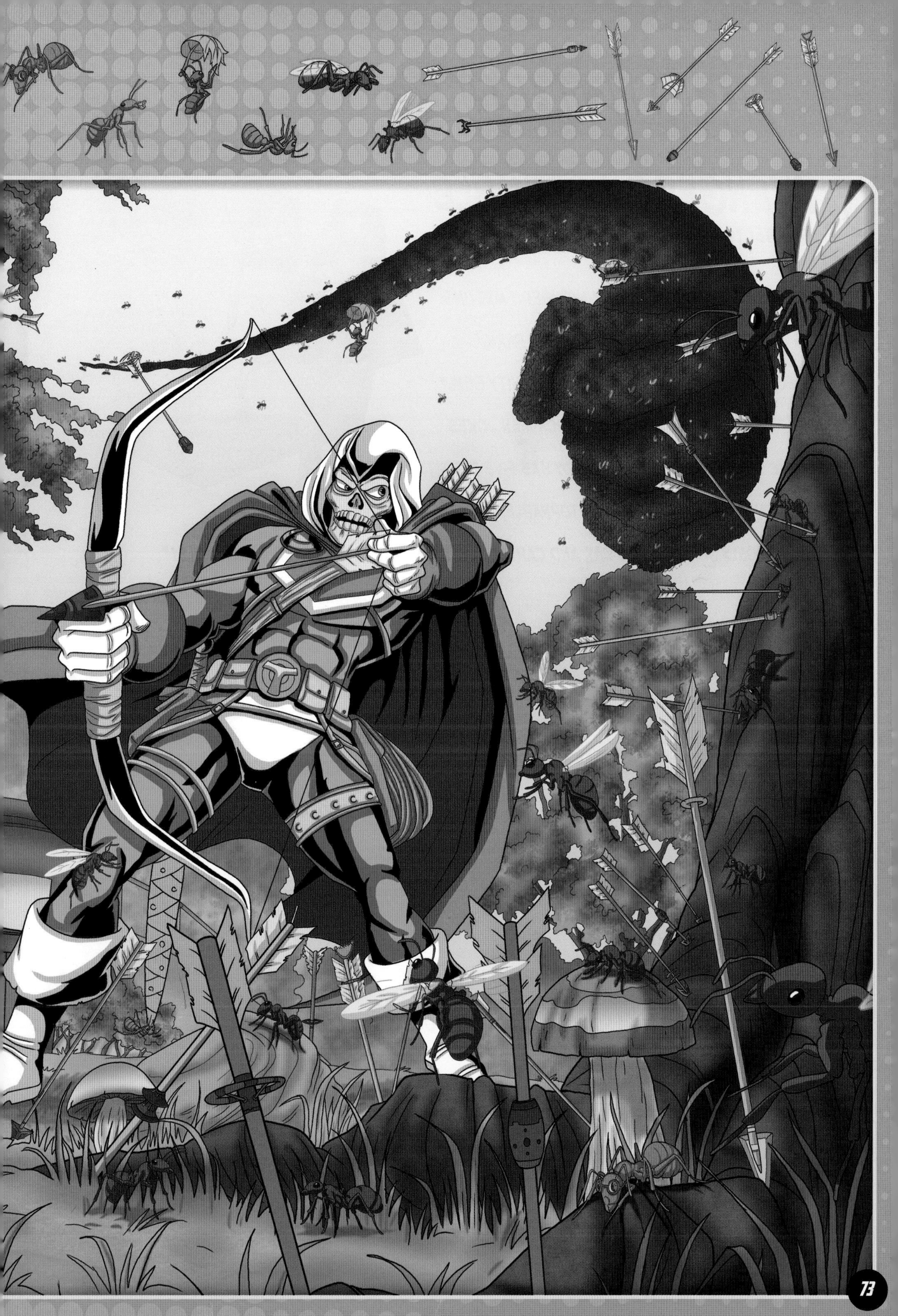

ALL HANDS ON DECK!

AVENGERS ASSEMBLE

"PROTECTORS OF NEW YORK...AND THE UNIVERSE"

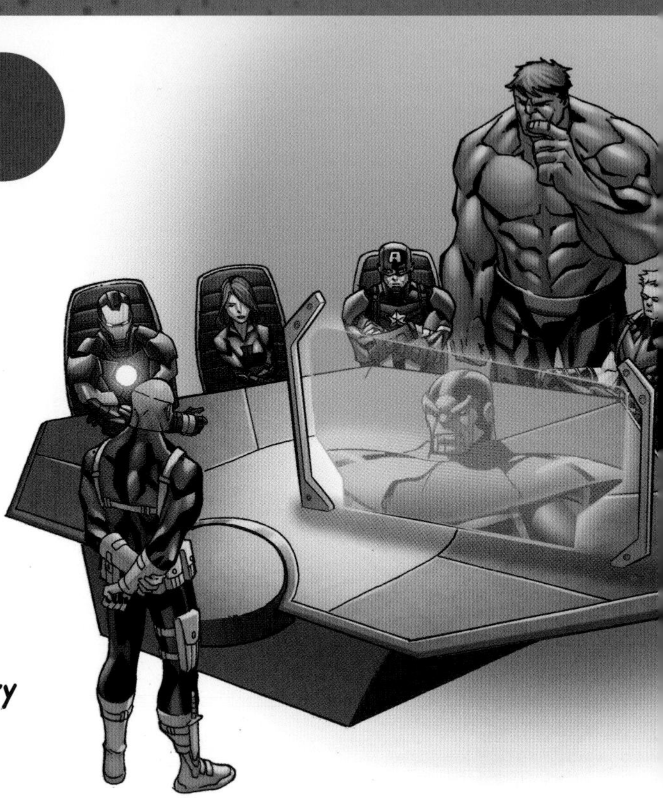

NICK FURY CALLS AN EMERGENCY AVENGERS MEETING.

"WE JUST SPOTTED THANOS IN CENTRAL PARK," FURY TELLS THE TEAM, "NEAR THE LAST INFINITY GEM."

"HEY, MAYBE IT'S A COINCIDENCE," IRON MAN JOKES.

FURY IS SERIOUS. "THANOS ALREADY HAS FIVE INFINITY GEMS. WITH ALL SIX, HE MAY BE UNSTOPPABLE."

THERE'S ONLY ONE THING TO SAY, AND CAPTAIN AMERICA SAYS IT. "AVENGERS, ASSEMBLE!"

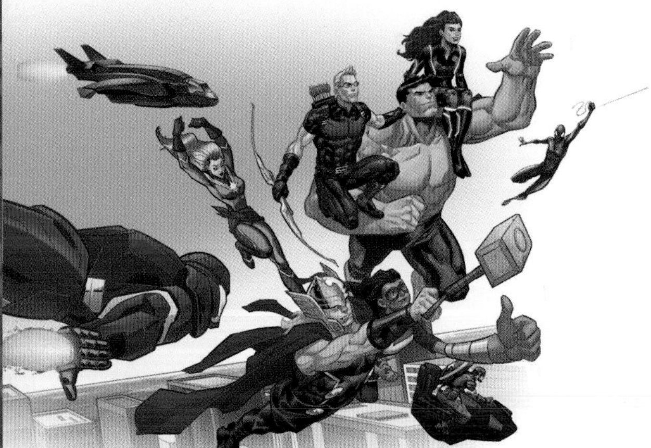

WAR MACHINE FLIES OVER THE PARK AND RETURNS WITH BAD NEWS.

"THANOS ISN'T ALONE," HE SAYS. "HE'S BROUGHT ALONG AN ARMY OF CHITAURI."

"WE'LL NEED ALL THE SUPER HEROES WE CAN GET," CAP SAYS. SPIDER-MAN AND MS. MARVEL TAKE THE DAY OFF SCHOOL. BLACK PANTHER FLIES IN FROM WAKANDA.

"EVERYONE READY?" CAP ASKS. "LET'S GET IN THE AIR."

CENTRAL PARK IS PACKED WITH CHITAURI.

"I CAN'T EVEN SEE THANOS," HAWKEYE COMPLAINS.

"FALCON," CAP SAYS, "GET A BIRD'S-EYE VIEW. EVERYONE ELSE—"

"SMASH," SAYS HULK, AND THE HEROES DO.

THOR SWINGS HIS HAMMER. MS. MARVEL SWINGS HER FISTS. SPIDER-MAN SWINGS THROUGH THE AIR. THEY EACH USE THEIR ABILITIES TO ZAP, SMASH, OR SLASH THE CHITAURI.

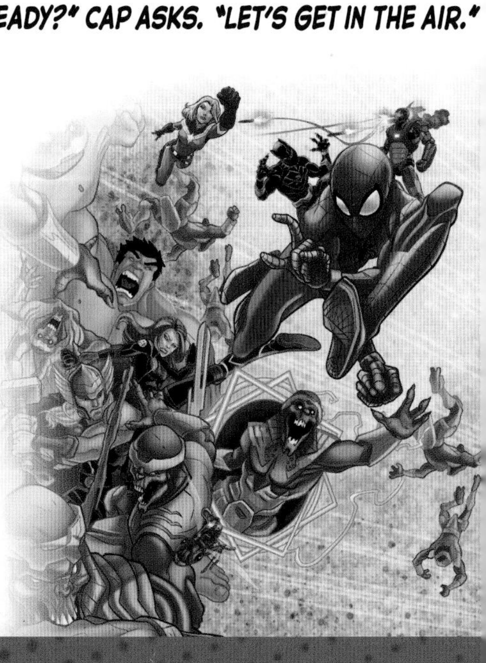

WITH THE CHITAURI GONE, THANOS STANDS ALONE—PLACING THE FINAL GEM INTO HIS INFINITY GAUNTLET.

"YOU'RE TOO LATE, LITTLE HEROES," HE TAUNTS. "I AM UNBEATABLE!"

"YEAH, I DON'T BUY THAT," IRON MAN SAYS, FIRING HIS REPULSORS.

HAWKEYE SHOOTS EXPLOSIVE ARROWS. BLACK PANTHER LANDS A MIGHTY BLOW. BUT THANOS STOPS EACH ATTACK.

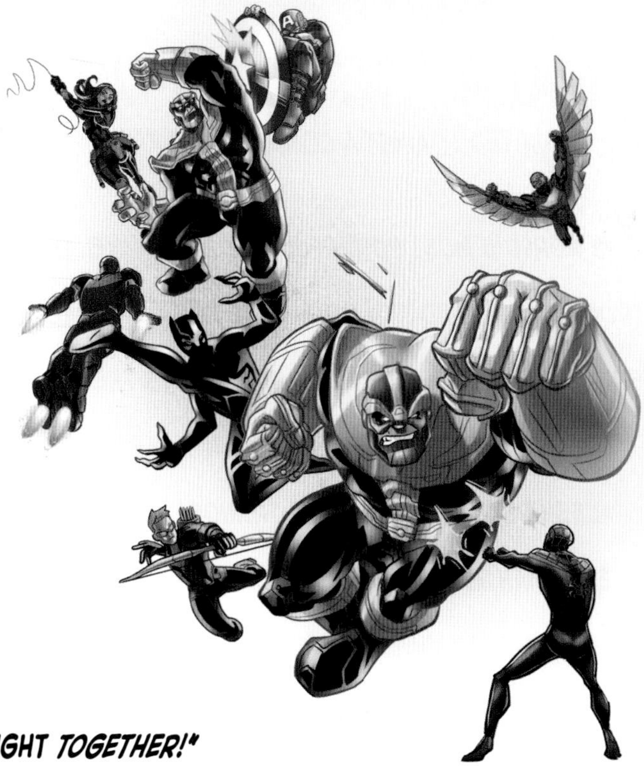

"AVENGERS," CAPTAIN AMERICA CALLS, "WE NEED TO FIGHT *TOGETHER!*"

WORKING AS A TEAM, THE HEROES ARE ABLE TO GRAB THE GAUNTLET OFF THANOS'S HAND!

THANOS KNOWS HE CAN'T BEAT THE AVENGERS WITHOUT HELP. HE FLEES, AND CENTRAL PARK—AND THE UNIVERSE—ARE A LITTLE BIT SAFER.

"A NOBLE BATTLE, WELL FOUGHT!" THOR DECLARES.

"WE DESERVE A PARTY," HAWKEYE SAYS.

"I THINK WE CAN MANAGE THAT," CAP SAYS WITH A SMILE, "IF WE ALL WORK TOGETHER."

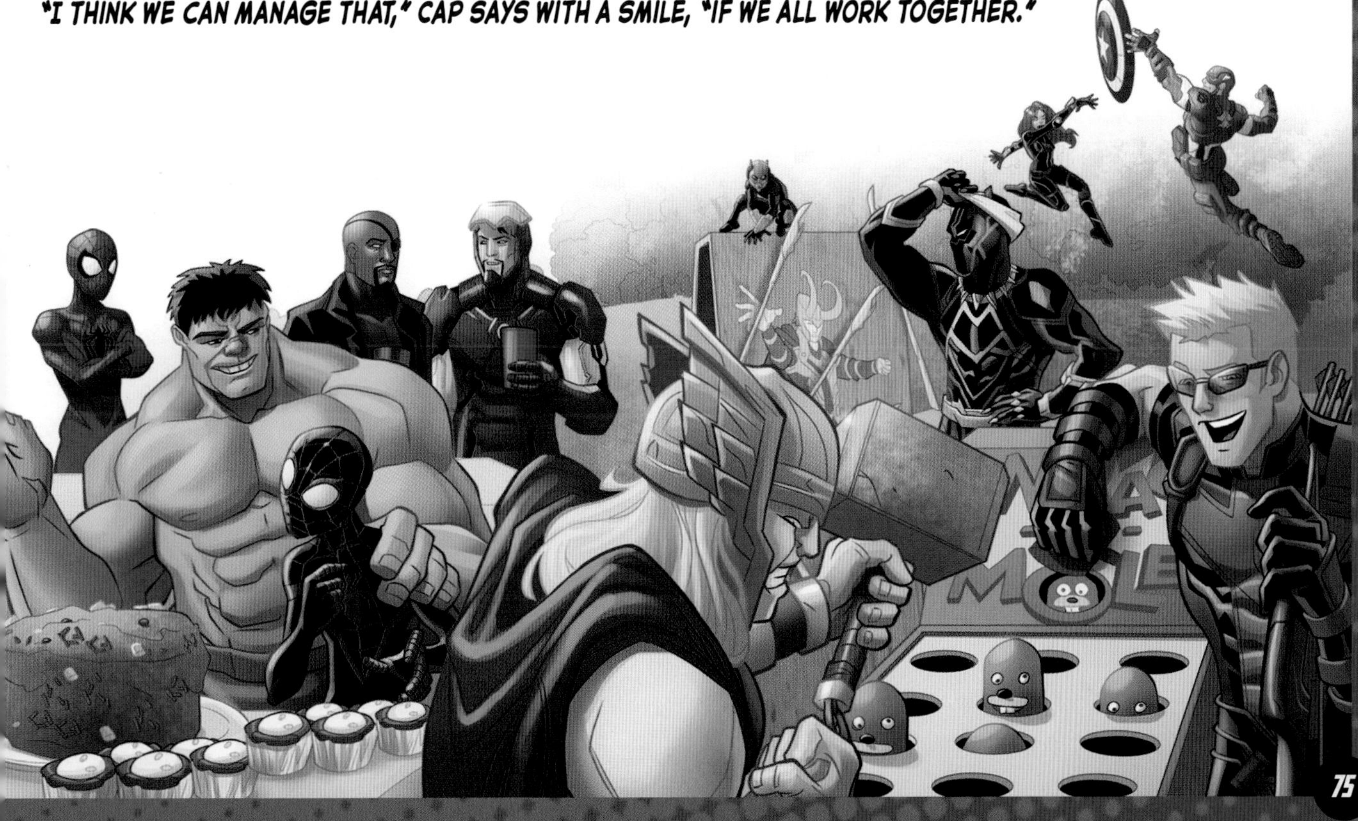

GALACTIC TEAM-UP

"UNITED AGAINST A COMMON THREAT!"

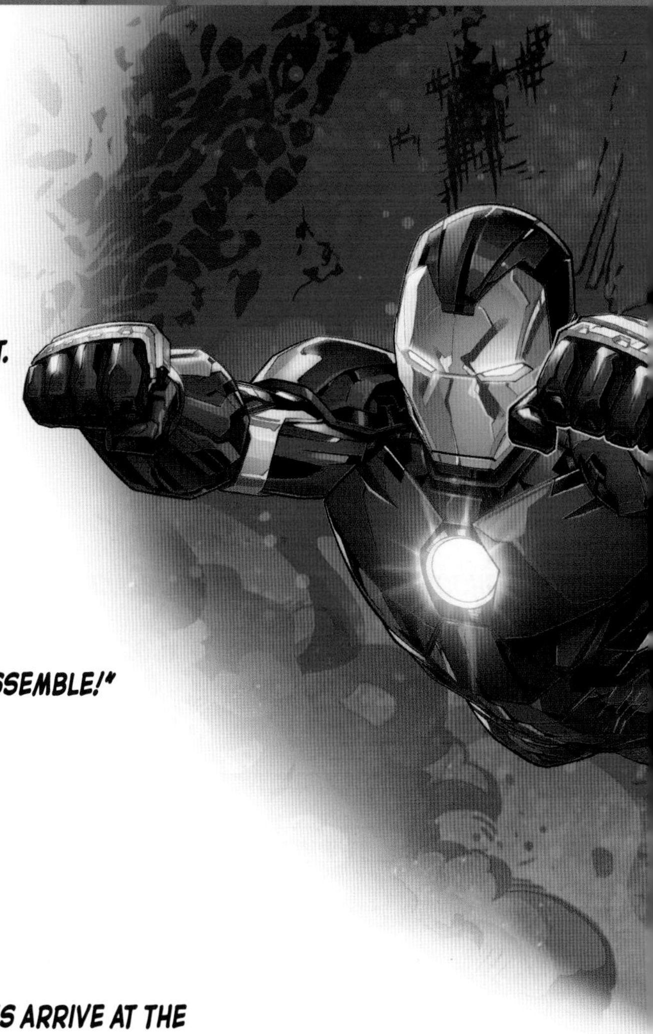

THE WORLD'S MOST POWERFUL LEADERS TRAVEL TO IRON MAN'S BRAND-NEW MOON BASE FOR A SPECIAL VISIT. SUDDENLY, A LARGE EXPLOSION INTERRUPTS THE TOUR!

IRON MAN INVESTIGATES. HE DOESN'T SEE ANY SPACESHIPS, BUT HE DOES SEE THANOS!

IRON MAN IMMEDIATELY CONTACTS THE AVENGERS.

"EARTH IS IN DANGER," SAYS IRON MAN. "AVENGERS ASSEMBLE!"

SOMEWHERE IN DEEP SPACE, THE GUARDIANS OF THE GALAXY INTERCEPT IRON MAN'S MESSAGE.

"THANOS IS ATTACKING THE MOON," SAYS STAR-LORD.

"GUARDIANS GATHER!" JOKES ROCKET.

THANKS TO THE *MILANO*'S HYPER JETS, THE GUARDIANS ARRIVE AT THE MOON IN NO TIME. THEY JOIN THE BATTLE JUST AS QUICKLY!

WHILE THE HEROES FIGHT THANOS'S ARMY, THANOS HEADS TOWARD THE MOON BASE. HE PLANS TO CONQUER EARTH BY CAPTURING ITS LEADERS!

"NOT SO FAST, BIG FELLA," SAYS CAPTAIN AMERICA. THE AVENGERS HAVE ARRIVED!

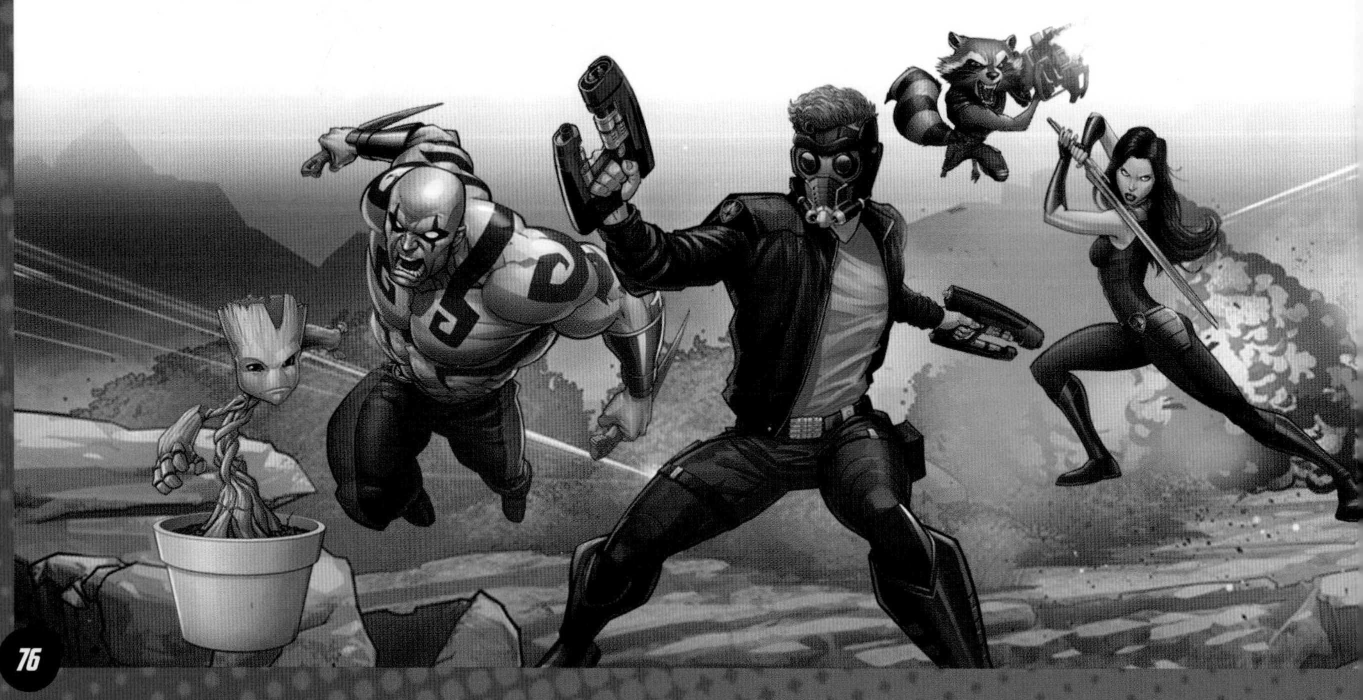

THE AVENGERS BATTLE THANOS WITH ALL THEIR MIGHT, BUT THE POWERFUL VILLAIN MOVES CLOSER AND CLOSER TO THE BASE.

IRON MAN SCANS THANOS AND NOTICES THE VILLAIN IS WEARING A SPECIAL BELT.

"THAT'S HOW HE TRAVELED WITHOUT A SPACESHIP!" SAYS IRON MAN.

IRON MAN GRABS THE TINY POTTED GROOT AND ZOOMS ABOVE THANOS.

"I AM GROOT," SAYS GROOT.

WHEN IRON MAN DROPS HIM, TINY GROOT GROWS!

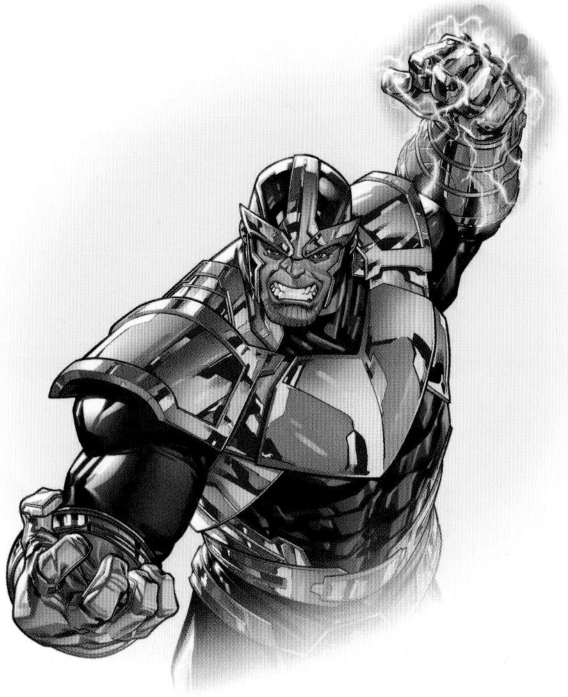

FULL-SIZE GROOT DISTRACTS THANOS LONG ENOUGH FOR IRON MAN TO GRAB THANOS'S BELT.

IRON MAN USES THE BELT TO TELEPORT THANOS AND HIS ARMY BACK ACROSS THE UNIVERSE.

EARTH IS SAFE—AND AS LONG AS THE AVENGERS AND THE GUARDIANS ARE AROUND, IT ALWAYS WILL BE!

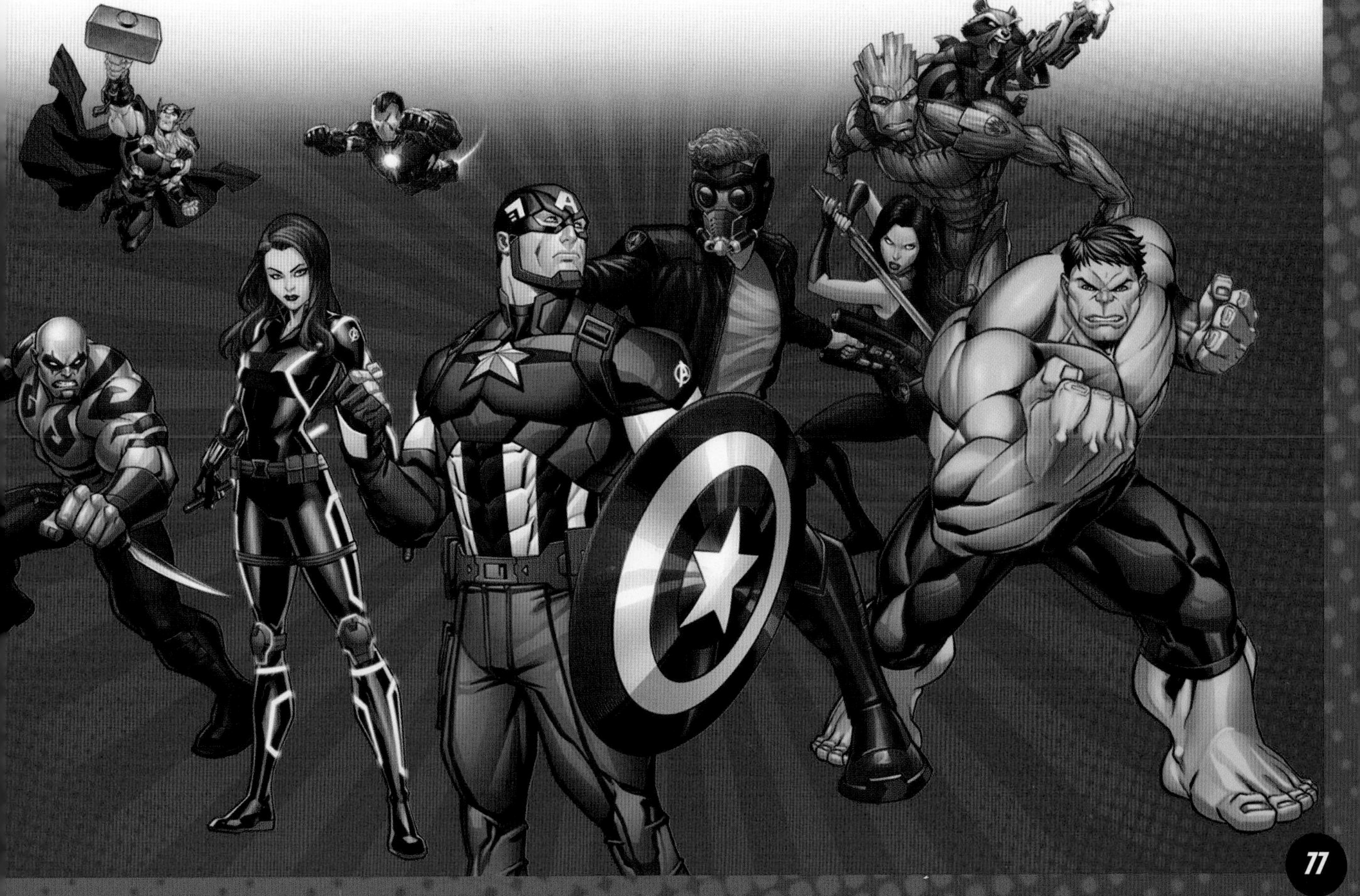

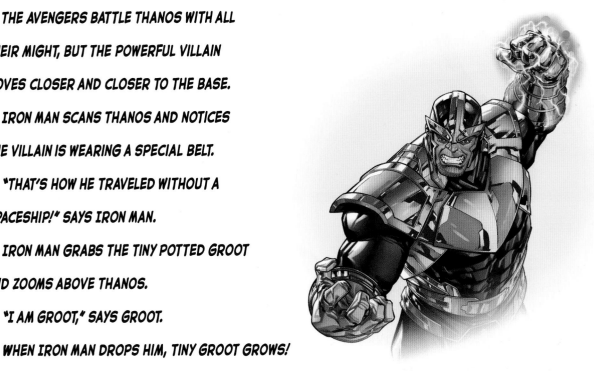

Picture Puzzle

When Thanos comes around, it's all hands on deck!

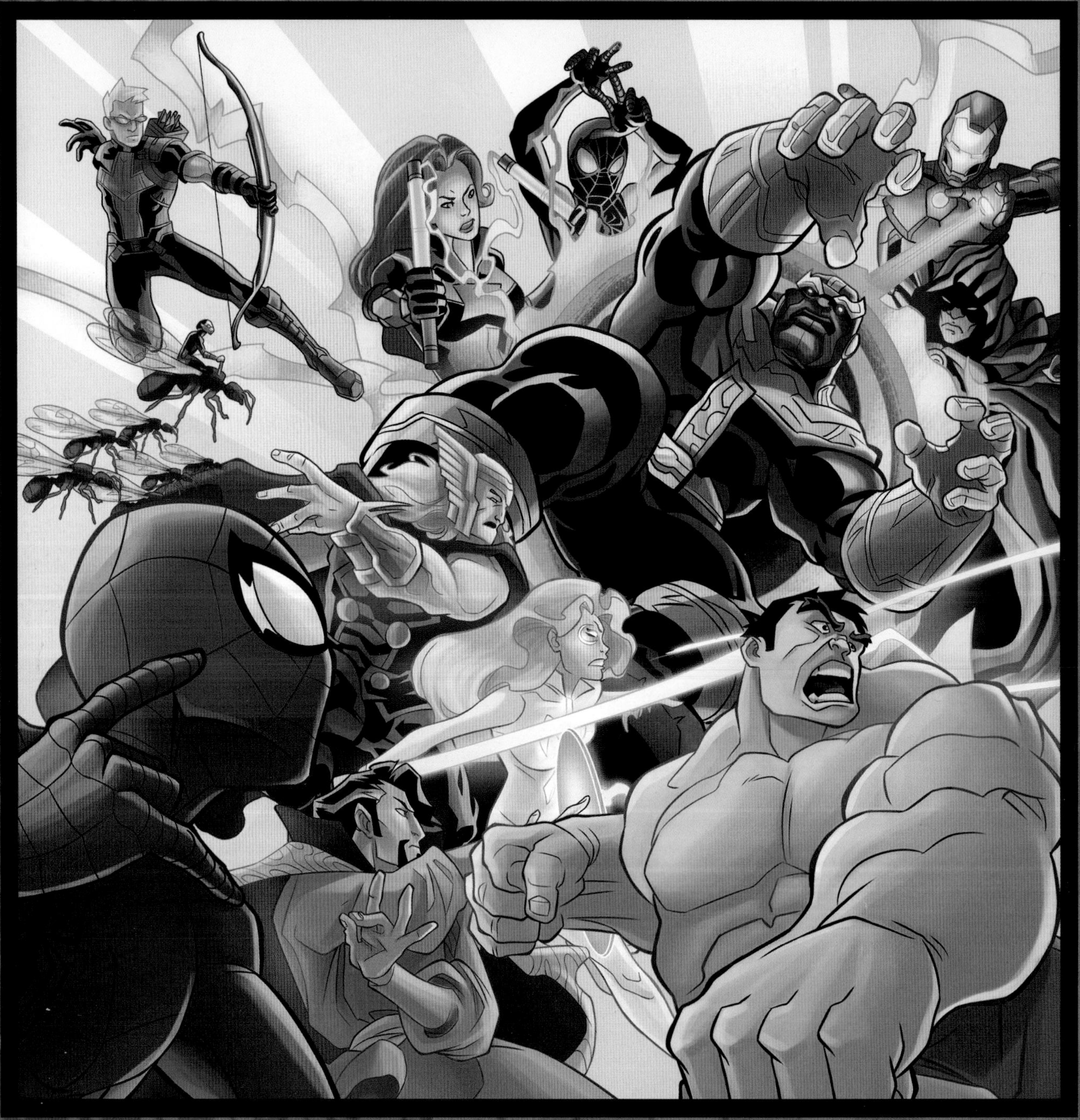

Do your part and seek 10 differences between these scenes.

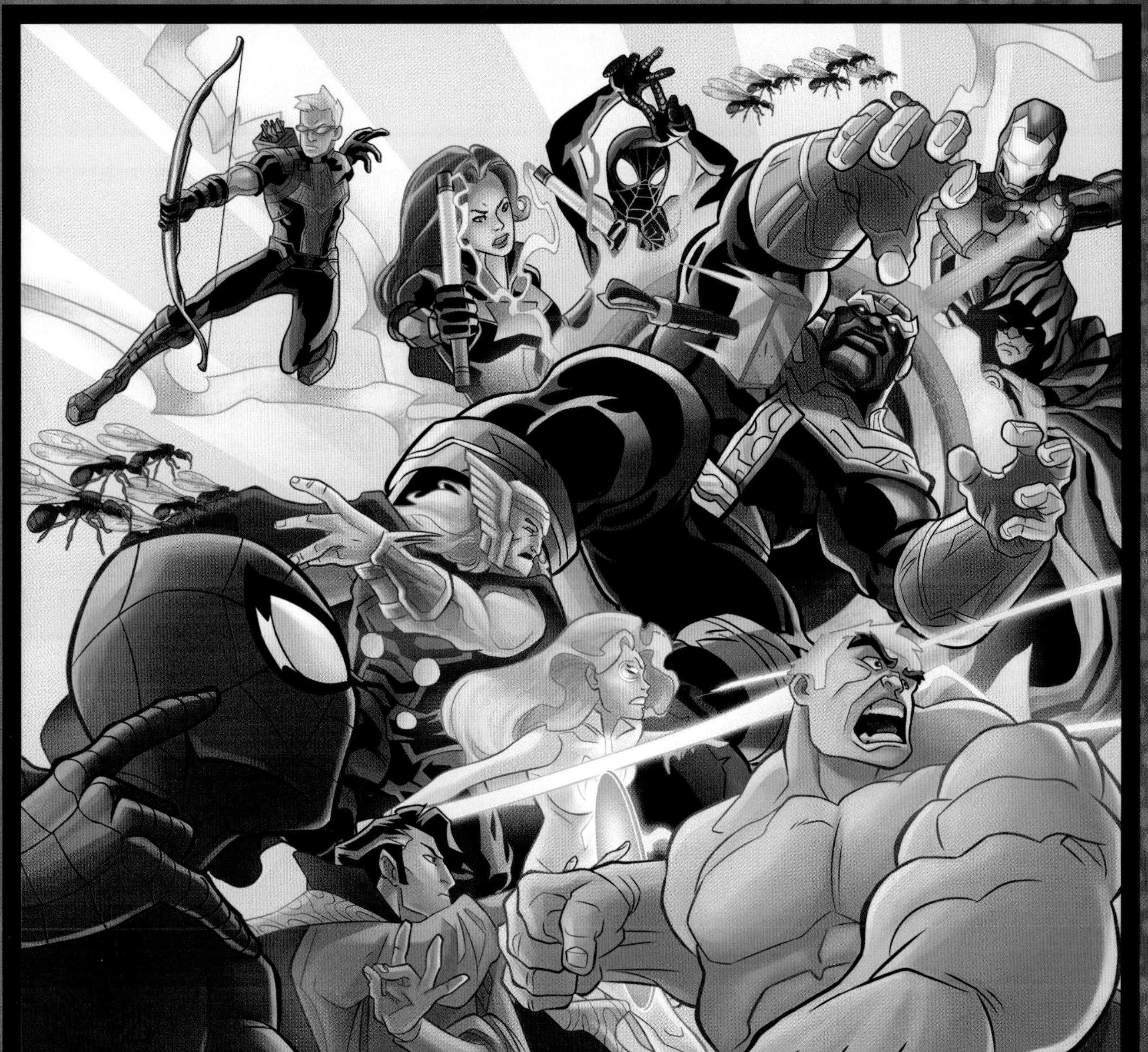

Answer key: direction Hawkeye is facing, ants above Thanos, arc reactor color, Ant-Man, Thor's hammer, color of Thor's buttons, Spider-Man's suit symbol, Doctor Strange's beard, Hulk's hair color, Miles's eyes

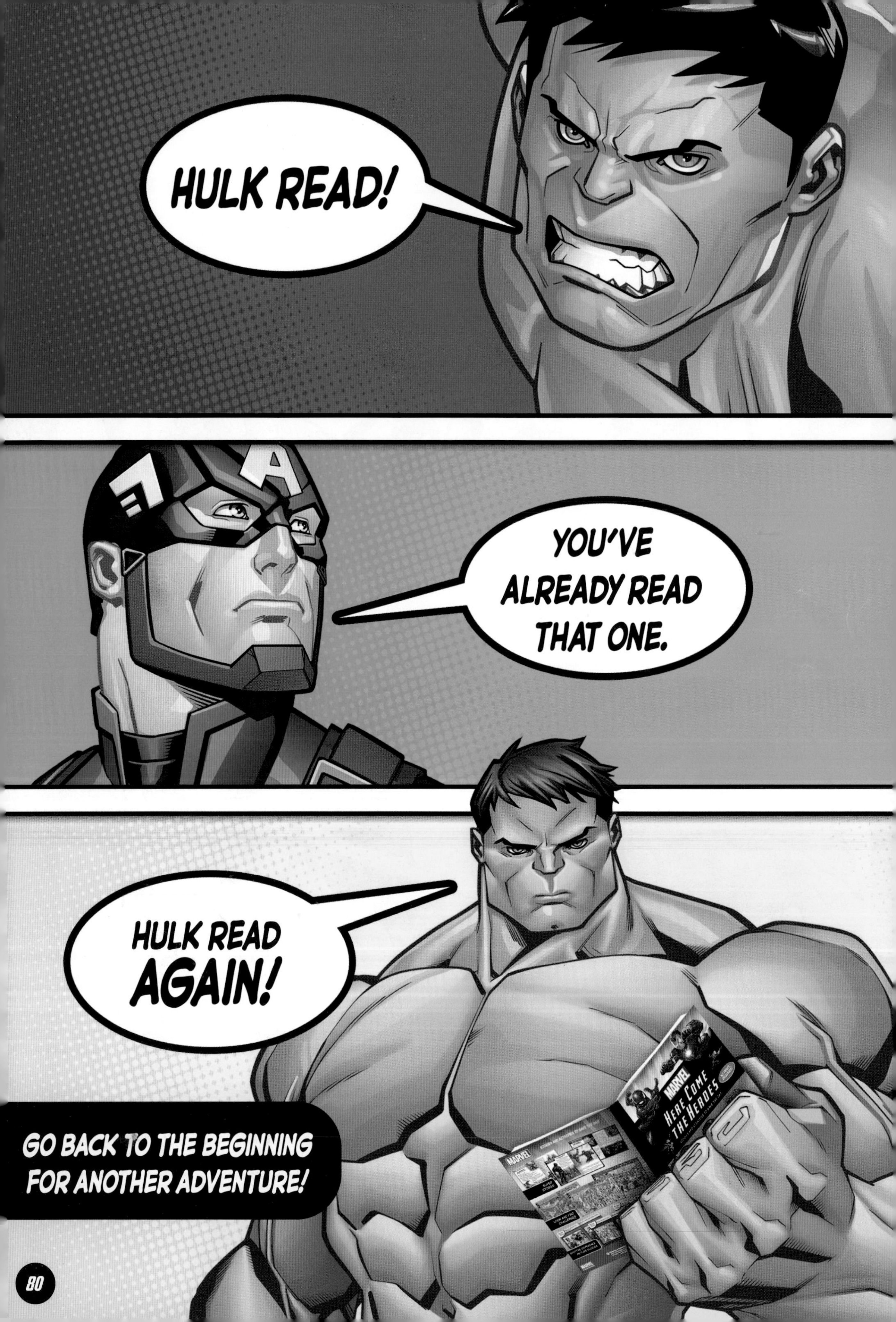
HULK READ!
YOU'VE ALREADY READ THAT ONE.
HULK READ AGAIN!
MARVEL
HERE COME THE HEROES
GO BACK TO THE BEGINNING FOR ANOTHER ADVENTURE!